SUNBURNT COUNTRY

Stories of Australian Life

EDITED BY B R COFFEY

FREMANTLE ARTS CENTRE PRESS

First published 1996 by
FREMANTLE ARTS CENTRE PRESS
25 Quarry Street, Fremantle
(PO Box 158, North Fremantle 6159)
Western Australia.
www.facp.iinet.net.au

Reprinted 1997, 1998, 2002, 2003.

Designer John Douglass.
Typeset by Fremantle Arts Centre Press.
Printed by PK Print.

Cover: *Loading Grain on a Three Springs Farm*, photograph by J E Newby,
coloured by P Stanway Tapp, *Western Mail* Christmas Number, 1930,
courtesy Shirley Taylor.

National Library of Australia
Cataloguing-in-publication data

Sunburnt country.

ISBN 1 86368 364 X.

1. Australian literature - 20th century. 2. Australia - Fiction.
3. Australia - Biography.
I. Coffey, B.R. (Brian Raymond), 1951 - .

820.80994

The State of Western Australia has made an investment in this project through
ArtsWA in association with the Lotteries Commission.

CONTENTS

BEGINNING

I was born in 1916 on the Western Australian goldfields, but my memoried life began when my father gave up mining and took on farming at Arthur River, in the Great Southern district. Until I was old enough to go to school I roamed about the paddocks and the bush as far as my legs would carry me and as long as daylight time allowed. The bush was a living presence that breathed around me and in me, and I was one of the creatures in her plenitude of life.

I met all kinds of bird, animal and insect life, at the close looking of a child. When I walked through the wheat it moved above my head. In spring the colour and smell of orchids were close to my eyes and nose, and a rash of everlastings pinked the ground. I paddled in the creek where the banks loomed over me with shadowy cold. In winter the rain stormed on the iron roof, rivered into the tanks and muddied the earth. I woke in the morning when the air shocked and the ground dragged heavy with dew. On the bushes hung perfect patterns of spiders' webs. On the far side of the woolshed, wheat seeds had burst through the ground overnight and tinged the paddock with an unfamiliar green.

When I walked in the bush the bobtail lizard flashed a silent threat with his blue tongue. Boodie rats and tammars looked with careful eyes. Hakea seeds split open like birds' beaks. Flannel flowers and tadpoles grew together in the swamp. The wind talked alternately strong and weak in the she-oaks, and ringnecked parrots coloured the gums. Plovers sat all one way on the fence, stubby tails behind the wind.

The farm was a country by itself. As the days grew I

explored in many places, ever with the delight of finding something new — a prickle of parrot bush, a swoosh of she-oaks, humps of granite outcrops, gravelly ridges, canyons of creek beds, a jam tree, green and round as a head, gum leaves wet and glittering in the sunlight.

Once I went too far and gulped with fear of never finding home. Would I be caught like Goldilocks in the bird man's net? Meet the fairy woman in the moonlight who spins a silver thread for a snare? Fall down a wombat hole and be lost forever in the dark underground? A tammar jumped before me and stopped. I followed him and followed him, and found the home gate and the house and my mother standing at the door shading her eyes against the setting sun. I ran in and comforted myself against her thigh.

In high summer my brothers and I went down to the orchard and lay under the hanging branches of fermented grapes and got drunk and vomited our way home as the sun went down like a dancing head.

We went barefoot everywhere and washed our hands and faces in the mornings only. One day I ran a splinter of dry wood into the bottom of my foot. My mother applied a linseed poultice which I left on for days, until the rag was the colour of the ground. When I took it off and looked at my foot, it was strange to see the skin white as salt where the poultice had been.

One day my two older brothers and I were put to drive a flock of sheep from one paddock to another. We worked without a dog and had to spread out to keep them moving. Andy was having trouble with a weak lamb that wouldn't keep pace with the mob. Two or three times he picked it up and threw it in among the other sheep to find its mother. We got the mob through and shut the gate, but still the lamb stayed with us, calling in a weak high voice. Andy said it must be a twin and its mother wouldn't take it. He carried it to a tree, took out his pocket-knife and slit its throat. The blood gushed out in spurts. We piled rocks on it to hide it, but the blood trickled through along the ground. Years later someone read me the story of Cain and Abel and the memory jumped when I heard the words 'What hast thou done?

Thy brother's blood crieth unto me from the ground.' It was murder and that living thing really was my brother.

I saw blood again soon after, and this time it was my own. My mother was getting the evening meal. I pestered her for bread and butter, and she tossed me a piece which landed on the plate upside down. I held it out, squawking that there was no butter on it. She stopped cutting the meat from the joint and made to hit my arm with the flat of the knife, but I moved and the knife struck edge on. I saw the skin open up clean with a V-shaped slit, and the blood spurted. My mother reached up to the shelf behind her, grabbed the tin of Zam-buk, picked up the baby's napkin, scooped up a large dob of the ointment, bunged the bandage on my arm and tied it tightly. For years after I was able to boast of the five-centimetre white mark on my arm, and weave romantic tales of how it came about.

I met death again but did not see the event. Our best two horses, Nigger and Tan, got into the shed during the night and gorged themselves so full of oats that, as Andy said, their bellies burst, and they were found dead in the morning. Dad fastened a rope to the stallion and led him as he dragged the corpses into the bush, where they were burnt under a pile of dry wood. When the fire died and the ashes cooled only their bones remained.

The loss of Nigger and Tan made more work for the horses that remained. On Sundays they were let out to graze in the home paddock. We were eating lunch when we heard squeals coming from outside. The stallion had mounted one of the mares. Dad went out to drive him off. I thought it unfair when they were only playing piggyback. I heard Dad tell Mother that he was too late but that it would make up the numbers. Only later when a foal was born did I understand what he meant, and I learned how life came, in the way all farm kids do. The foal was given to Andy and he rode her once a week to the settlement to pick up the bread and the mail.

Now and then strangers came to our place. I did not know that people could be black until a group of myalls, seeming to emerge from the trees themselves, walked up to our house carrying spears, standing on one leg, picking up stones with their toes, talking in a strange tongue and looking with dark eyes. My mother gave them Dad's tobacco and some flour and they went quietly away back into the trees. We never saw them again.

Red-haired Hetty from the next farm came blubbering and stumbling across the home paddock, a pair of binoculars around her neck. Her two little brothers had got lost in the bush. Hetty was a grown-up young lady and she frightened me by crying like a kid. Dad came out and put his arm around her shoulders and they went off together to join the search. My mother stood at the door for a long time and watched them go until they disappeared over the rise. Then she lay down on her bed and she cried. Why were all the grown-ups acting queer? I picked up the cat and went to the shed and sat down among the bags of chaff, and found a nest of little newborn mice but could not stop the cat from eating them all.

Dad was a great singer of songs. He had taught himself to play the piano and could read music as well as play by ear. He was reckoned a good dance pianist, and was hired for the socials that were held from time to time in different parts of the district. At home, as well as the piano, he played the piccolo, banjo, violin, squeezebox, tin whistle, mandolin and mouth organ. On winter nights he piled the fire high, brought in a dead tree, lay the butt end in the grate and its length along the floor. As the evening wore on, he shoved the unburnt shaft up along to keep the blaze alight, while we grouped around the piano and sang about the doings of Barney Google 'with the goo-goo googly eyes' and about the Greek who kept a fruit stall with all kinds of fruit — 'but, yes we have no bananas, we have no bananas today'. There was a mildly rude one with the refrain:

All the monkeys at the zoo
Have their faces painted blue.
Horsey, keep your tail up,
Have yours painted too.

And one about the girls who were invited to

Roll 'em down, girls, roll 'em,
Roll 'em down and show your pretty knee!

There was a long tale of impossible adventures in which the hero boasted 'I've bought diamonds fifteen a penny there/ I've travelled everywhere, nowhere and anywhere/ I'm the top-notch curl of this wide, wide, wide, wide, world.' He met up with an astonishing alligator: 'From the tip of his nose to the tip of his tail/ Was forty-five thousand miles!' He told of cannibals, 'funny looking animals', met while travelling the length and breadth of Patagonia and Tickolonia.

Then there were the sad songs Dad seemed to like the best, mostly songs about partings:

Oh, it's time for parting
And my tears are starting.
Leave me with a smile.
Maybe it's forever, so while we're together
For a little while,
Hold me like a flower, for one little hour —
Leave me with a smile.

For hours, days and years, some unknown girl had to suffer us 'yearning just for you' and to accept that we would be loving her always. Although we had never seen the sea, we sang about it, and with all our lives before us, we retired to some out-of-the-way corner and 'with a pal good and true, let the rest of the world go by'. Then at the end of the session we cheered up, put on 'them golden slippers' and doo-dahed happily with the Camptown ladies while the piano almost rocked over with the vamping chords.

My two older brothers and I started school together when the little one-teacher building at Minding opened in the early 1920s. Dad blazed a trail with the axe five kilometres for us to follow through the uncut bushland. In the winter we squelched in the mud and crossed the creek on a log. In the springtime the spider orchids grew along the track by the thousands and everlastings spread for miles. In summer bull ants, boodie rats, bobtails and snakes showed themselves, and once, a spiny anteater.

One day we wagged it, built ourselves a little bough humpy and sat in it and ate our lunches too early. We got home to find our grandmother come to stay while our mother was away finding us a new baby. When my brothers saw Grandma they escaped, but she cornered me and demanded to know if we had wagged school. I obeyed my brothers and told her we had got all our work right and had been let off early, but I knew she was not deceived.

There were twelve kids in the school. I sat next to Alice, at a flat bench on a five-foot form with a narrow backrest that dug into my shoulders. Alice was the first girl I ever spoke to. She was a bold girl. On my second day she asked me about my dick. We bargained that I would show her mine if she showed me hers. When the teacher was at the back of the room I popped it out under the desk and Alice peeled down her drawers and gave me a quick look. At lunchtime the boys demanded to know what it looked like and I was made to draw a diagram on the ground with a stick. My sketch of a circle crossed by a straight line was greeted with howls of derision. An appeal was made to Robert, the oldest boy, who had sisters. He declared that I had it right. But he was disliked and was not believed. The oldest and the youngest knew the most. After this I wondered about our teacher, who wore a dress and had long hair like Alice.

Once, a town girl came to stay at a nearby farm. She turned up at our school and I thought her the most wonderful creature. She spoke differently from us, had golden hair and her name was Gloria. She was my model for all the princesses in fairy stories I read thereafter.

A new boy came to the school. He sat at the front bench and separated me from Alice. I would not lend him my crayons. So he flattened my plasticine model with his fist. I swore at him in deadly words I had heard from my father, but not so loud that the teacher could hear. When we came in from lunch, she told me to stay in after school. I knew that Tom had potted on me. At the end of the day I tried to sneak out, but Miss held me and sat me in front of her while she busied herself with a piece of sewing.

'Tom told me you swore at him. What did you say?'

I sat dumb, knowing that, though my father swore when he was struggling to get the horses into harness and when he burnt his hand at the forge, they were words unfit for a teacher to hear. Miss persisted, so after a while I said, 'I just swore at him.' She went on demanding to know what I had said. I became desperate as I could see my brothers getting further and further away from me on the track home, and I feared I would not be able to find my way on my own. What if she kept me in until it grew dark? I burst out, 'I called him a bloody bastard, Miss!'

I saw the pink of her face begin to turn red. I grabbed up my school bag and dashed out the door, across the paddock and onto the home track. My brothers were waiting for me down at the creek. When I told them what had happened they staggered about in helpless laughter. Next day the story spread among the kids and grew in the telling. For some weeks I was the hero of the school. I had sworn at the teacher and she had been afraid to cane me!

A day came when the teacher did wrong. On the last day of the school year we were told to clean up the schoolyard of all rubbish. We were happy and strung out the job, as we had got out of some school work. Then she decided that the wild oats and other dried grasses must be burnt. The older boys protested. The school was on a two-hectare plot, fenced off from a farm paddock which was now alive with wheat ready for harvest. Strong words passed between the teacher and Robert, the oldest boy in the school, until she smacked him on the wrist and told him to carry on. She ordered everyone to break a green bough from the roadside trees and stand as guardians to the fire. Patches of grass were successfully burnt, but not for long. A tongue of flame shot through the fence and caught alight on the wheat. The fire swung to left and right as the wind changed and in quick time the whole crop was ablaze.

Miss shrunk into a frightened girl, gave a kind of choking cough, and rushed into the school. Out of the babble of voices as the kids rushed about someone called out, 'I told the silly bitch ... I told her.' The change in our teacher disturbed me and I wanted to see what she was doing. I sneaked up to the school door and looked in. She was sitting on her chair, fists clenched and staring straight ahead. She looked at me, with a face that reminded me of our cow Daisy when she was sick, then she put her head down on the table, threw her arms out, and burst into terrible crying. I was so frightened I had to run away and push in among the crowd of kids, who had got together under the trees on the far side of the school grounds. The paddock all around was black and smoking, and far away the fire was still blazing. The kids talked about what would happen to the teacher. Perhaps she would go to gaol.

We waited a long time for the bell to ring but all was silent from the school building. Robert went over to have a look. He called us to come. The teacher had gone, leaving the door open. We all went in, packed our bags very quietly and went home early, our minds oppressed by a feeling that we had been guilty of taking part in a dreadful event.

At the beginning of the next school year my brothers and I went to a new school. We also had a new home. We had left the first farm because the owner would not renew the lease. Andy said it had something to do with Hetty who was always coming to our place to see Dad. When the time came to leave, Dad made a number of trips on his own with the wagon to carry our furniture and gear. Then Andy, Jerry and I went with him to see the new house. We passed over a river and along a swamp where we chased and caught three little ducklings, one for each of us. We slept on the floor that night and shut the ducklings in the house with us. In the morning they were gone. Jerry said Dad must have hunted them out because they shat on the floor.

The new house was iron-walled and iron-roofed like the other and also had three rooms and a kitchen. There was an orchard with yellow plums which Dad called greengages, and almonds, but no grapes. The land was more cleared, there was less bush to roam in. But there were some high trees near the house. I liked to lie on my back under them on hot days and watch the clouds taking the leaves and branches away on a long road in the sky. There were wattle trees that bled gum which we chewed, and my brothers made glue from it. At the front there was a patch of sunflowers. They reminded me of the girl who had been turned into a flower and, because she loved Apollo, kept her face always to the sun from dawn to dark.

Our new farm was called Wonga Wonga. It was named for a large high granite outcrop that sloped away on one side to level ground that was always damp. The old-timers said it had been a meeting place of the myalls when they wanted to have a 'wongie'. We used it as a playground. We sat on small flat slabs of rock and went scooting down the long slope to catapult onto the ground below. None of us ever broke a leg or an arm because we knew the spirit of the rock would look after us.

The house at Wonga Wonga was on a height about two kilometres from our grandparents' farm, which lay in the valley with the creek down below us, and was called Maybell. We often walked down to their house because we loved our grandma who had a kind voice and gave us nice things to eat, but wouldn't stand any cheek. The house had a garden around it on all sides with flowers nearly always in bloom, and there was a shade house covered with dolichos creeper, with a seat inside, and a fence covered with grapevines, and winding gravel paths round the garden beds, and here and there pyramids of rocks. But our crabby aunts would not let us hang about for long, so we went to the machinery shed and the stables and the chook yard, and so through the thicket of parrot bush back home, and sometimes saw a kangaroo or boodie rat, and once a death adder that made us run for our lives.

Andy and Jerry were getting old enough to be called up by Dad to help with farm jobs, so I was left on my own and was supposed to fetch and carry for Mother, but I escaped when I could. Our mother now seemed always to be sick and spent most of her time in bed. We boys got scratch meals for ourselves and Dad cooked a hot meal now and then. He was a good cook, especially when he made a roast. We came to rely on him for everything we could not do for ourselves, and when we talked at school about our dads we found that we loved him more than the other kids loved their fathers.

We were pleased when our aunts remarked tartly that 'they think the sun shines out of him.' Our dad had offended them by marrying our mother and going off to live with her instead of staying home and working for his own father and mother and sisters, as Uncle Josh did. Aunt Marion said, smiling, that 'our Josh is married to his car.' Our dad didn't have a car and Jerry said that only bachelors could afford them.

We had not been long in our new house when Mother ran out one day screaming that there was a snake inside. She told me to run, run, down to Granny's place and tell Auntie Gladdie to come quickly with the rifle. Gladdie worked like a man and could drive every kind of farm machine, but she did not shear or kill sheep. I liked her because she had a pretty face and loved a joke when you were with her on her own. She called Aunt Marion, and we all three came fast, fast, up the rise to Wonga Wonga. We found the snake by the water tank and beat him out till he wound himself around the wire clothes line. 'With cool daring', as my story book said, Aunt Marion picked up the clothes prop and pushed the forked end under the snake's head, and made Gladdie a steady target. With one shot she blew its head apart, but the bullet passed through the iron wall of the house and scared us all. Mother came out carrying the baby. Luckily she had been lying down, so no one was hurt. The snake was boiled up and fed to the chooks.

One day when everybody was out Mother told me to bring the big iron tub we used for a bath. I dragged it in from the outside shed, bumping and clanging it up to the doorstep. It was too wide to go through the bedroom doorway so I left it in the living room, and went out to play. I heard strange noises coming from inside so I went back in, and saw my mother standing in the tub with only her top covered above the waist and blood running down her legs. She waved me away. I knew where Dad was from the sound of the harvester. 'She's dying, she's dying', my feet hammered it out on the ground. I must have shouted as I ran.

Dad jumped down from the machine, handing me the reins. 'Get up there and hold the horses. Don't let 'em move.' How could I stop them if they took off? They shook their heads and flicked their tails as the flies worried them, and then began to move forward. I screamed at them to stop. I stood up. I pulled on the reins and in a fluster stepped on the cutter control clutch. The spinning hand crank grazed my chin and the harvester front sank quickly down until it thumped on the ground. It stopped the horses, but because I thought I had broken the machine, I walked back very slowly to the house. Dad was helping mother up into the sulky. He didn't ask me what had happened. He only said, 'When Andy comes back, tell him to unharness the horses and take them back to the stable. And tell him to get tea. I'll send someone to look after you till I get back.'

Dad and Mother were both away for some time and a strange lady came to care for us. But she was not like a lady, not like our aunts. She was giggly and girlish and had golden hair. Was she Gloria grown up? I asked her, 'Are you going to be our new Mum?' She laughed and said I could be her sweetheart if I liked. I said yes, I would, but did not like to ask her what I had to do about it. We went to the orchard to pick yellow plums and had great fun when they toppled out of the dish and we sat down together to gather them up. She played with me like our mother never did and I hoped we would go on like this forever, but she left when Dad came home and I never saw her again.

Our new school at Arthur River was part of a little hamlet that had a post office, a small shop, a community hall, a small hotel attached to a house and, further down the road, two houses and a church. All the buildings were of local stone except one house which was brick on a stone foundation. The settlement was on the main road from Perth, which we had learned was our capital city, big enough I thought to have perhaps a hundred houses!

We started school there after the Christmas holidays. We had further to go than to our first school, too far to walk, so we went in the spring cart pulled by one of our horses, a quiet old plodder called Tom. The track took us close by Maybell and our grandma was always at the fence to wave to us, and sometimes to ask us if we had taken lunches which she knew we had to get for ourselves. Mostly it was 'doorsteps' filled with jam, sometimes a bit of cold mutton splashed with tomato sauce, and fruit from the orchard if it was the season.

From Granny's we went over the dry riverbed at the stony crossing and on along to the main road and the school, a distance of ten kilometres. This was all right in the summer, but in winter the depth of the river made it impassable. We had then to go the long way round, sixteen kilometres by the bridge. We started doing this after a scary incident one morning at the stony crossing. It had been raining all night and Dad told Andy to note the depth of water in the river as shown on the measuring pole. 'If it's over two-and-a-half feet,' he said, 'you'll have to come back and go by the bridge.' But Dad had not taken into account the force of the water flow, which had carried away much of the riverbed, so that the depth was greater than registered on the marker. Andy urged the horse in, we got halfway, water flowed over the floorboards, Tom lost his footing, we began to float and move sideways. The downstream wheel came up against a large boulder, Tom got his front feet on the ground, he pulled us up and onto the other side and we got away safely. It rained on and off during the day and we had to come home by the bridge, wet and miserable, but full of boast at the tea table of how we could have been carried in our cart-boat to the sea.

The school day began with music. It was the first time I had heard group singing. The teacher, Miss Casey, struck the table with a tuning fork, put it her ear and sang a note. The children took it up and then the song began:

> *Sweet and low, sweet and low,*
> *Wynd of the western sea*
> *Low, low, breathe and blow*
> *Blow him again to me.*

Our teacher had a strong singing voice and the fifteen voices together had an appealing sound, and I wished for the time to come when it would be sung again and I could join in. But even more wonderful was the chorus of the spoken word:

Lift up your heads O ye gates,
And be ye lift up ye everlasting doors,
And the King of Glory shall come in.
Who is the King of Glory?
The Lord of Hosts, He is the King of Glory.

I learned it quickly and never forgot. Dad was a great reciter of lyrics and ballads and he had prepared my ear for the magical sound of words.

The hours in school seemed long despite the morning and afternoon playtimes, and lunchtime. But good things happened. If we heard a car coming up the long gravelled hilly road that ran past the school, we stood on our seats, with the teacher's permission, to look out of the long high windows. Once an aeroplane flew overhead and we were let out to see this marvel that flew like an airborne car with wings, so quickly out of sight.

One day the free stock arrived in a big pine box. Two older boys were given the job of breaking it open. Out came things that looked and smelled like new toys: shining red pencils, the red-covered Oxford readers full of brightly coloured pictures, smelling of new print, boxes of Reeves pastels with colours I had never seen before, new pens for the older children and white china inkwells, slate pencils for the Infants, a round globe to tell us about the earth we lived in, rulers to make straight lines, compasses that the older ones could use to make circles, packets of ink powder, strips of cardboard for manual models, coloured cottons for the girls, a bell for the teacher.

The Oxford reading book delighted me with its red cover, its bold print, its decorated first capital letters and its imaginative and repetitious stories. Miss Casey encouraged my fondness for reading and one Friday let me take home a Blackie's reader, but I must keep it clean and bring it back on Monday. This was one of our teacher's strict rules, that borrowed books must be returned next school day. She had many rules and saw to it that they were obeyed. My brothers did not like the teacher and when I told them about the Blackie's, they ordered me to kick it along the track to punish the teacher. The book to me was a valued gift. I tried to keep it in my bag. But they snatched it out and booted it in the air. To keep mates with them I gave it a feeble kick, but was so disgusted with myself that I did not read anything in it.

On Monday I tried to sneak the book into the cupboard, but the teacher called on me to show it to her. I saw how Andy and Jerry grinned behind their hands when she was annoyed at a dirty page and a torn cover. I would never again be given a book to take home. But when the inspector came he said I was a good boy for reading well. The teacher secretly gave me a pat on my shoulder. I knew she had forgiven me. Dad said Miss Casey was a good teacher, but the boys did not like her because she was strict with them and seemed to favour the girls.

One day, led by an older boy, we all put our thumbs and fourth fingers together to make a 'long bacon' of twenty hands in the direction of the schoolroom where she was seated at the table eating her lunch. We had a great belief in the malevolent power of this symbol. Something bad would happen to her in time.

Towards the end of the year an elderly red-faced man with white hair and a beard like Abraham came with a box full of lemonade, cola beer and raspberry creaming soda. We all got book prizes. Even Dan, who could not count above ten and who stumbled badly in his reading, got one for 'regular and punctual attendance'. As part of the wind-up an inter-school cricket match had been arranged. We were to play against Widgiegarrup and the game would be followed by afternoon tea for the parents and a Christmas tree for the kids. I was glad to see that, for once, our mother was coming with us. We all climbed into the spring cart for the long journey to Widgie. The road was rough and we had lost our best carthorse, so we arrived late for the start of the match. Andy was called up almost straightaway to go into bat and he got out for a duck against the enemy's famous demon bowler. But Andy got his own back later when he bowled a googly and got their best man out. We lost the match but, as the spokesman for the parents said, 'We ask not if you won or lost, but how you played the game.' We liked that and said it many times afterwards when it seemed right.

We drank tea and lemonade under the trees, and then went into the hall for the Christmas tree. One by one the kids were called up to get their presents from a red sweating Santa Claus. When 'Jackie' was called, mother sent me up to get mine. The red man asked me, 'Is your name Jacqueline?'

'No,' I said, 'it's Jack.' Why isn't he giving me my present? I wondered. He thrust it into my hands and quickly called the next name. 'Struth,' said Dad, 'what have you done, Mother? He's got a darned doll.' My brothers scoffed and badgered me about it all the way home, so that if Mother had not taken the doll from me I would have thrown it out of the cart. She put it on a high shelf in the living room and Dad said it would come in handy if the next one was a girl. Next day I stood on a chair, pulled it down, kicked it all round the home paddock until I had broken its legs and arms, then threw it into a bush and felt better. No one ever asked me where it was.

(From *Challenging Faith*, an autobiography, 1993.)

CONNIE MILLER

A GLORIOUS SUN

Western Australia! Here we were, at the bottom of a wobbly gangway, and actually setting foot on the furred grey planking of Fremantle's Victoria Quay ... Being hugged and kissed by a big, red-moustached man we hadn't seen for almost two years. Laughter, and tears. And some hesitation from both my brothers, six-year-old Alan, and ten-month-old Arthur whom Father was now holding for the first time in his life.

How firm it was underfoot, after seven weeks aboard the 7660 ton SS *Gothic*, a small ship for the one thousand seven hundred and seventy passengers she had carried. Almost half of them, including us, had disembarked at Fremantle. Only too thankfully, for since leaving Durban the old *Gothic* had tossed about unmercifully.

It had been pleasant at first, before Durban. Even in the Bay of Biscay where everyone expected the ocean to be angry and rough. But the late summer days were mild and the evenings beautiful, with twilight turning imperceptibly into dark. Mother let us stay on deck as long as possible, not taking us downstairs until our baby brother had to be fed.

A man had fallen overboard in the Bay and had drowned. I learnt of this only from hearing people talk on deck. Mother hadn't mentioned it and I forbore to question her. At the age of eight I had already discovered there were some things you didn't question mothers about.

Another subject I hadn't brought up, probably because it didn't really interest me, was that of Lord Aberdeen. He was travelling among the emigrants and his presence there was causing some speculation. Indeed, irreverent passengers had made up a ditty about him, which they sang in quiet corners of the ship:

> Lord Aberdeen, Lord Aberdeen,
> The queerest man, Was ever seen.
> He paid two pounds, For a ten pound trip,
> To sail a board, This awful ship!

At the time an adult emigrant paid £19 for the journey to Australia, £10 being, subject to certain conditions, refunded later. I thought, well, Lord Aberdeen must have his own good reasons for travelling cheaply.

Sighting the Cape of Good Hope was a great excitement. Here was a foreign country I'd read about in my *Oliver and Boyd Geography Book*. We could see flat-topped Table Mountain, and we were all ecstatic because it meant Durban and getting off the ship were now quite close.

Alan and I loved Durban. Thanks to a coal strike we were there almost a week. Each morning Mother took us across the wharf and into the city, or to the long beach with its shark-proof enclosure and its wide stretch of sand that reminded me of Blackpool, or to the beach front's delightful restaurants where, after the monotonous shipboard food, we feasted greedily on fresh meat and vegetables and fruit. Not forgetting the sandwiches and cakes and fizzy drinks.

For days we romped and paddled and gorged. We visited the museum and the native markets. Mother bought a miniature ship and other toys for Alan and, for me, oddly attractive bangles of tight-coiled metal in silver and bronze tonings. And a gilt-edged, easel-shaped brooch which bore an enamelled picture of the museum.

Each morning on our way to the beach we passed Zulu rickshaw men. Big, splendid men with bulging arm and leg muscles. They gleamed with paint, and wore peacock-coloured feather headdresses that outdid the magnificence of their decorated vehicles. They leapt and shouted to attract a customer's attention, and their limbs shone like polished copper, their muscles rippled, their metal and ivory necklaces glittered and jingled, and the sun drew multicoloured lights from their ostrich-plumed headgear. But Mother, timid of such goings-on, refused to be tempted.

Often, when the coal strike was over and we returned to the ship tired after a long day ashore, we heard fearful cries and screams from the coal-carrying natives who, on being released from their compounds, were now voicing their delight ... Delight? When being released meant the beginning of a wearying spell of toil, carrying hods of coal up the gangplank and down into the furnace room of our ship? Hearing their cries then, I knew only fear.

There were other moments of fear on the voyage. During that final slow progress across the Indian Ocean hordes of sharks followed us well out of Durban, leaping and snapping, their jaws wide. And sometimes when I was alone, when the fierce wild westerlies were behind us, I'd watch the ship's funnel and masts sweep frighteningly across the dark infinity overhead, until nausea sent me rushing down to the cabin with its bunks and bunkside receptacles. In the end it had become so rough that women and children were forbidden to go up on deck at all.

One incident, before Durban, had horrified me. A family of children and their mother were near us on deck. The mother had been scolding one child for some misdemeanour, and suddenly she took up the little one, held her over the ship's railings, and threatened to drop her into the sea. The child's screams were frightening.

Being a bookworm I found the cabin pleasant enough, to begin with. Among the cabin's luggage were issues of the English *Woman's Weekly*, to which Mother had subscribed since its first copy was published in 1911. She had stitched the copies together to make a couple of thick volumes. The young people's pages, with their stories of two families of children, the Blacks, and the Whites, intrigued me. And some of the adult fiction held my interest. Especially *That's My Child!* It was a tale about two little brothers who, at birth, had gone to the wrong mothers. I believe it was the first printed story that made me cry. Then, thanks to the economy-conditioned and (after having enjoyed fresh farm food for most of our lives) tasteless food the shipping company provided, I enjoyed the recipes. I spent hours copying into an exercise book those I considered the most mouth-watering.

Mother had a little methylated spirit stove and could make a cup of tea whenever she liked. She kept a tin of condensed milk on a ledge above the cabin door. Alan and I knew it was there and I am sure Mother must have known why the condensed milk disappeared so quickly.

But, after the injunction that women and children must stay 'below', the gloom, and above all the sense of anxiety and fear that seemed to permeate the below-decks area made us all long for the tedious voyage to end.

Now, it had ended and we were on dry land once more. Already I was able to put from my mind the more unhappy aspects of the voyage: the hypnotic fascination of watching the tall masts trace incredible arcs against bruised clouds; the sickening sensation that accompanied each plunge of the vessel into valleys of dark ink overhung by terrifying mountains of pitted lead; the smells of rank potatoes and of burnt porridge that I'd come to associate with certain of the ship's alleys at particular times; and the recent fortnight of fetor and gloom and stridor below decks.

They had all gone. A new land lay before us.

From Gage Roads where the ship had waited at dawn, the coastline looked strange to our English eyes. We had wakened to lightning, thunder and rain. The buildings of Fremantle and Cottesloe, hazy above a ribbon of pale sand, thinned out on greying hinterland that vanished into a misty and indefinite horizon.

But by the time we docked at Fremantle the rain had cleared, the sun was shining and the wonderful clarity of the antipodean light sharpened all outlines, defined shapes and bulks, and made our awareness of a 'new' country doubly intense. I expect I was tired; what I saw didn't impress me much.

Mother and we two older children were tired. Delighted that the seven-week journey was at an end we had been awake and up very early, eager to see Western Australia. We had watched as the little boat carrying Customs Officers and the Doctor had chugged steadily towards us. But after the exciting business of the men clambering up a rope ladder at the ship's side, we'd had a wearying wait for medical inspection and clearance.

Now all that was over. We were in a dimly lit railway station and stepping into a little brown train whose windows were rather dusty. And for a few minutes, with each, I suppose, trying to sort out his tumultuous thoughts, there was absolute silence in the train's compartment. Then, with a whistle and a lurch and a hiss of escaping steam, the train began to move. It pulled away from the comparative murk of Fremantle Station and chuffed into the amazing September sunlight.

Silent, I leant on the window's edge and gazed at the sky. Except for tiny white puffs of cloud far to the east it was blue, an unbelievably clear bright blue, all over.

The train crossed over a river bridge and, stopping noisily at minute brown stations, it went on through the alien countryside, this new, open countryside that had been our homeland for only the past few hours. At a flat section where the railway lines clung to the coast, the Indian Ocean stretched out and away south, west and north. After its heaving and crashing during the previous few weeks it looked strangely quiet, its low swell breaking and foaming in great lacy festoons onto a wide, white beach of stark emptiness and wonderful purity. And the ocean was blue like the sky.

At Blackpool and Southport, the only beaches I had ever really known, the sea was never like this. Or maybe, there, the sea had passed without undue notice in face of all the other attractions: the donkeys, the piers, the helter-skelter, the giant wheel and the tower. There were none of these, here. And no rows of two and three-storeyed houses from one of which, a short time back, in socks and sandshoes and with wide-brimmed straw hats topping striped galatea outfits, Alan and I had set out each morning with Mother or Ruth for an entire fortnight.

There was another difference. This sand gleamed. And way out past the festooning waves, the sea looked bluer than the sky; a deep, satisfying ultramarine that shone and glittered on the horizon. Sand that was silver in the sunlight, and a sea that glittered like diamonds — maybe this new country was going to be very special!

'Better sit back a bit, Connie.' From the opposite seat where he was nursing my baby brother, Father smiled at me.

Now we were drawing away from the sea, and past one station appeared a row of houses, each house back from the road and in its own small garden.

'They're teeny little houses,' said my brother Alan, pointing.

'You mean, low,' Father laughed. 'People here don't need an upstairs. There's more room, so they spread out, instead.'

Almost drugged by the bewildering changes, I asked no questions.

At Perth Railway Station we waited on a brown-painted wooden seat while Father arranged about our luggage. Here, too, the light touched everything with dioramic intensity. The two long platforms of dingy asphalt almost shone, and between the lines smoke-grimed rubble had taken on rich shades of burnt umber and bright sienna, speckled with the citric green of tiny blades of grass. A bit down the line in the direction from which we had come, trains billowed brown smoke and shunted fussily into a motley collection of brown sheds. On the station's walls distributors of Bonox, Zambuk, Bee Tea, Mother Siegel's Syrup and Hutton's Hams vaunted their products via colourful enamel plaques. The acridity of coal smoke and hot oil tickled our nostrils ... But the bustle and crowds and racket of the railway station we had left on a dull morning of London's July were missing.

Father joined us. We left the station, passed horse-drawn cabs lined up alongside a picket fence bordering the station yard, crossed Wellington Street and its tramlines, walked through the gloomy cavern of Central Arcade and crossed Murray Street, then free of tramlines. In cheerful Baird's Arcade we had our first Australian meal.

Weariness had overcome us three children. The baby was asleep in Mother's arms, six-year-old Alan was blinking drowsily, and for all my two years' seniority I could scarcely eat. Certainly Mother and Father talked. But I had come to the limits of my receptiveness and I was able to take in nothing of what they said.

The meal must have taken rather a long time. All the lights were now on. Outside, clouds had gathered again and we walked from the Arcade into comparative darkness and a fine drizzle of rain ... Waiting, once again, at the Railway Station for more business concerning luggage and then climbing aboard a tram for its journey to the Oxford Street terminus in Leederville, and finally climbing down alongside a two-storeyed brick building in a dim-lit street. Standing in now heavily falling rain, but too tired to voice complaint, and hearing Father say the last tram to Osborne Park had left.

Osborne Park, where we were going to live! A moment of re-awareness flashed through my mind.

Was this Park to be anything like the Dunham Park we once had driven through on our way to visit an uncle and aunt near Altrincham? Would there be the same trees, elm and oak and holly and beech? And round-eyed deer playing hide-and-seek among them?

I was too tired even to ask about that.

Walking, then, between Mother and Father. Father with Alan on his back and carrying in his free hand the bulky, two-piece cane dress basket with leather straps; Mother carrying baby Arthur. Walking to the end of Oxford Street. Turning left into Scarborough Beach Road; then right, along Main Street. Left along Hector Street, and right once more along King Edward Road. Walking five long, dragging miles, in utter blackness and pouring rain, at the end of a tiring and exciting day. Walking through a tunnel with walls of black trees, black shapes even darker than the streaming sky.

Then, in the Stygian gloom we left the road and were moving through a strange, barbed-wire gate. Alan began to cry; and Mother, too close to the wire, tore the new gaberdine raincoat she had bought in Stockport a few months earlier.

Awareness of another strange shape, a round one, near a house. It was a corrugated iron water tank. Scrambling up the ramp, and entering the house. Such a queer one, set up on legs almost as high as I was. Walking into an odd room lined with whitewashed hessian. Watching, through the haze of approaching sleep, as Father lit a fire in the funny kitchen range. And being conscious, but barely, of the sudden crackle and flare-up of the pieces of dry blackboy he was using, and of its sweet, resiny smell.

Going into another whitewashed hessian room. Undressing. Crumpling on to a mattress laid on the floor. Being wafted into immediate sleep by the rainwaves of sound on the corrugated iron roof.

I awoke next morning to one of the most dazzling and captivating scenes of my life. It was the seventh day of Australia's spring in the year 1912.

Outside, surrounding the house except where its front faced the plank and limestone of King Edward Road, and running down to the brook I soon came to call a creek, an immense golden carpet lay before me. A carpet so golden and so immense its beauty held me spellbound.

And from above, from a sky higher and bluer than any sky I'd seen before, a glorious sun blazed down its incredible radiance. Silent, aflame with ecstasy, I stood there, lips apart, taking in the sweet fresh air.

(From *After Summer Merrily,* an autobiography, 1980.)

KIM SCOTT

STINGRAY

Billy, Liz and their students took the bus to the beach. The trip
was in many ways, perhaps, a form of trade-off. Later the students would write about it. So, there they were — Scrap Metal
music blasting on the stereo, eskies of food and cool drinks,
fishing lines — all chattering and laughing. The new, and
somehow soft, bus seemed incongruous with the hard light, the
dust, the shimmering trees and bush, and a track that always
jostled and shook you up.

They stop just once, for a tree that had late bush apples.
Something like a radish, but injected with air. Like a Chinese
Apple, like a red heavy tough bubble, stick-bashed out of a
scrubby tree. Billy enjoys the collecting. A kid in the bus shouts
out. The bus stops and whoosh! everyone's off to get bush
apples. Figures all through the bush. Appearing, disappearing.
A shadow in coloured shirt flits from trunk to trunk; a flurry of
them become the kids throwing sticks up into a tree and, in vir-
tually the same motion, plucking the bush apples from the air as
they fall, and briefly bounce.
    In the bus, shimmy-shammying through sand and rustling
leaves, the kids check each tree is where it should be, and read
the tyre prints to see which cars have been where, and name
sites. There's rock paintings in there, I think. They stop for a bit
to look.

We climbed and climbed and we went right up to the top of the
rock. From there you look out to the sea and you can see all the
beaches and feel the wind. It is a lovely view. We told Sir and

Miss if they wanted to see some better rock paintings so we took them right around the rock. They liked them. Then Jimmy went into a cave and we saw paintings of people, animals, tools and Wandjinas. We also saw some bones of long time ago. But then we thought it might be a Law cave and we were frightened. So we got out, and we did want to go to the beach anyway.

At the beach everyone dispersed along the shoreline in small groups. Except Francis of course. And he's not right, you know. He's been a little bit sick ever since he was a baby. And maybe he's a bit spoilt. He's different; big thick glasses, little bit deaf. He sat on the beach in the shade of the bus and listened to AC/DC on the Walkman that Moses bought for him.

Billy and Deslie went together. Billy was hoping to learn something about fishing. Walking calf-deep in the tepid water near some mangroves Deslie grabbed Billy's arm. 'See, Sir? See? See. Stingray. Good eating sometimes, them ones.'

Eventually Billy did see. A stingray, some fifty centimetres across, was motionless between where they stood and some rocks before them. 'You watch it, Sir. I get stick.'

Deslie crept back from the mangrove's edge with a thick stick the length of his forearm. Billy pointed unnecessarily to where the stingray remained. Deslie slowly raised the arm holding the stick. He threw it, moving rapidly towards the stingray as he did so. Billy saw the stingray as if flying on the surface of the water, splashing, straining, racing towards open sea. Deslie snatched up the stick from where it was bobbing in the water. He ran through the deepening water in the direction of the stingray's retreat, the stick above his head. He threw it again, picked it from the water and, running and splashing hard in the thigh-deep water, he threw it a third time. He stopped where the stick had landed, looking around him. He bent over and, with his back arched awkwardly to keep his head above water, began feeling around in the sand. 'Here somewhere, Sir.'

Billy looked away, a little embarrassed for Deslie's sake. It had escaped. His eyes followed the shoreline a few hundred metres to where the others had gathered on the rocks not far from the bus. They were fishing there, and some gathered oysters before the rising tide made it impossible to do so. Billy turned around and Deslie was walking towards him. He held the tail of the stingray in his teeth and his left hand gripped its jaw. His right hand broke off the barbs at the base of its tail.

'Deslie, you're fantastic.'

'Good eating, Sir, these, when they're fat.' He held the stingray flat and belly up on a rock, and cut a small opening with one of the barbs he'd saved. The skin opened as if from a scalpel, showing white flesh. Deslie poked it with his finger. 'This one no good.' He dropped the stingray back into the water and kicked at it. Sluggishly, it swam away.

They walked further around the coast. Deslie asked Billy to work out compass directions using the sun and his watch, the way he'd shown them at school.

Billy hesitated, 'It's only approximate, Deslie, and I need a protractor to reckon it accurately.'

Deslie laughed. 'I don't need to do that, eh? Do I, Sir? I don't need to make those reckonings. I know this country, I'm here, I'm Deslie.' He pointed to the ground beneath him and rapidly stomped his feet, and they laughed and stomped together, as if dancing in their joy.

Billy maybe felt a little bit silly then. He was meant to be the teacher. And walking back, under Deslie's direction, through the twists and curves of the mangroves and the tide rushing in again, he thought of how Deslie no longer used his childhood name because someone of that same name had died in the recent past, and of how Deslie was not of this country, really, any more than Billy himself was. Yet Deslie seemed so confident of who he was. At least, more so than Billy; take away his job at the school and what's left?

They all crouched in the shade of the bus and lunched on fish, oysters, sandwiches from school, cordial. 'You ever hear them spirits, them devils in the mangroves, Miss? You know 'bout them?' asked Margaret. 'They got long long hair, and the men, long beards. You hear them, when it's quiet, if you careful. 'Bout sunset time. Little sounds you know. Them men ones sneak up behind you and steal you away. The women try to whistle, warn you. You know Walanguh, old Walanguh? They took him when he a baby and he did stay with them. That be why his hair all white.'

They were all watching Billy and Liz, hands frozen in the act of delivering food to their mouths.

'True? Is that true?'

'Yes, that what they say. It true I think, you hear them. My daddy he saw one, one time, at Murugudda.' They all quietly agreed.

They were in the bus, with its motor idling, when Deslie remembered he'd left his fishing line on the rocks near the mangroves. He ran to collect it. They watched him running back to the bus through the soft white sand, grinning at them. Behind him the rich blue sea suddenly erupted. A huge manta ray burst into the air close to the shore, and they could see the ocean cascading from its back and beneath it the torn and foaming whorl it had left. For a moment it hung, impossibly, in the air, then fell with a great splash. They could breathe again. Liz felt the bus should have burst into cheering. Deslie looked at them, behind him, at them, and ran faster, not laughing now.

(From *True Country*, a novel, 1994.)

C O N N I E   E L L E M E N T   &
R O N   D A V I D S O N

THE GHOST IN THE
RAINWATER TANK

'What duty have you been on, Margaret?' I asked my friend as she joined the line stretching across the courtyard to wait for the tea bell to ring.

'I've been on charlies,' she said with a marked lack of enthusiasm.

Being on charlies was not a high-ranking duty. Girls thus engaged were always treated with condescension by friends holding superior duties such as officers' table, reception room, laundry or kitchen duty. Being on charlies brought with it a deep sense of inferiority, for charlies were enamel chamber-pots which the girl on charlies distributed nightly to every dormitory. They were placed discreetly out of sight beneath the beds. Each morning, the contents were emptied into a bucket and, after the pots were piled on top of each other, they were carried to an isolated spot near the dressing-room. There, the pots were washed, wiped and stacked before being consigned to a cupboard.

'Serves you right,' I said unfeelingly.

'Why does it serve me right?'

'Well, you went and got saved when you promised not to.'

'I didn't mean to,' Margaret replied apologetically.

'What do you mean, you didn't mean to?'

'It was a mistake.'

'Don't be silly. How could it be a mistake?' I asked.

'Easy,' said Margaret, eager to reinstate herself in my

affection. 'I thought Lieutenant was asking for singers — not sinners — to come forward. I thought if I sang nicely enough, I might get into The Company. She was so happy to see me that I had to let her save me.'

'Never mind, Matron's reading the new duty roster tonight,' I said. 'We might even get laundry duty. That's fun. I'm tired of being on toothbrush duty. The kids fight you all the time. Although it's much more important than being on charlies.'

I told Margaret about toothbrush duty. First, you reported to Lieutenant and she gave you the toothbrush board, a jar of carb soda and a notebook with all the kids' names in it. There was a loop on the top of the board through which you placed your head so that your arms were free to dole out the carb soda and the toothbrushes, and to tick off the names of children after they had cleaned their teeth.

Strips of tape were tacked in loops across the board and into each numbered loop was inserted a toothbrush bearing the same number.

In the notebook were listed names and numbers of all the orphans and each reported for her toothbrush. I fought many a battle as my clients complained about the quantity of the carb soda I poured sparingly into the palms of their hands, questioned whether I'd given them the correct brushes, or grumbled because moisture had oozed from used brushes above and dampened theirs.

I was constantly accused of double-dealing with the toothbrushes. Wars raged with unabated fury. The major cause of mix-ups was smudged numbering which made for considerable trouble when subsequently I failed to identify a brush correctly. Brush owners had an uncanny knack of identifying their own even though the uniform shade of cream must have made such identification difficult. When the battle reached fever pitch, Lieutenant Bradfield acted as mediator and solved the problem by boiling all the brushes and starting again.

I carried out toothbrush duty with a fervour our more fanatical officers would have envied, feeling not a little power drunk as I stood outside the washroom checking the numbers in the notebook. Having identified the would-be defaulters, I shouted their names enthusiastically. I repeated them until shame sent each defaulter running to apply for brush and carb soda. At last, when all teeth were cleaned, I merely wet my brush, ticked off my name and applied for dismissal, teeth unbrushed.

Margaret looked unimpressed despite my efforts to emphasise the importance of my duty.

'Wouldn't it be good if we were placed on laundry duty together? Stamping blankets is fun,' I said.

'I don't want to go on laundry duty, because there's a ghost up there,' Margaret declared.

'Where?' I asked.

'In the rainwater tank just outside the laundry. All the kids know about it. It throws the bucket at them.'

'It's not fair,' I declared, changing the subject abruptly.

'What's not fair?'

'Me being in pop each afternoon, and I don't see how I can ever get out.'

'Why not?'

'I'm in pop now because I told a kid about seeing a ghost in the dormitory. Well, if I said I didn't see the ghost, I'd be telling lies and God would be angry, and when I died, He'd send me to hell. Just because Lieutenant didn't see the ghost, she reckons my story isn't true.'

The pealing of the second tea bell interrupted this line of thought. 'Attention! Left turn! Quick march!' called Lieutenant Bradfield, then she stood at the salute as we marched into the dining room. As we passed her, the salute was returned with varying degrees of enthusiasm. Quietly, we filed into place behind our chairs and waited. As the presiding officer struck the opening chords on the piano, we sang grace:

> *Be present at our table, Lord.*
> *Be here and everywhere adored.*
> *These mercies bless, and grant that we,*
> *Shall live in Paradise with Thee. Amen.*

Then at a given signal, we pulled back our chairs to seat

ourselves before our regular evening meal. It was always four half slices of bread topped with margarine, treacle, syrup and jam, one of each. We called it bread and scrape. The topping was scraped on, then off again. This was followed by a cup of weak tea.

The meal was eaten quickly, then girls seated at the inside of the tables turned their chairs around and faced the officers seated at the far end of the hall. Tonight, it was Lieutenant Bradfield's turn to read the Scriptures.

As the evening prayer meeting began, I was restless. Although I enjoyed the community singing immensely, I often found the sermons tiring. I had heard the same theme expounded so many times in so many different ways. It was always the same theme: CHOOSE! CHOOSE! CHOOSE! Choose between God and the devil! Choose between the rose-strewn path leading to hell and the thorny road to heaven! Salvation or damnation? What was it to be? To step to one side was to betray my fun-loving friends; to step the other way was to betray my guardians. If only there was a middle course! It was hard to be good.

I thought that maybe officers were different from orphans, as they were so overwhelmingly confident that death would ensure their Promotion to Glory. And they seemed equally certain that the kids would burn eternally in hellfire, despite the fact that they spent many hours begging, pleading and beseeching us to seek salvation before it was too late. I stared at each of the officers in turn. That way, I thought I might be able to see what made them so different from us. Sure enough, I detected a faint glow of light surrounding each head.

Lieutenant Bradfield was only now beginning to master the art of projecting her voice. She was battling to emphasise the power of the passage she was reading and project it down the long, beautifully decorated dining room.

And it came to pass on the third day in the morning that there was a thick cloud upon the mount, and the voice of the trumpet exceedingly loud, so that all the people in the camp trembled. And Moses brought

forth the people out of the camp to meet with God,
and they stood on the nether part of the mount. And
the voice of the trumpet waxed louder and louder
and there was thunder and lightning and God spoke
unto Moses saying ...

'Connie, will you please stop fidgeting!'

Our enjoyment of any such statement was, of necessity, deferred. We were too scared of Matron to laugh openly, but many throats were cleared and many an elbow nudged a fellow orphan's ribs as the lesson proceeded.

At last, the closing hymn was sung: it was Matron's favourite, 'Choose Ye Today'.

Only with an effort did we contain our excitement as Lieutenant Bradfield sat down and Matron rose. Keenly conscious of the suspense, she shuffled and reshuffled her papers. She then cleared her throat and began to read the new duty roster.

'Hazel — No. 3 dormitory; Evelyn — officers' table ...'

We waited anxiously as each name was called and its owner locked glances with a mate to register triumph or disgust.

'Laundry duty — Maude, Margaret, Edna, Dolphino, Mollie, Connie ...'

I echoed the words as if they were sacred: 'Laundry duty!' This was the promotion I had long coveted. It meant freedom, if only fleeting, from the tyranny of the bell that heralded every phase of the day. It meant getting up at five o'clock in the morning and eating breakfast picnic-fashion in the laundry with as little interruption as possible. I knew it would give me a great rise in status. It would be wonderful to be able to peep out of the laundry door and grin patronisingly at those less fortunate who were left to stand in line waiting for the breakfast bell to sound.

Then an unwelcome thought intruded: what about the ghost?

'Margaret, that ghost — it isn't really true is it?' I whispered at lights out, which automatically brought with it an order of silence.

'Yes, of course it's true,' Margaret answered happily. 'You're not scared of it, are you? I'm not and I'm on laundry duty, too.'

'Of course I'm scared,' I spluttered, without noticing that Margaret had changed her views about fearing ghosts.

'Never mind, I think it's a kind ghost,' said Margaret. 'The kids reckon it likes to play. It only throws the bucket at you. It doesn't do anything else.'

As the early morning light filtered through the dormitory windows, Lieutenant Bradfield walked from dormitory to dormitory to awaken the laundry duty girls. I rubbed the sleep from my eyes as her torch shone in my face.

'I want you to go ahead and light the copper fires. Here are the matches. Hurry. I want you to have the water warm by the time the other girls join you.'

I fondled the small box. Striking a match had become an ambition I had hoped some day to attain. It was also a tribute to my trustworthiness. And this I thought I had forfeited for all the time when I stubbornly refused to say that my ghost story was false.

The crisp morning air served to increase my elation. This was adventure indeed, one that could only be equalled by great adventures like joining the French Foreign Legion I had heard my brother talk about. However, I was scared as I tiptoed through the shadowy hallways. Ghosts might lurk in the shadows and, if Margaret's gran could be believed, they differed as much in temperament as mortals did. It was wise to be wary.

Lieutenant Bradfield always said that prayers and hymns were the weapons good Salvationists used to frighten away the forces of evil. Spontaneously I broke into song as I stepped out onto the asphalt path:

> *Jesus Saviour pilot me,*
> *Over life's tempestuous sea;*
> *Boisterous waves obey Thy will,*
> *When Thou say'st to them be still.*
> *Wondrous Sovereign of the sea,*
> *Jesus Saviour pilot me.*

The song lifted my spirits, but as I reached the laundry door and peeped in, the large mangle standing in the corner draped with sheets looked like a ghostly creature with outstretched arms waiting to grab me.

'Choose!' it seemed to be saying. 'Choose! Choose between me and Matron! You can't follow us both.' I thought for a moment that it may be easier to follow the mangle than Matron.

To follow Matron was so difficult. She told us: 'Obey! Obey! Obey! Open your eyes! Close your eyes! Stand up! Sit down! Kneel! Don't dare be impudent!' And yet she often used as her closing hymn:

> *Dare to be a Daniel,*
> *Dare to stand alone,*
> *Dare to have a purpose true,*
> *And dare to make it known,*
> *Hold the Gospel banner high,*
> *On to victory.*
> *Satan and his hosts defy,*
> *And shout for Daniel's band.*

How could we shout for Daniel's band when we were ordered not to speak? It was easy to be brave and imagine yourself facing a savage lion while singing with ninety-nine other kids. But to be all alone with ghosts in a silent laundry, with no witnesses to your courage, was much more difficult.

It was comforting to know Margaret was on laundry duty. After all, she knew all about ghosts and she was saved, even if only by mistake.

Summoning my ebbing courage, I stepped into the laundry and, keeping an eye on the mangle, I gathered some coke, wood, chips and paper and carried them toward the coppers. I then bundled them into the grate and struck a match. As the kindling burst into flame, I huddled close to the copper and watched the flickering shadows about me. The shadows made it seem that ghosts were everywhere, but the warmth was comforting.

I had never sat before an open fire before, but I knew that hunters lit fires to protect them from marauding animals and it sure kept dingoes at bay. I took refuge in the thought that perhaps ghosts also were afraid of fire. Why couldn't Matron and Lieutenant be more understanding about ghosts?

It was hard not to talk about such an interesting subject even if only to oneself, and I thought it was better to talk while there was still time. Only the other day, Matron had said that soon it would be possible for her, at the flick of a switch, to hear every word we were saying around the orphanage.

I was pondering the dangers that this machine would pose for me when Lieutenant Bradfield's voice broke in on my thoughts. 'Good girl,' she said, 'I see you have the fires burning. The other girls will be here soon. I want them to stamp the blankets in these troughs. I have already placed the soap suds and water in them and I want you to fill the rinsing troughs with rainwater. Bring it in from the tank outside. It is much softer for rinsing, and ...'

With great daring, I interrupted. 'Please Lieutenant, can't I stamp the blankets just this once?'

Lieutenant clicked her tongue impatiently. 'You know I don't make the rules. I am a Solider, just the same as you are. I am on duty and, like you, I must do as I am told. Besides, if I give an inch, you children take a yard!'

'But Lieutenant, there's a ghost in the tank,' I pleaded, throwing caution to the wind. 'It threw the bucket at Edna one day. Truly it did.'

'Really, Connie, you're incorrigible! When will you learn? Ghosts do not exist so they cannot hurt people.' Gently, she pushed me towards the tank. 'Come on, there's no time like the present.'

As Lieutenant returned briskly down the path I stared at the tank. Duty was duty; to fail and forfeit the prestige I had just gained was unthinkable. I knew I would never be able to convince Lieutenant about the ghost.

I turned the bucket upside-down and sat down and pondered my dilemma. Soon I heard my friends coming up the path and I hurried to greet them. Their progress was slow because each girl was bent almost double, the better to carry the bundle of blankets tied in a sheet and slung on her back.

39

'Good morning, Margaret,' I greeted my friend. 'How about changing duties with me?'

Margaret swung her bundle from her back and faced me. 'Why?' she asked cautiously. I decided to be frank.

'Because I'm on tank duty and I'm scared.'

'Well, I'm scared too!'

'But you shouldn't be because you're saved. Besides, if the ghost is really in the tank, you should be able to convert it.'

'Think you're smart, don't you?' Margaret sniffed. 'I'm not going on tank duty, so there!' and, turning, she stooped to drag her bundle up the steps into the laundry. The others were already taking their shoes off in preparation for their job.

Perhaps, I thought in desperation, I'd better kneel down here and now and get saved. But hard on this thought came the realisation that God knew everything and any prayer for conversion now would be rejected on the grounds of insincerity. Maybe tomorrow night. No, that wouldn't do! The ghost had to be faced now, and maybe tomorrow morning after breakfast Matron would again be intoning the two words she always used with such a wealth of meaning: 'Too late!' Too late if the ghost had already killed me. I would meet so many sinners and have the brand of sin imprinted on my soul.

I thought again about Margaret. It wasn't fair of her to get saved after saying she wouldn't, and, to make matters worse, she was revelling in luxury in the laundry. Indifferent to my misery, she climbed up into a trough singing happily:

> *I feel like singing all the time,*
> *My tears are wiped away,*
> *For Jesus is a friend of mine,*
> *I'll serve Him every day.*

Quickly, the tune changed to provide a more thrusting tempo as the girls drove their feet into the blankets. They now sang:

> *With banner wide unfurled,*
> *We'll tell to all the world:*
> *The blood of Jesus cleanses white as snow.*

And the Aboriginal twins, Sally and Mary, talking the alto, reiterated in a lower key:

Yes, I know. Yes, I know.

Drawn irresistibly by the singing and the sound of splashing feet, I picked up the bucket and walked into the laundry, impulsively ignoring the work I should have started. I leaned against the pine table and stared enviously at my friends. Two girls stood facing each other in each of three troughs, their frocks tucked tightly into the elastic of their combinations. They clasped each other by the shoulders, their knees rising and falling to the rhythm of the tune they sang, the white foaming suds billowing high about their thighs.

'You'll get copped.'

The singing ceased as they saw I was inside and Margaret paused to call a warning. 'You'd better start carrying the water.'

'Yes, you'll get more pop,' said Edna.

'I won't,' I replied defiantly. 'I dare you kids to come and march around the table with me rather than following orders. Come on. I dare you.'

The stamping feet slowed then stopped as the girls stared at me. I stared back. A variety of expressions flitted across Margaret's face. She, too, was beginning to have problems choosing. What would be worse, breaking her conversion or refusing to accept a dare from a mate? At last, she climbed slowly from the trough and wiped her feet on the rough hessian towel provided for that purpose.

Quickly, the others followed.

'Quick march,' I ordered as the last girl stood in line behind me. They lifted their knees in the exaggerated marching style of some of our officers as I began to bellow a parody of a popular hymn:

> *Steadily forward march,*
> *To Jesus we will bring,*
> *Sinners of every kind,*
> *The Lord will take them in.*

41

The rich, and the poor as well,
It doesn't matter who,
BRING THEM IN AND CHAIN THEM UP,
AND TELL THEM WHAT TO DO.

Lieutenant Bradfield's piercing voice brought the march to a halt and seven pairs of eyes stared at her in dismay. 'What is the meaning of this? Have you any excuse to offer?'

'Please, Lieutenant, it's the ghost,' I muttered miserably. 'I was only trying to get the other kids to help scare it off.' My voice trailed away. I threw a pleading glance in Margaret's direction, but her word wouldn't do, either. She had just broken her conversion.

But Lieutenant was again speaking, and in a tone that brooked no nonsense. 'You girls go back to your work. Connie and Maude come with me. Bring a bucket.'

'Now, Connie, fill the bucket,' she commanded as we faced the tank.

I looked intently at Lieutenant's face. It was no use. There was no relenting there. I reached out to turn the tap. As I did, the bucket leapt into the air and an invisible hand seemed to snatch me up then drop me roughly on my back on the gravel.

As I awakened, a million glistening diamond shapes clustered in a heap before my eyes. Slowly, they detached themselves, one by one, from the glowing mass and began to float away and dissolve into the darkness that had enshrouded me. At last, I managed to focus and I realised I was the centre of attention. Margaret was staring alternately at me and at Lieutenant Bradfield whose face was ashen with shock. Lieutenant tried to speak, but the words would not come out.

Finally, she managed to speak. 'We'll all be killed! We'll all be killed!' she gasped. 'I must find an electrician. Don't touch the tank!'

'What's an electrician?' I asked Margaret as the Lieutenant rushed away.

'Dunno,' said Margaret. 'I expect he's someone who kills ghosts.'

I was ecstatic. I would soon be out of pop. Lieutenant must

know now that ghosts existed.

Margaret was less elated. 'What did you make me break my conversion for?' she complained. 'I won't go to heaven now that I'm not saved.'

'Never mind,' I reassured her, 'it can't be a very nice place. Lieutenant seemed awfully scared of going there just then.'

'Am I am backslider now?' asked Margaret. I agreed that she was and I think we both agreed that backsliding was not all that bad a thing. Margaret smirked as she savoured the fresh experience. She said brightly, 'Let's dare the other kids to touch the tank.'

(From *The Divided Kingdom,* an autobiography, 1987.)

THE BOAR

In September, just after my twelfth birthday, Frank wanted a boar pig for his six breeding sows. He had bought the sows and they all had little ones which were now being weaned. Some had already been weaned and were getting into the porker stage. Frank borrowed a large black boar from his brother-in-law. This boar was very savage and every time I went to feed the pigs he tried to attack me. I had to be very careful; he had large tusks and he used to froth at the mouth. I had to jump from pigpen to pigpen to dodge him when feeding them. I was scared stiff of this boar and he seemed to know it. As soon as I went near the pigpen he would have his eye on me.

One morning early in October, when the weather was getting much warmer, I was passing the pigpen to get the horses in. The boar seemed worse than ever. He never usually bothered me when I was just passing, but for some reason this morning he left the sows and ran down to the fence near where I was walking. He was frothing at the mouth and making a kind of roaring sound.

At first it didn't worry me, but then he tried twice to get through the fence. The pig fence joined the race where I had to bring the horses, and if the pig did get through my chances against him were nil. I reached the corner of the piggery; beyond that point there was bush and trees. The boar followed the fence along to the corner. I felt gamer now — I had the trees and scrub to run to if he got out.

Being a boy, I couldn't resist heaving a rock at the boar. When I did this he made one terrific charge at the fence and came straight through and after me. I ran for a large tree leaning at about a forty-five degree angle. It was a she-oak tree with a lot of small limbs attached to its trunk and, with the boar right on my heels, I bounded up it. I had never known my luck. I was just in time — another two yards and he would have had me.

The boar tried to climb the tree but without success. So there I was, up in this tree. It was the nicest tree I had known, and I was pretty safe as long as I could stay where I was. But what about the horses? The sun had begun to rise. The boar at first sat on his haunches looking up at me. Then he rooted a furrow under the tree big enough for his body and lay down.

I was trying to think of a way out of this pickle that I was in. The sun was getting well up into the sky, and guessing by the way my bottom and legs were aching, I had been there about an hour or so. I broke off some small branches and used them as spears. Each time I speared the boar he would get up, walk around the tree, let out a roar, then go back to his furrow and lie down again.

Then, looking down to the house, I saw Frank walking towards us. This horrified me and I wondered how I could warn him about the boar. I made up my mind to call out to him when he got within hearing distance. But Frank had other ideas. He took no notice of me, although I was yelling at the top of my voice. I paused to hear what he was calling out to me and I heard him saying, 'I'll give you bird's-nesting when I send you to get the horses.' I called out to him that the boar was loose and that he was here under the tree, but Frank was too riled up and kept coming. Then all at once the boar got up and bounded towards him. As soon as Frank knew the danger he turned and ran for the house.

It was downhill and if anyone had told me that Frank could run as fast as he did I wouldn't have believed them. He had a little luck because at one stage the boar almost grabbed him. Frank was running along the side of the track and there was a heap of stones about two feet high. Frank jumped this but the boar, being so intent on getting Frank, didn't see the stones and struck them with his front legs. He fell heavily and that saved Frank.

Frank got inside the house and slammed the door shut. I got

down out of the tree and set off for the horses. Then I heard two loud gunshots almost together and I wondered if he had shot the boar. When I returned to the house I saw the boar lying dead about ten feet from the door of the house. Mum had told me several times about Frank's temper but this was the first time I had seen him properly raged.

My feelings had changed several times during the few minutes of the race between the pig and old Frank. At first I felt amused, then my feelings turned to fear as the boar was catching him, then relief when the boar fell. The fear again gripped me until Frank dashed through the door and shut it. When this happened I felt complete relief.

Frank never said a word when I returned to the house for my breakfast. He looked terribly upset. When Mum gave me my breakfast she asked me what had made the boar get through the pig paddock. I said that I didn't know but that he had seemed extra savage that morning.

Old Frank usually never took the team out until after the midday meal. That morning he went over and told Jack Connor, Mum's brother, what had happened. When he returned he was very upset and I heard him say to Mum that her brother was a dirty scoundrel. She didn't like this and they had a real go-in. At first I thought he was going to hit her but he didn't. He went over to the stable and harnessed the horses and took them out ploughing — he wouldn't stop to have his dinner.

When I went in to dinner Mum remarked, 'Now Bert, you have seen Frank in a temper. What do you think of it?' I said that he goes pretty mad and she said that if he ever got that way to keep away from him. She said that he soon cooled down and that he would be all right again that night. I asked what her brother said about the shooting of his boar. She told me that he had made Frank pay ten pounds. He thought that the boar was worth that but they knew it had only cost him two pounds. Mum said, 'Jack is like that. He would take his own mother down if he could.'

When Frank came in that night he had gotten over the whole upset and was quite jolly. He said to me, 'What went through your mind, Bert, when the boar was chasing me down the hill?'

I told him about my changed feelings. He laughed and said that he had never got to the house quicker and that the boar nearly had him once, but fell behind. He could almost feel the boar's teeth. He didn't know what had happened because he didn't have time to look behind. I told him about the rocks and said that I felt sure they had saved his life. He said, 'Oh well, it's over now. Did Mum tell you what that miserable sod valued that boar at? To think that I nearly lost my life.'

The next morning he sent me over to the plough to get a swingle bar and a set of chains. He brought a harnessed horse up to the house and fixed a chain around the pig's head and dragged it into a timbered paddock where we piled up logs and bushes over it and burnt it.

(From *A Fortunate Life,* an autobiography, 1981.)

GAIL JONES

KNOWLEDGE

On the remote and tiny island off northern Australia where my mother and father worked as missionaries there was one area of beach I was prohibited to visit. It was, my father explained, some kind of cleansing beach, a place where the Aboriginal people, in times of intolerable distress or guilt, walked into the sea, cast off their clothes, and then, after whatever due ceremony or act of communion, re-emerged naked to the world and mysteriously renewed. I would know this special beach, my father warned, by the odd litter of clothing thrown back by the sea, and if, by chance, I ever came upon this beach, this unusual beach of littered clothes, then I must turn the other way, and walk back to the place from which I had come.

Even then I understood that it was nakedness not sacredness that caused my father's warning. He had no particular respect for Aboriginal culture; indeed he was doing his utmost to dissuade the people from their tribal ways. It was with contempt and with a peculiar contraction of the lips — which seemed to signify an almost physical sensation of disgust — that he spoke of their dances and fights, their sucking at turtles' eggs and scooping at the bellies of fish, their laborious body painting, their elaborate funerals, their night-time descriptions of their own cosmogony. The things that fascinated me he regarded as primitive and in need of conversion. He would shake his grey head and with a melancholy tone of false solicitude lament that the Aboriginal people were insufficiently intelligent to see the wisdom of his ways. To me this opinion was inexplicable: it was only later that I realised that contempt, like hatred, actually explains everything.

This story, I suppose, is of a pair of gloves. They arrived one day at our island community along with dozens of miscellaneous items of cast-off clothes. From time to time white people in the South would send, without warning, large canvas bags which were stamped in red ink with the mysterious legend AIM. The arrival of these bags was always a pleasure and even though I was not permitted to participate in the sharing I enjoyed watching the people unpack and distribute each item of clothing according to scrupulous and cunning codes of fairness and need.

We gathered beneath the mango tree that grew behind the church, sat ourselves down in a rough circle upon the dirt, and a nominated woman — usually Mary Magdalene — would, with great solemnity and purpose, cut open each bag and reveal its gifts. Unseasonable sweaters (left behind after football matches), copious floral frocks (discarded, presumably, after slimming routines), tee-shirts (washed unwisely to a state of unflattering shapelessness), trousers (from dead men), shoes (out of fashion), skirts, blouses, even suspenders: all sprang from the AIM bag, carrying with them their ghostly implications of invisible lives lived in faraway places. Mary Magdalene would dangle each item for a brief inspection, and then after laughter, exclamations, suggestions and contestation, nominate decisively the new recipient. Being a person of suave and subtle command she was rarely contradicted.

On the day of the gloves I recall that there were two other unusual items on display. The first, which was greeted by a shriek of embarrassed giggles, was an extraordinary gown which I took to be a wealthy woman's nightie or petticoat. It was pearl-coloured, diaphanous and intricately gold-threaded, and Mary Magdalene flung it over our heads to a young woman named Rebekah, who was about to be married. Rebekah, I remember, held the lovely petticoat across her hips, shyly exhilarated; and then catching by accident the gaze of her lover, buried her face in its folds, mock-virginal and pleased.

The other item of clothing, one even more fabulous and strangely dislocated, was an ancient fox fur, the type that women in magazines might wear draped at their necks. This object caused a general stir of consternation, and Mary Magdalene seemed wholly unsure of its use. She held the fur at arm's length and sent a small child to summon old-man Francis Xavier for his wisdom and advice. He arrived, examined the fur, and declaring in his own language that it was nobody's totem, flung it ostentatiously to the waiting dogs. Commotion erupted as the animals tore at the fur and above us black flying foxes shuddered in the mango leaves and shifted their shapes nervously in response to the din.

All of the clothes had apparently been displayed and distributed, the flying foxes had resettled, the dogs, disconsolate, lay resting in the dust among little fragments of now unidentifiable fox, when Mary Magdalene upended the last of the AIM bags to reveal a pair of gloves. They plopped gently at her feet, like two pathetic hands in weary supplication; they were white and embroidered and struck me as objects of the most astonishing delicacy. I had never in fact seen a pair of real gloves before, and they were so ingeniously hand-like, so redolent of another order where even fingers are clothed, where one touches fastidiously and points and caresses beneath a smooth enveloping surface, elegantly drawn on, digit by extended digit — drawn on, no doubt, to the accompaniment of whining violins and curling wreaths of blue-grey smoke — so redolent were these gloves that I longed to possess them. They were distinctively otherworldly, foreign, adorable. Wallpapered interiors opened in my mind. There were velvety surfaces, embossed upholstery and high-toned tinklings from prismatic glass. And from somewhere unseen in this private province a copper light entered, bringing peach tones to the furniture and pretty moon-shaped shines to the surfaces of paperweights and burnished vases ...

I knew from experience that such impractical objects as gloves would not be valued by the community, and, as it happened, I was absolutely correct. There were a few faint murmurs of curiosity, but no one seemed to think that they were at all worth claiming.

To my surprise, however, Mary Magdalene took up the gloves and with no consultation stuffed them pre-emptively in the front of her shirt and declared the clothes distribution over. There was no sense in which this was a crudely appropriative gesture; she simply took the unwanted gloves and efficiently dismissed us.

My heart began to swell in self-conscious anger. There were inner functions and disturbances which registered — how shall I put it? — the childish beginnings of the sin of covetousness.

I am not sure, even now, why the gloves so entranced me, but I think it may have been connected to a visit to the cinema. Once when I was seven, or perhaps six years old, I flew with my mother in the small mail plane south-west across the sea to the town of Darwin. The actual purpose of our visit was a new set of maternal dentures, but to me it centred entirely on a promised cinematic occasion.

The movie that we saw — illicitly, given my father's beliefs — was in black and white, but utterly impressive. It was like a kind of dreaming, fluid and non-participatory, effortless and ineluctable. And there, dreaming awake, in the warm embrace of darkness, I saw in gigantic projection the most brilliant of scenes and occurrences. An unknown city. Houses of impossible and imposing solidity filled to the brim with objects from storybooks. There were singing and dancing and beautiful Audrey Hepburn. There were men with heads thrown back as they smoked slim cigarettes, women in hats and gloves who peered over their sunglasses, cars without roofs and scarves in the wind, gyrations on dance floors and bristling intimacy, and one long orchestrated kiss, breathtakingly held. I sat wholly agape, stunned by what my mother later called 'civilisation'.

(And she forbade me absolutely to tell my father of the movie. Our own little secret, she whispered in my ear).

When I saw the gloves from the AIM bag perhaps I recalled certain images from the movie several years before. More puzzlingly, though, I was simply consumed by an unpremeditated desire, by a kind of imprecise longing, stringent as hunger. For days I could think of nothing but the gloves, and moved through the community annoyed and preoccupied. Mary Magdalene, whom I had loved, became the special object of my anger and ill-feeling, yet I did not ask her for the gloves — somehow it never occurred to me — I simply resented her possession.

At night I lay beneath my mosquito net listening to the Aboriginal songs arising through the dark from the campsite beyond our fence. Clapsticks struck and voices rose. I listened to the cycles of tribal chants telling of ancestors and rainmaking, and I thought, not as usual of the conjured images of the songs, of sweeping monsoons bending low the pandanus, of the spearing of dugong or the transformation of sisters into stars or birds; I thought instead of a white woman who, with long gloves, moved in slow motion down a curved flight of stairs and accepted a triangle shaped glass in a gesture of haughty and experienced seduction. This woman of my imagining wore a diaphanous petticoat and a fox fur at her throat, but her distinction, her supremacy, her all-time claim-to-fame, was marked most specifically by her dazzling gloves. I heard the voices through the night, mythological and familiar, and constructed, as though in some kind of strict competition, my immaculately gloved woman to contest and denounce them.

The gloves disappeared for several weeks but then reappeared conspicuously at Rebekah's wedding. Weddings were insisted upon by the mission authorities, but the people of the island treated them with a mixture of vague derision and half-hearted enthusiasm.

Mary Magdalene attended the wedding wearing my pair of white gloves. I remember thinking how ludicrous and misplaced they looked, how they were unsuited to black skin, how rather than clothing or ensheathing her arms they appeared stuck on and superfluous. My envy was huge. I sat in the middle row between my friends Rachel and Hepzibah and became gradually aware — quite unexpectedly — of something anomalous and odd in my situation. It was not anything which I could comprehend or even identify, it was some minor revelation of disjunction or difficulty, a feeling which, in my pique, I was able to hastily attribute to Mary Magdalene's too-flagrant exhibition of my gloves. But as I sat in the pew, suddenly everything appeared particularly concentrated and clear, so that now I remember the wedding scene in each exact, perspicuous detail.

A yellow light fell brightly through the doors of the church — for it was little more than a shed, mostly open at both sides — and lay across the earth floor, not quite reaching where my father stood. There was an altar decorated in Aboriginal designs, with X-rayed fish and patterns of crosshatching, and above it a wooden cross, robustly hewn. My father stood before the altar with the bible in his hands; he was robed and authoritative, and spoke in an unusual and extremely loud voice, as though the church were not of bark but some vaulted and echoing cathedral of marble and stone. I remember thinking for the first time: my father is annoyed; this is a voice of annoyance; this is unholy, improper.

Before my father kneeled Rebekah and Jacob Njabalerra, she in the communal wedding dress which I had seen several times before and which now barely contained her swelling stomach, he in a new-secondhand AIM shirt of cowboy checks. Both Rebekah and Jacob were bent low before my father as though receiving remonstration. My mother, I noticed, was seated in the very front row of the church and she too was bent over. Her head was bowed and submissive and I somewhat precociously thought: this is as she always is, my mother bowed thus, hunched before my father. The nape of her neck appeared exposed and pitiable and my unclear sense of disjunction resolved around its image.

I instantaneously felt what I can only now describe as the profundity of dissent. I hated my father. I hated his voice as it married the couple. I hated the rustle of his robes and the largeness of his hands. His deliberative actions. His presence. His face. I was pleased to be sitting at a critical distance.

It was at this point that Mary Magdalene turned and smiled indulgently and waved a gloved hand at me. Sitting next to her Joseph, her older husband, also abruptly turned, as though curious to see what had caught his wife's attention. He too gave me a wave, spontaneously complicit with Mary Magdalene's offering. Beside me Rachel and Hepzibah snickered a little, but I was caught in a moment of confused response. Anger and envy competed with shame. I felt ungenerous and mean. I raised my arm to wave back to Mary Magdalene — it seemed so proper an action, so reciprocally incumbent — and felt the burdensome gloved woman poised on the staircase inside my head begin to insubstantially waver and disperse. I smiled at Mary Magdalene and she continued to smile at me. I saw the lustrous and shining dark of her half-turned face and thought — I remember now — how beautiful her skin was, how it caught, with perfect ease, bows of glaze and illumination from even that shadowy and church enclosed air.

I did not entirely relinquish a hankering for the gloves — my cinema woman's residency was much too tenacious — but reconciled with Mary Magdalene and resumed fishing and gathering food with her. We never spoke of the gloves at all, and I believe she may have guessed that these were the particular, shameful cause of my previous bad humour. It was a subject which remained between us like an invisible canoe. We moved slightly apart, were gentle with each other and tentative in our behaviour. It was as though we balanced a weight, each aware of the poise and cooperation of the other.

Within weeks after the wedding, however, this poise was lost: Mary Magdalene was cast into a terrible despair. Her husband Joseph had been beaten with a nulla-nulla in a fight, and at his death she collapsed into a state of voluble grief, one so extreme in its expression that I dared not approach her.

The mourning cries trailed throughout the campsite. Even closed in our house I heard traces of her voice, eerie and miserable and continuously plaintive. I knew too that Mary Magdalene would be cutting her breasts with stones and tearing distractedly at her hair as she had done, several years before, when her only daughter had died. There was of course also a chorus of other women mourners, but her single voice rose above them and attested a more immediate and individual pain. I could not bear the wailing. I thought of the ash-smeared face and the blood upon her breasts, the body doubled over at a diligent self-mutilation.

Yet it was at dinner time, I remember, when in my own copycat misery, my own version of imagining Mary Magdalene's awful condition, that I insulted finally and irreparably the paternal order of things. My father sat above his meat, stabbing and sawing, and then announced with undisguised impatience and anger:

'Why doesn't that woman shut up? Why must she go on?'

And since I knew the correct answer from Rebekah Njabalerra I could not remain silent.

'Because she fucked Peter Moorla before he killed Joseph.'

There was a dreadful, static silence. My father swallowed his mouthful. My mother hung her head, wretched at my mistake and blushing excessively. And then father arose, thumped at the table, and shouted in a voice I still continue to hear:

'You know nothing at all! Nothing! Nothing!'

He struck the side of my head with such rude intensity that my ear dramatically exploded with blood. Then he strode from the room and was absorbed almost instantly into the gathering darkness.

I did not see Mary Magdalene walk into the sea but I know that she did because I found the gloves at the clothes beach. And although I did not see her I believed I could reconstruct in every single detail exactly what happened.

In the movie in my head she approached the waves very slowly, hesitating at first as though somehow assessing their qualities. Then she would proceed, moving deeper, until the water flowed in gentle eddies and soothing circuits around her body. Her clothes would become liquid and begin to rock against her skin. Then she would submerge entirely, and after a second or two arise, her black skin glistening and bright with rivulets of water, to stretch up her arms and remove her large, loose dress. Then, last of all, she would pull each white glove from each black hand and set them floating beside her, like phantom remnants of another body or some unimaginable life form. She would stay for a few minutes naked in the water, her cut breasts stinging with the salt water, her hair streaming out behind, and then walk back through the waves, slowly and ritualistically. In my vision it was a dark and monsoonal day, so that the sky was grey and the water deep purple. But the remarkable feature of the scene was that despite the lack of light Mary Magdalene's skin was almost blazing with silver. Her nakedness was magnificent.

I cannot exactly recall when I discovered the clothes beach. I had walked much further than usual in the direction I suspected, when I came unprepared and unforewarned upon it. There, in a little bay, feeling at once vaguely treacherous and certainly transgressive, I suddenly saw them. One glove was draped rather tremulously in the mangroves and the second lay, at a small distance, beneath it in the sand. I contemplated the gloves, so vibrantly white, so innocently tide-cast, and realised at once that I knew something with certitude. I knew that the gloves were incorporated into another realm. They were no longer recoverable, no longer desirable, no longer in fact white. The gloves on the clothes beach — formerly so invested with my movie-tone visions — were absolutely transfigured, remade Aboriginal.

(From *The House of Breathing,* short fiction, 1992.)

SIMONE LAZAROO

CHANGING SIDES

At my high school, as in colonial Singapore, a sharp eye for the symptoms of others' unfortunate pasts was an asset in proving one's own superiority. A group of girls lined up at the main school entrance every morning to smoke and sharpen their critical skills on other students. My father observed when he dropped me off at school one morning that these girls were itchified, ripening too early.

But it dawned on me as my second year wore on, that these were in fact cool girls. Truly cool girls actually paid heed to concealing certain aspects of themselves tastefully, whereas these hotly itchified girls did not.

Itchified girls spoke in sentences highly dense with swearwords, tossing them loudly over their shoulders to snare a bit of admiration for themselves. Itchified girls with their blonding rinse and make-up a few shades too bright, were like Grandmother Blessed Miracle in her peplums and fishtail hemlines: having unwittingly put something disgusting from their past on the table for all to see, they tried too desperately to regain acceptance.

Truly cool girls were the ones who had their hair streaked professionally so it wouldn't look too obvious when the roots grew out. They reapplied their non-running mascara and subtly coloured foundation in the toilets every recess, and classified others using high status slang rather than swearwords.

'Wears *high heels* to school. And her lipstick ...'

'A tart.'

'But her brother.'

'Oh, he's, he's a skeg. A spunk.'

They hissed and laughed between themselves, their gossip flushing only just as audibly as the most discreet lavatory cisterns. You needed an unnaturally sensitive nose to even suspect any socially unacceptable pasts were hiding under their beds.

Towards the end of my second year of high school I was still sitting with students who bought their uniforms secondhand, wore lace-up school shoes and did their homework diligently. We were more loosely affiliated than either the cool or the itchified girls.

We spoke in different accents from each other.

We sat together because no one else would have us. Most of us hid some of our unacceptable pasts under our bed or in our lunchboxes. (Although I'd tried hard to give away all things Eurasian, salted plums and saltfish pickle were addictions I continued to administer furtively.)

While we dags might steal an occasional glance from behind our books at the cool and the itchified, they stared at us with blunt gazes and passed comment loudly, the criteria for judging already agreed upon.

'She's a Pommy, that's why her skin's so white. That's why she wears socks with her sandals.'

'My brother says, he'd rather do it with a woman with hairy legs or bad breath than with an Asian.'

So bewildering, to have what came naturally to you diagnosed as symptoms of abnormality. Again and again I tried working up the courage to protest, but again and again I lost my nerve.

My unspoken protests contracted into short alarming stabs of pain in my gut that began visiting me at random moments of the day. There was only one cure that I could see: to be cool like Sue, rather than to guard against early ripening. I was not sure how long this decision had been coming to me, but knew there were several darknesses about my appearance that I would have to alter if I wanted to obliterate my origins and be accepted by Sue and her friends. I would have to aim for as close to their iridescence as depilatories and chemical warfare on my natural colouring would allow.

I tried my new diguises out at home, secretly in front of the mirror at first. I figured it would be better to begin with the least desperate measures. Less chance of appearing itchified. If the most dangerous disguises could be worked up to gradually, perhaps my father could be persuaded to accept them, and perhaps I would be interpreted as cool by my peers.

I plucked my eyebrows.

I streaked my hair, whose pigments were so tenacious that the blonding rinse would only convert it to a dark brownish red.

I shaved my legs, which were so Asian unhairy that the razor had nothing much but skin to pull against.

I went to the dinner table that night with everything red from either plucking, shaving or dyeing, the skin underneath my brows, the colour of my hair, my legs. A tandoori chicken.

I waited for my father to shout at me.

He said nothing. I took heart from this. Maybe changing to a new disguise wasn't going to be as difficult as I thought.

I tried for a blonder rinse.

I applied layer after layer of mascara, following the advice of *Dolly* magazine, using a hairdryer between each application to help my lashes dry quicker. They felt as brittle as the bristles on my hairbrush. I was pleased at this hardness, my new face to wear.

SPOILS

I bought myself a western shirt and even tighter jeans with the earnings from my waitressing job. The first day I wore them around the house, it didn't appear my father would react.

So I put on my new Dr Scholls scuffs. *Kerlack kerlack* I clattered across the tiled floor in front of him.

'Ah yah!' He looked up from his newspaper, annoyed at being interrupted. 'Why you getting about looking so cartoon these days, huh? Itchified, lah! Looking like you want to make si-si!' [Si-si: to urinate.]

'She needs to try out these things,' my mother suggested

'She will be soiled goods before she is sixteen!' he shouted.

'If she does try out a few relationships before she marries, all the better! Then she won't make the same mistakes I did!'

My poor father. Australia had gotten into his women. They had turned on him.

They put on new unwomanly disguises, dressing like itchified cowboys, speaking as if they saw a future away from everything he knew.

AN INVITATION

When Sue had jammed lilly pilly berries onto her barbie doll's breasts, I had been taken aback by her boldness, and I'd suspected hidden knowledge. Now we were in high school she'd take up a pen and draw on the wooden desk tops; waves closing in like the eye of a cyclone; disembodied surfie hairdos (the fringes that defied gravity, the streaks that spoke of a life in the sun); eyes with brows thin as wires and eyelashes jagged as sharks' teeth; bosoms like huge puddings slung in skinny hammocks of bikini tops.

She left messages on the desktops too. *Barbara sux more than eggs* she wrote, and *Stewie wanks to the max.*

Nothing could be more maximum than max. I was overawed by her.

Imagine my surprise when she rang me at home one warm Saturday morning.

'Hullo banana boobs. Sue here.'

I was too stunned to reply.

'Wanna go to the beach with me 's arvo?'

I just managed to refrain from saying, *I'll ask my parents.* I thought hard and fast: my father wasn't home and my mother wasn't so strict about letting me go out unescorted.

'Okay,' I drawled, hoping the time I took to reply would be construed as coolness.

'I'll meet you at the train bridge at Leighton in an hour.' She didn't give me time to reply.

That meant half a mile on foot and twelve miles on three buses, all in an hour. Though their tightness aggravated my occasional stomach pains, I put on my new jeans. In my panic to be on time, I ran all the way to the bus terminus at the shopping centre, my school bag thumping the backs of my knees and pushing me forward to my Australian destiny when I was almost out of breath, *On, go on. Be cool.*

The further away from home I got, the more thorough the gardens and houses became in their efforts to make statements of wealth and style.

Asbestos fences gave way to pillared and wrought metal ones.

The low dronings of swimming pool filters grew more concentrated as the plantings of palms and conifers did.

The car parks and walkways surrounding the shopping centre were empty. Without the activity of expectant customers around it, the concrete-faced buildings sat like monuments to the dead or larger-than-life hermetically sealed eskies, locked, guarding their unmarred contents for changes in fortunes and in the weather.

I was the only passenger on the bus. Several kids I recognised from school glided past my slow bus in the back seats of Mercedes and Volvos.

At the highway, I had to wait fifteen minutes for the bus which went through to Fremantle. While I waited I examined my new jeans, Woolworths own brand, and knew they would not guarantee me Sue's approval. They rucked up above my knee with perspiration. Graeme Donaldson shot me a bemused and derisive glance from the passenger seat of a fast-travelling Volkswagon loaded with surfboards. I was glad to hide on the bus when it arrived.

I finally got to the railway bridge at Leighton, courtesy of a sequence of MTT buses whose schedules were never designed to connect. By the time I arrived at this destination for cool kids, I was sweating over how uncool my own journey was compared with theirs.

THE ASIAN IN ME

Bodies sticky with tanning lotion picked up granules of sand and shell grit. Behind them foam leapt almost fluorescent against the light-infused sky, so that I had to squint. I couldn't see Sue anywhere.

I tried to keep my anxiety in check.

I felt around in my school bag for the packet of cigarettes I'd taken from my mother's kitchen cupboard.

I'd never smoked in my life before. I'd taken them to impress Sue.

I walked a little way down the beach.

She lay under a broken-spoked beach umbrella, looking slightly comatose, mining the sand with her heels.

I breathed a supressed sigh of both anger and relief.

'Got a lift with my brother, he surfs. Couldn't be buggered waiting around the bridge,' she said out of the corner of her mouth, not even looking at me.

I found the brevity of her aqua-coloured bikini quite alarming. I felt hot, overdressed and overloaded. The pain in my gut was so strong I had to work at not walking doubled over.

I put my bag down.

'Brought some cigarettes.' I looked around me and added in a lowered voice, 'thumped them actually.' No need to tell her where from.

I was hoping this pronouncement would impress her. Instead she turned her head to one side and made a small coughing sound, as if she was affronted and wanted to be so privately.

I felt myself blushing.

Neither of us referred to the cigarettes again that afternoon.

'Wanna go for a swim?' Sue asked through her mouthful of hair.

She stood up and observed me while I took my jeans and shirt off.

I was wearing my sister's one-piece bathers, made of material as thick as carpet.

I nearly ran to hide myself in the sea.

We swam around in separate aimless circles.

I waited until she left the water and started walking back towards the towels before I emerged from the water. I ran towards my own towel and wrapped myself in it while she still had her back to me.

A young man in red speedos jogged past us.

'Hey girls like a ride on my ten inches? It's big enough for both of you,' Sue parodied in a low voice.

Sue's jokes made me feel shy about laughing, as if I didn't really understand what they were about. I felt myself blush but managed a snigger. We subsided into the sand on our stomachs for some moments, leaning our chins on our forearms, looking at the crowd in the surf through half-closed eyes.

Sue rolled over onto her back. 'Ya wanna go see a film? With some guys I know? Gotta car.'

'Okay.' I didn't want to think about getting permission from my father. Lying on the beach like that with a girl like Sue, I wanted to pretend that nothing mattered. I felt as if I had stepped into a place of limitless light and potential, away from my home where the hidden and dark past lay waiting to sabotage my bright future.

When Sue finally spoke again, she spoke as as if she was depending intently on my reaction to her question, but her eyes were averted: 'Do you think girls who have *done it* are sluts?'

I was alarmed by her question. I had never thought about such things in these terms, but something beseeching about her tone of voice warned me that it was important that I reply, as sincerely as I could, 'No.'

Sue looked at me gratefully. 'I always think of you as being such a dag, but it's just that you're so calm and quiet. You know, I am like this ...' she smacked one hand vertically against the other and upwards, like a storm wave colliding against a rock '... and you are like this ...' she motioned gentle unbreaking waves using one hand held horizontally, fingers spread, palm down. 'It must be the Asian in you.'

So, it still showed. Despite my bleachings and other modifications for the market, my Asianness showed. Perhaps that explained the rolling and gripping in my gut. Perhaps, to spite all my efforts at external improvement, my gut harboured my repressed Asianness like it would a disease.

The evening I asked my father for permission to go to the pictures with Sue and the guys with the car, my twin sister sat listening.

My twin sister has always been much more delicate in appearance than me, and never more so than when I was in third year high school toughening up my hide. She had finely attenuated fingers so flexible that they arched backwards slightly, even in repose. Her eyes were dark, shaped like bay leaves and tilted slightly up at the outer corners.

The other curves of her face, too, seemed as constrained and idealised as Sanskrit script, making the typical expression on her face difficult to read. I thought this had something to do with her looking more Asian than I. I'd seen the feature articles in the newspapers and on the television, full of observations on *the inscrutability of our Asian neighbours.*

I disliked the tension her appearance caused me. I was glad she was going to another high school. What I didn't realise was that the expression on her face was a veil of her own making, to protect her against the fecklessness and cruelty of playground taunts.

I read her face from the corner of my eye. If I looked at her straight, she would tighten her mouth and close her fine fingers. Had she always behaved like that?

Her delicate, inhibited mannerisms jarred with the slanging and swagger of the cool kids I'd seen at high school.

I wanted to slang and swear better than any of them.

I practised two finger forks and saying 'suck eggs' while I gulped down my food.

It pained me that my sister's mannerisms just weren't going to be an asset to me out in the playground.

It was the same with her not-talking.

'Is anything wrong with you,' I'd ask her, in the manner of a flat statement.

'No.' She would blink as if sheltering from harsh light, opening and closing her hands on her lap, closing the conversation.

The way she was threatened everything I wanted. I wanted to have the tough kids draw me into their guffawing, gum-chewing group. I wanted to burn at the beach. I wanted to lead the way in slashing school uniform hems. I wanted to be cool like the surfie chicks and the singers on Countdown. ('Cool' means 'healthy' amongst some Eurasians.) I wanted to squeeze the middle out of a Chiko Roll into my mouth as an allusion to worms and several bodily acts whose names I wasn't sure of.

All these Australian things I wanted to do, and yet I was stuck with a sister who wouldn't even drink Choc Milk.

I became full of disgust for her goodness and politeness. She didn't have to worry about doing things that would conflict with my father's ideas on what a good Eurasian girl should and should not be allowed to do.

My feet started burning again.

I chose my moment to ask permission from my father nervously, after the kofta curry pot had been cleared away and the family was finishing off the meal with my mother's carefully cut pieces of fruit.

'Dad, can I go to the pictures?'

'Which picture and who with?'

'Something to do with life in a nice little country town,' I answered, deleting the bit about the surfing and itchified behaviour, and hoping he wouldn't insist on me answering his second question.

'And who with?' he repeated.

I was going to try a version of the truth out on him, say, *Remember that nice girl Sue? Her and some friends, they drive an old Holden but they're all very polite.*

'It doesn't matter,' I muttered instead, seeing the impossibility of him allowing me. My father snorted and walked down the passage with the newspaper under his arm.

I looked at my sister fiercely. She shrugged sympathetically in her graceful, barely-there way.

She was eating her piece of fruit noiselessly and carefully, taking time after each bite to turn the next piece over in front of her and observe it from all angles. I looked at her long enough for the fire in my gut to race up to my tongue.

'You're slow. You're so slow you need to have your nose pulled around to the back of your head to smell your own thoughts. You stare at your food while you're eating. You drink *water*. You're too scared to blow your nose loud.'

She looked at me with her unperturbed look. I hated her unperturbed look. I wanted to make her swear dirty things. I wanted to make her hawk her spit. I looked at her small feet, curled one on top of the other under the table.

'*Asian* feet!' I sneered. Not even any nail polish or bunions from wearing high heels.

I jammed my chair leg down onto her toes.

Her knife and fork clattered down onto her plate.

She closed her eyes tight and opened her hands onto her forehead in such a weary gesture of despair that I was appalled by it, but she didn't utter a sound.

Sorry, I wanted to say as the first tear rolled down her face in an almost desultory way, *I don't know what is happening to me*.

Oh, the pain in my belly.

'Stand up for yourself!' I shouted instead. 'Say "get stuffed" or "Why don't you go suck eggs". Go on! Say anything you like! Just quit being such a dag!'

She opened her eyes and looked at my forehead for perhaps fifty seconds, as though she was noting something general about the weather there.

'I know you're bad and angry like me,' I continued. 'I've heard you shouting in your sleep!'

She closed her fingers up and put the underside of her wrists on the edge of the table.

Like all the old aunties back home.

I felt the muscles in the middle of my chin pucker.

'Go *on*. Stand up for yourself.' The last syllable fell off my tongue lamely, like it had nowhere to go. I wiped my nose on my sleeve. 'Gutless and clean and smelling like Mr Sheen! Where's your guts, hey? Betchou don't have any.'

Tears rolled down her face, but I narrowed my eyes against them, with all the desperation and denial of someone who wanted to burn on the beach; to be like the others.

That night just before bed, the Asian disease exploded inside me. It felt as if a bucket of scalding liquid had been flung across my insides.

My father drove me to hospital a short while before I began losing consciousness.

As I struggled out from the effects of anaesthetic in the recovery room, no one knew I could hear the cool kids, who'd become doctors in white coats conducting their diagnoses on us huddled patients.

'And that one's a wog, that's why his skin's so oily. Their skin's always oily you know. And that hairy.'

We wogs shifted slightly on our benches underneath our hospital blankets. We tried not to take up space. We didn't protest. We were on pain-killers so we couldn't feel how hurt we were. We stayed manageable.

The next morning the surgeon brought me a copy of the scan he'd had taken upon my arrival at hospital.

'Your appendix,' he explained. 'You were lucky.'

My insides, I thought, looking at the white ghosting of organs on the black background. Even more complex than my exterior. Even more inscrutable.

'A redundant organ. Serves no purpose,' the surgeon concluded.

I closed my eyes. How perfectly his words described the Asian in me.

(From *The World Waiting to be Made*, a novel, 1994.)

JOHN LANE

REVELATIONS

Five years of living in an Australian institution found me almost on the threshold of manhood. A few more months and I would be sixteen, working on some remote property far removed from the familiar facade of Fairbridge. But even with this approaching inevitability, I had not given it much thought. Experience had taught me to live for the day, and the day was pleasant enough spent in the Pinjarra bush with the ring of the axe and the swish, swish, swish of the saw. Seldom anything happened out of the ordinary; certainly nothing of note since Ken McCullough's daring drive. So when I arrived home one evening to find a letter from England on my bed in unrecognisable handwriting I opened it with a great deal of apprehension. But I had only to read the first few lines before I felt faint with shock.

I read the letter through the first time, mechanically, incapable of grasping the implication of its message. It was only after reading it for a second time that the true meaning emerged from the confusion that I felt. The one fact that seemed likely was that I now had a maternal mother. To say that I was totally unprepared would be the understatement of all time. It was like reading an unusual novel; a sequence of highly unlikely events leading the reader along to a premature unfinished ending. And the bizarre thing about it all was that the story was written by my own real mother, the woman who had given me life; and not only my life; for I had sisters — and who else?

It is difficult to recall my feelings at that moment. Perhaps turmoil could best describe them, although no single word could adequately explain the thoughts that fought for recognition in my mind. Ideas tumbled about in my brain like laundry in a tumble dryer. When it stopped spinning, a feeling of elation overwhelmed me as the realisation grew that I was no longer alone in the world; that at last I could say that magic word 'family'.

As I re-read the letter again and again, emotion registered in a number of different ways. In turn I experienced bewilderment, excitement, compassion and even a measure of disbelief.

Naturally, Mrs Greenish was delighted for me when I told her the incredible news my letter contained but advised me to discuss it with Canon Watson, a suggestion to which I readily agreed, and an appointment was made for the following day.

When the Canon had finished reading, it surprised me to see the distinct lack of enthusiasm on his face. I would have thought that he, too, being a true Christian, would have been happy with the news. But when he talked it over with me, he sowed the seeds of doubt in my thinking. He put forward several questions for consideration. Why had my mother waited fifteen years before contacting me? Had she known about my leaving England over five years before, and if she hadn't, how did she discover my present address?

'And another thing,' the Canon pointed out, 'you are about to go out into the world as a working man; you will be earning a wage. Be careful that your new-found mother is not after some financial assistance.' The Principal concluded by saying, 'By all means Ramsbottom, acknowledge your mother's letter, but my advice to you is to be watchful in your future relationship with her. I sincerely hope that you will find happiness in the knowledge of your discovery, but do not rush into anything you may regret later.'

When I thought about Canon Watson's advice, I must admit there was a lot to think about, and now that the initial euphoria had subsided, amongst its replacement was a distinct feeling of disappointment that my mother had not sent me even one card in my whole life.

Nevertheless, I immediately wrote back to her Manchester address saying how excited I was to learn that after fifteen years of being an 'orphan', I could now boast of having relations and would she reply soon to tell me about the rest of the story. In that first letter to her, I wrote a brief synopsis of my life story, in particular about my love for my foster parents who had given me such a wonderful childhood. I explained how I was on the threshold of a new life somewhere in the vastness of Western Australia, and that I would save up to come back to England some day and see her.

It was true, and only natural that I wanted some day to see her, but it was also true that if I ever returned to England my first call would be on the Nobeses, the people who had been my only parents.

But it soon became clear to me that it would be many years before I could afford such a trip. With Mr Greenish failing rapidly, Mrs Greenish broke the news to me that I had been found employment on a farm at Gnowangerup in the Great Southern part of the State. My employer was to be a Mr Monty House who ran a mixed farm of about a thousand acres, so I was to get good all-round farming experience. My starting wage was to be twelve shillings and sixpence per week, half of which was to be sent back to Fairbridge by the employer to be held in trust until I was twenty-one. I was to be provided with a complete new range of clothes which included working gear, suit, overcoat and trilby hat. All I had to do with my half-wage was to maintain or buy new clothing, buy a bicycle with which to get into town to spend a weekly two shillings to see the picture show. And, of course, I was going to save for my big trip.

Fortunately, my meals and accommodation were to be provided by Mr House, otherwise I would have been concerned about my solvency. But I still had a few weeks to wait, so that problem was put out of my mind. Of far more importance was the question of whether I would receive an answering letter from my mother before I left.

During the intervening few weeks I spent a lot of time thinking about the sequence of recent events that had overtaken me. Only a few months before I had been a forgotten orphan with only an occasional short letter from my foster mother to remind me that there existed at least one person who cared about me. Then, in the space of a couple of months, not only was I writing to an intelligent young lady penfriend, but out of the blue I suddenly discovered that I had a real live mother and a host of other relatives including sisters. But what concerned me was that there was no mention of a father. What of him? Where was this Mr Ramsbottom who had so gratuitously permitted me to suffer cruel inventive taunts from pitiless boys and mindless adults? And there were other questions ... Was my mother genuinely concerned for me? How much had she suffered? How long did she keep me after I was born?

The answers came in a letter from my mother only a few days before I was due to leave Fairbridge. It arrived in a bulky square envelope. Mrs Greenish handed it to me with a sympathetic smile, her face pale and strained with the loss of her husband only two days before. Hurriedly I raced to my room, closed the door noisily behind me and tore open the envelope.

My Own Dear Son Jack,

I write these lines to you with great remorse and shame. To have to meet you and tell you face to face, I am afraid I could not bare to.

Well, I was born on 15 January 1894, rather delicate, had to be kept alive on the blood of raw meat for a long time (I believe). My mother says that I was the best baby she had and I grew up to be a nice child. Mother was very strict with us all until we grew to 14 years of age; trained us to clean and scrub and wash. Away to Sunday school from being tiny tots. As I grew to my early teens it was Chapel morning and evening — Sunday school afternoon. We are Baptist in religion. I was baptised when I was 18 years, then I became a Sunday teacher. I was trained to be a waitress and was very happy at my work. Wages eight shillings and what tips were made; was a home girl — tipped all my money up; that, we all had to do. Sixpence a week pocket money until 21 years of age.

At 20 I met my first boy — at 21 I had a lovely party. We were going to be engaged at his next leave, but he went to France and married a French girl. But he got let down — she could not bare him any children. That was his punishment, and me — a broken heart.

I must tell you I have always been of a very nervous and afraid to go forward disposition, and still am. However, I was still working at this first class cafe when one afternoon two gentlemen walked in for tea and one of them knew me well, being the husband of the daughter of my parents' best friend. I was introduced.

They were Ministry of Supply officers — they were in uniform, the war was on. I got friendly with the one I was introduced to and he took me around. To me he was the perfect gentleman, until one evening he betrayed my trust, and I did not see him again until I found out I was going to have his child. Until then I was a virgin.

He acknowledged it. He was of very wealthy stock and it was settled out of court for a sum of money, but to my surprise he had a wife who was awaiting a divorce. However, time went marching on — then Barbara arrived. Mother took over the entire charge of the baby, and the £250. Then I met another bitter sorrow. From church, they crossed me right off the membership. I was grieved indeed — so all the family stopped going.

Time went on and I was still working and looking after Barbara and having things rammed down my throat. Then one Saturday evening my parents brought some friends home for a musical evening — they were all members of a concert party. We had a lovely home, plenty of music and plenty of drink, though we were never allowed to touch anything. My parents' friend and her husband brought her brother along one evening, quite a nice smart man about my own age; he was an accountant and they were quite a nice family.

However we got friendly and he knew about me having Barbara and we started going around together. I found I got fond of him and a little later on I found I was going to have a child by this man, and his name was Harry Mills. Need I tell you that he had no honourable intentions towards me. He made Barbara the excuse and denied everything, so I just could not be bothered with him any more.

I had to leave home. I went to Ramsgate in Kent. I worked until as long as I could, as a waitress, then I went to hospital and there you, my Son was born — perfect and beautiful.

How I loved you!

I got well and I transferred to Manchester hospital, and then my parents had to claim me from there. I went home — went out to work to keep us both — got in touch with Harry Mills again to see if he was going to help maintain you — but frankly refused. My life was hell on earth at home so I packed up and with my son Jack, — you, we travelled back to the county where you were born — Kent. Being a holiday and seaside resort, I could only work the summer season. I had to take what digs I could find, that would look after you while I was working. It was a horrible place for both of us to be living in.

Then I met a man there. It was my day off duty. I had taken you down to the beach and I was feeling down in the dumps and homesick. However, I kept seeing this man when I was at liberty, and told him that you were my baby — and about Barbara. When he decided to marry me I thought it might be one way out (to my sorrow). Well we came back to Manchester and went to my parents and were married from there, and lived there.

If ever there was a human beast — he was it.

Never, in all my experience have I ever met such a man. Then, after a few months, one morning I came down and found that a solid marble clock was missing from the dining room. I got my mother out of bed and we looked around and found that other articles had gone. We went to his place of work, and found that they did not know such a man. Then we went to the police and got a warrant for his arrest. I did not have a photograph of him but the description I gave the police tallied with someone they were after from other parts of the country. But he was never found, and I have never seen or heard of him from the day he walked out on me.

But the worst had happened — I was left expecting a baby. That was Norah — our Norah Buckthorpe.

Then I had to go to work again until the baby was born, then I got well again and had to start working once more. I got a foster-mother for you on condition that I could see you every night and have you to myself on weekends. You were only there about three weeks when I discovered that the master of the house beat you and put you in the cellar — they only wanted the money for drink. So one night, I watched and waited for them going out. Then I brought you away. I had got the place from the Ministry of Health. They were registered as foster parents. I got them taken off the Register. However, I had a hell of a life at home.

So my mother got busy among her friends and with influence, got you in Dr Barnardo's, and Norah at Mrs Mathews at Blackburn. But believe me, my hands were forced; I had not a say in the matter, and what my mother did she thought it the best — that you would get an education.

Then I became the slave and drudge of the house, and going out to work, tipping my money up and drudging at home after a days work. But I still stuck to my parents, and have done till recently.

So now my Dear Son, I have opened my soul and mind to you, but please do not think I have been all bad. No — I never went dancing or drinking or cursing. My only recreation was swimming and life-saving. But you can rest content that, You, Norah and Barbara are pure — free from all complaint and disease; you were never tried to be got rid of. I am proud of you my dear, and not ashamed of you. It's myself I am ashamed of for putting too much trust in people. But even today, I am just the same disposition, ready and willing to help anyone — any person in distress or trouble. I have tried to redeem my sins by trying to do what I can for others. The old saying is 'Reward is in Heaven' — well I trust so. There will be peace at least, and I don't care when that time comes. When God is ready to take me — I am ready.

So now my Dear Son, have no fear about your birthright, but I am extremely sorry for all the anxiety I have caused. I ask you my Dear, to forgive me. If you are ever in any trouble and you just have enough to get over to me, come to me. I shall be waiting with open arms. Darling, if only I could express myself plainly I am sure you would not judge me so.

I want to ask you my Son for one photograph of yourself, just in case you decide to disown your Mother. If so, please answer this and tell me so — then I shall understand.

For now, I will say cheerio and God bless you, ever and ever. There is more I will tell you next time if there ever is one,

Your Sorrowing Mother xxxxx
(I Love You all)

On the back of the first page was a postscript.

I guess you think I had forgotten you, but I admit

this is the most dreadful job I have ever had to do because, I know that I have to hurt you, my own Son.

Long before I came to the end of the tension-packed pages, tears distorted my vision and trickled down my cheeks. I felt only sadness — deep and overwhelming compassion for the woman who had endured so much. And the woman who had struggled and fought her way through a wretched life, had relived it all in the humility of her confession, was my mother.

It was so bewildering, unbelievable almost. If so tragic a sequence of events had appeared in a novel, they would have been read with scepticism. But what I had just read was true. It had to be the truth; no woman would ever condemn herself so courageously if it were otherwise.

Right there and then I vowed I would go to her as soon as I saved the fare even though it seemed an impossibility on the paltry wage I would be earning. In the meantime, I would write to reassure her of my gratitude for her frankness and honesty, and that I would never entertain the thought of disowning the woman who have given me life. I would let her know that although I had suffered heart-wrenching separations from loved ones in the past, time had helped heal the scars, and that there had been so much to be thankful for in my life.

I would tell her I was well and strong; that I had learnt new skills, new sports; that I could swim and save life, and that in a few days I would be leaving behind my boyhood, donning long pants and going out into the world as a young man to be a farmer.

I pondered on her latest name of Mrs Jones that had been revealed in her first letter. She had said nothing of her husband. I hoped that now, at last, she had found happiness in marriage and enjoyment in life.

Slipping the letter back into the envelope, I placed it in the far corner of my desk drawer. No one must see it, not even Mrs Greenish. The pain behind the story would be meaningless to other people. Better to keep it between mother and son.

The twenty-third of September 1938 was a milestone in my life. It was the day my childhood finished. It was my turn to leave Fairbridge. Exactly five years and four months before I had chugged into the village on the back of an old lorry a bewildered and unhappy little boy. I would never forget the turbulence of that day. Yet over the past five years, not only had I survived that initial shock, I had weathered the initiation into a vastly different environment, graduating through the tough disciplined ranks of the barefooted urchin brigade right up into the senior boy's status. Today was the day I would shed my short pants to become a man. At any rate, I was dressed the part.

Self-conscious in my neat blue suit and new shoes, I entered the main dining hall and strode to my place at the long central table for the last time. For over twenty years several hundred old girls and boys had gone before me, each one the centre of attention. Knowing now that all eyes would be upon me, I suddenly became aware of a new-found esteem; a realisation that a whole new life lay ahead of me, that destiny was sweeping me into the uncertainties of the future.

The order to stand and say Grace brought me back to earth, and as I settled into my place on the form to help pass the porridge plates along the table, I wondered if it would be the last time I would sit down to a breakfast of bread with dripping and jam. Little did I suspect that in the not too distant future, I would spend many sleepless nights craving for just one mouthful of the food I was sick of eating that morning.

After breakfast there was time enough for me to take one last stroll along the top road to the church. It was an opportune moment to let my gaze wander towards the white painted railings that enclosed the grave of Kingsley Fairbridge, the man who had made it all possible for me and thousands of other British foundlings to be given the chance of a quality of life that most certainly would not have been available in the orphanages of Britain. Here at Fairbridge, we were an ever-expanding family of brothers and sisters sharing a unique experience that would survive for as long as children of Old Fairbridgians lived.

Lifting my gaze beyond the Founder's grave to the giant

granite outcrops of the Darling Ranges, I was reminded of how their rugged beauty differed so much from the softer lines of the Cotswolds. Inevitably, my thoughts drifted back to the carefree days spent in exploring the woods around Eastcombe together with the special charm of the Toadsmoor Valley. I pictured the family group climbing the winding secluded track through the hills and on into Stroud. The happiness of those early childhood years enveloped me in a flood of nostalgia until the conflict of competing loyalties suddenly thrust itself upon me.

Now there was my new-found Family to think about. Again, doubts crept in, new questions surfaced. What had my real mother said? 'There is more to tell you next time.' Had there not been enough last time? Just how much more could there be? She had sought, and I had given her my assurance and understanding. The only exception had been the question of my name. For the life of me, I couldn't understand why I hadn't been given my father's name of Mills. My mother would have done me a big favour if she had done that instead of saddling me with the family name of Ramsbottom. That name might be familiar enough around Manchester, but to wear it through years of institutional life is a fate no child should suffer.

No other thought could have brought me back more quickly to the realities of the moment. It was only after a lengthy period of familiarity that the taunts and insults dried up. Now that I was leaving my friends to meet strangers in the outside world, I knew I'd have to go through it all over again.

With a wry smirk, I headed back towards Scratton and the waiting school vehicle. In a sudden burst of angry frustration, I aimed a savage kick at a cluster of dandelions sending the severed heads flying. At the same time I choked out a frustrated warning: 'Look out Australia, here comes that little Pommy bastard Jackie Ramsarse.'

(From *Fairbridge Kid,* an autobiography, 1990.)

A WORKING GIRL

At the age of fifteen I was in the embarrassing position of being a year over school-leaving age and having never been employed. Mum escorted me around the shops and factories, making applications on my behalf, but employers took one glance at the great gangling girl standing mutely at her mummy's side and firmly shook their heads. The situation became so impossible that I was ashamed to show my face in public where I was sure to be tackled by some indignant matron for being a 'lazy big lump living off your poor mother'.

However that situation changed somewhat when Mum approached the manager of Charlie Carters and spoke the magic words: 'We are Catholics.' Charlie Carters and Freecorns were Fremantle's first self-service food stores. Carters preferred to employ Catholics. The opposition, Freecorns, dittoed with Protestant staff. The same was said of Perth's two large stores, Boans and Aherns. It was rumoured at that time — only rumoured, mind! — that Boans store had thrown down the gauntlet to Aherns, threatening to dismiss any Catholics on their staff if Aherns continued to employ RCs only. So there!

My first job was only part-time, Saturday mornings only. But at least, as Mum said, it was a step in the right direction. So the following Saturday morn I was put to work stacking the shelves in the self-service section. Clad in a white canvas apron I bustled about, keeping the aisles clean and replacing the items which became depleted. There were quite a few girls working on the checkouts whom I recognised as church members. When I smiled at them, however, they turned away. Perhaps my position was too lowly for them. It was quite obvious that the whole staff was thoroughly cowed by the Head Lady. And no wonder! With her buxom form firmly corseted beneath her tailored garb, her red hair firmly set into rigid, corrugated waves, and her protruding green eyes darting behind thick-lensed glasses, the lady was indeed a fearsome sight. At first glance I sent up a prayer to Our Lady and all the Saints to protect me from such a one.

At the end of that first day I received my few shillings pay in a small white envelope. So overcome was I that — white apron and all — I ran all the way home. Mum was waiting for me, standing with arms akimbo in the middle of the path as I came puffing towards her. 'Your first pay envelope, Pearlie?' she said as I placed my earnings proudly into her outstretched hand.

Alas, my pride — and my job — were short-lived. My downfall came one morning when I began work and was immediately accosted by a pram-pusher who asked me where she could find the packet tea. Unfortunately, during the week many of the grocery items had been shifted and tea was one of them.

'Ya don't know, do ya?' snarled Madam Pram-pusher. 'Wadda ya think ya doin' here, anyway?'

Ignoring my stumbled explanation that the tea was not on its usual shelf, she pushed past me and copped my toes under her pram wheels. Later I noticed her talking to the girls at the checkout and gesturing angrily. My heart sank. I knew she was dobbing me in.

Later, I was confronted by two men, one carrying a sack, the other with a long list. 'Where's the flour, girlie?' one of the men asked. 'We have to fill this here sack with tucker.' Observing their tanned faces and broad-brimmed hats, I guessed that they were country workers like my Uncle Happy.

'If you'll give me the bag I'll fill it for you, Sirs,' said I in my best businesslike manner. I did just that. I filled their sack with packet and tinned goods, ticking the list as I went along.

'Cripes, thanks luv. You're a little corker. We'd have been here half the morning if it hadn't been for you.'

My chest swelled with pride when I heard the two men laud my praises at the checkout. 'Great little toiler ya got there. Filled our tuckerbag in no time. A real humdinger, ain't she, Blue?'

After all that praise, I'm in for good, I thought smugly. Which goes to prove that pride goeth before a fall because when I reported to the Dragon Lady on the Friday — which all part-timers were obliged to do — I received the biggest letdown in my working life. 'Ah yes, YOU!' The Dragon Lady's buggy green eyes narrowed to slits as she eyed me from head to toe. A vision of Sister Bridget came to mind. Blood rushed to my face, a lump swelled in my throat and I could feel the downward pull of my mouth. With bowed head I stood trembling before the Boss Lady ...

'The girls in the checkout have told me about YOU! YOU don't know your job. YOU turn customers away because YOU don't know where things are. Why should we pay YOU if you are not doing your job. Well, have YOU anything to say for yourself?' I could not speak. With my head down I swallowed hard and stared mutely at her large pointy-toed shoes. Above me I could hear the Dragon Lady breathing so heavily with rage that she actually snorted. I also was aware that the checkout girls behind me were listening avidly.

'Well, I suppose I'll have to give you one more chance. But you'd better improve because I'll be watching and if you don't improve — out you go!' She finally let me go.

Fighting back my tears, I ran to the church where Mum was working. At first I couldn't see her so I went first to my 'heavenly' Mother. I pressed my head against the rail before Her shrine like a child who buries its face in its mother's lap, and let the tears flow. My mother was so outraged when I told her what had happened that she forbade me to — as she put it — crawl back.

'It's better to go without than have that kind over you. That sort of person delights in taking a rise out of the working class.' It did not occur to either of us that the Dragon Lady was herself one of the working class.

After that I did my own job searching. From nine o'clock in the morning I'd go from shops to factories asking if there were any vacancies, but always received a negative reply, until my quest led me to a small sewing establishment in High Street. A middle-aged foreign man interviewed me, asking if I'd had any experience as a machinist. Of course I had not, but after a moment's meditation he said, 'Okay, we teach you. Come nine o'clock tomorrow and bring lunch.' Unfortunately my would-be boss was not present when I reported for work the next morning. In his place was a wiry, small lady with snapping black eyes.

'Whadda you doin' here?' she asked. I told her that the boss had promised me a job. 'Oh yeah! Well I'm sayin' that there's nothing for you here, so git!' I got!

Dame Fortune finally smiled at me, though. I answered an advertisement in the 'Situations Vacant' column of our daily, joining a long queue of hopefuls outside Brown & Dureau's factory in Henry Street, Fremantle. I was not chosen at first, but a week later the manager sent for me. Several of the girls he had employed left after the first few days.

'Young people don't seem to want to work these days,' Mr Bull, the manager, grumbled. It wasn't hard to see why. The job proffered was not in B & D's factory, but across the road in an empty storage shed. Mr Bull and some of his associates had invested in a new venture, marketing olive oil and brilliantine which retailed under the brand name 'Natty'.

Now at the side of Mr Bull's new factory was a lane, at the end of which was a tin shed. Inside the shed stood a copper, a heap of chopped logs and a couple of cement troughs. Outside the laundry stood crates of empty bottles. Our job was to fill the copper with bottles and water, then light the fire underneath, bringing the water to boil. After the empties had been boiled we scoured them thoroughly and scraped away the old labels. The bottles were then rinsed in the troughs and upended in crates which we carried into the factory, where our fellow workers filled them from big drums. Two at a time, we all took turns at the copper; a cosy job in winter, but pure hell in the summer months. This new business boasted a staff of six girls. The head girl was one Dorothy Chadwick, whose father, Tom Chadwick, was a Councillor for the City of Fremantle. He also served in the vestry in the Beaconsfield Church of England. Dot and I became friends. I spent many happy hours in her home, in the company of her Mum and Dad, and her sisters, Grace and Ruby.

The year was 1939 and war had been declared on Germany. There was an army camp in the same area as the Chadwick home and a young soldier named Charlie Stevenson became a constant visitor. Charlie was a welcome addition to our youthful gatherings. It was a treat to watch him wiggle his ears. My first beau was Charlie's mate, Private Mervan Howe. Even though Mervan was a nice boy the romance did not last long. He simply could not compete with Nelson Eddy.

My weekly pay came to about fifteen shillings. When Mr Bull wanted his car washed he gave Dot and me five shillings each to do the job. When Christmas Eve came around the boss gave each girl a large box of Black Magic chocolates. Giddy with delight, I once more ran all the way home holding Mr Bull's gift before me for all to see. Never before had I been presented with a whole box of chocolates. Once emptied, I held fast to that box for many years, filling it with my treasures: my best lace-edged hanky, my scarf, a velvet cravat and a one-and-sixpenny brooch from Woolworths.

We soon became acquainted with the boys who worked at Brown & Dureau's across the road. When Mr Bull was absent from his office they would sneak across the road and fill their 'empties' with Natty brilliantine. They need not have been so furtive. Natty had a strong, distinctive odour. One could smell those sleek-haired lads coming a mile off.

As the war progressed, the arrival of cargo ships became erratic and there came a time when Mr Bull had to let all his bottling staff go because he had no more drums of oil for us to bottle. A few weeks later, however, a shipment came in and he recalled his 'best girls' and I was proud to be counted as one of them. He warned us, though, that the work was now only temporary. 'This could be our last shipment,' he told us sadly. But then, just as we were working on the last drum, Mr Bull came into the factory with a beam on his face and rubbing his hands with glee ...

'I've been giving this idea some thought,' he said. 'Many of the young men working as stores hands have left to join the forces. So I'm going to give their jobs to the lads who are packers, and in turn have you young ladies take their places. And, should more shipments of oil arrive, Dorothy and Pearl can come over and fill the orders. How does that strike you? Do you think you can pack porridge as good as the boys?' Happy to know that our jobs were secure, we gave him the affirmative at the top of our voices.

The young men who worked at Brown & Dureau's were: 'Dogga' Manson, a hulking six-footer who was an incorrigible tease; Keith 'Doc' Davies, one of nature's gentlemen; Alec Dunning, who got himself into trouble for writing rude words on the inside of 'Three Bear Porridge' packets; and Keith Paudius, whom the foreman dubbed as 'Flash Gordon' because he was always late for work. Next to the foreman, the head man was Bob (Magpie) Smith. His nickname suited him well. He was tall, thin, with slick black hair parted in the middle. His face was long and narrow, so was his nose which came to a point above a small pursed mouth. His eyes were dark and held a darting, inquisitive look. The foreman, Sid Gissing, middle-aged and slightly bald, was a bachelor who lived with his aged mother. They occupied one of a row of cottages in Adelaide Street, Fremantle. (Mrs Gissing lived to an age at which she received a telegram from the Queen.)

These are among the few years I can look back on and recall happy times. I had a steady job, young friends and, for the first time in my life, a real house to live in — even though I still had to share a bed with Mum.

Mr Bull was so pleased with the success of his plan that he hired more girls to pack porridge. One, named Edie Curedale, a brown-haired lass with a radiant smile and infectious laugh, became a good friend. At first, working upstairs had one drawback. In the middle of the floor was a railed opening through which the sacks of porridge were hauled from below. The lads had a habit of calling one of us to the rails on some pretext or other. Like innocent lambs we went, until Sid, the foreman, happened to enter the scene. One upward glance made him aware of what the boys were up to. He sent the wolves scattering and forbade us girls to go near the rails.

'Is it dangerous, Sid?' Edie asked.

'More than you know,' Sid replied.

Since entering the work force I began to realise that the big event of the week was not the Saturday night pictures, but the Saturday night dance. On Monday mornings I would listen spellbound to my fellow workers as they romanced about the gowns they wore and the boys they danced with. When I first asked Mum if I could go dancing too, she said, 'Definitely not!' Surprisingly, however, Grandma took my part and so did Uncle Harold.

'She'll be safe,' he told my mother. 'Both young and older groups attend those dances.'

So Mum relented, and the following Saturday I attended my first dance without giving a thought to the fact that I could not do ballroom dancing. I sat alone in a corner of the room watching the couples execute intricate steps of The Gypsy Waltz, The Pride of Erin and the foxtrot, my spirits sinking lower with each number. Just as I was planning to leave I saw Harold making his way towards me.

'Aha! I thought so,' he said. 'Come on Nippy, I'll teach you how to dance.'

He was a patient teacher in spite of the countless times I trod on his toes, almost sending us both tumbling to the floor. At halftime he left me to refresh himself with a cold beer. 'That's the end of the dancing lessons,' I thought. But to my surprise, and relief, he came back. By the end of the evening I had mastered the steps of the most popular numbers. Harold also walked me home, teasing me as usual and whistling the tunes we had danced to. To my Uncle 'Dibbie' I owe many a happy evening twirling around the dance floor in the old Fremantle RSL hall.

And an even greater surprise awaited me when I came home one Friday night and placed my pay-packet on the table.

'There's something for you in the bedroom,' Mum told me.

There certainly was! Spread across the bed was the most beautiful evening gown. White taffeta shimmered softly beneath folds of misty white organdie. The bodice had a sweetheart neckline and puffed sleeves. Sprayed across the front of the gown's long, full skirt, handworked pink roses bloomed on a green-leafed trailing vine.

'Brockman's let me have it cheaper than its original price

because the hem was a little soiled,' said Mum. 'I have sponged the stains away.' She had also transformed an old pair of white sandals into elegant dancing shoes by applying two coats of Silver Frost paint.

On Saturday night I gazed in wonder at the image in the mirror before me. The little princess had emerged, all grown-up now in her frothy white gown with pink roses. A delicate spray of tuberoses adorned her hair which had deepened from childhood fairness into honey gold and fell in rich profusion around her shoulders.

'Is that really me?' I gasped. Mum, who was standing behind me, nodded.

'That's you, Pearlie,' she said smugly.

In the dance hall, girls who were unescorted sat in line along benches placed alongside the wall (hence the word 'wall-flower', descriptive of those who sit and wait in vain). When the MC cried 'Take your partners for the next dance', young men moved en masse across the floor towards the girls who tried to appear nonchalant, yet waited hopefully for a bow, an extended hand, and a 'May I have the pleasure of this dance?' Some of the more dashing types would run halfway across, slide gracefully on the polished floor and come to an abrupt halt before the lady of his choice, extend his arm with a flourish and query: 'Dance?'

Oddly enough, it was the Saturday night dance that sparked a showdown between my mother and me. Since beginning work I had handed my unopened pay envelope over to Mum. She, in turn, would give me money for the pictures whenever I wanted to go. My workplace was within walking distance so there were no tram fares to pay. Intermission at the dance created an embarrassment for me because I had no money to join my friends when they went out for refreshments, usually a milkshake or a spider (a soft drink topped with a serve of ice-cream). Our group included Edith (Edie), Dot Chadwick (now engaged to her soldier boyfriend), Magpie, Dogga and Les Fowler, who was really good looking and a smashing dancer. In fact Les and I were judged a perfect match when we danced the Minute Waltz together. At intermission I would answer my friends' invitation to join them at Culley's with: 'No, I don't want a drink. I'll just sit here and get my breath back.' My discomfort increased when, realising that I had no money for refreshments, my pals offered me a 'shout'. I refused because firstly, I was too proud, and secondly, there was no way I could return the favour. So, one evening when we were walking home from Grandma's after a happy time together with my grandparents' neighbours, I broached the subject of pocket-money. Mum was quiet as I explained how embarrassed I felt when I could not join my friends in a drink. By the time I had ended my petition for ninepence a week pocket-money we had arrived home and prepared for bed. Mum's tight-lipped silence should have warned me there was trouble afoot; but I was completely taken unawares when she suddenly charged me with clenched fists and began pummelling my back and shoulders with all her strength. She then took me by the scruff of my neck and threw me outside. Clad only in a pair of sleeveless Celenese pyjamas, I huddled on the verandah, shivering in the crisp night air and sobbing desperately as my mother hurled abuse ...

'You THING! After all I have done for you! You'd take the bread out of my mouth for the sake of your fancy friends. You useless rotten THING!'

Worse than the pounding and Mum's abuse, was the feeling of guilt that weighed heavily upon me. Mum had gone without clothes for herself to buy me a lovely evening gown and I still wanted more. It seemed hours that I sat on the verandah step, weeping and moaning and frozen to the marrow, until the door opened and my mother's strident voice rang out, 'Get inside here, you rotten THING, before I come out there and drag you in.' I'm sure the whole neighbourhood had heard the rumpus.

Ever had to crawl into bed alongside someone who had punched and upbraided you and made you feel ashamed and worthless? Believe me, it's the ultimate humiliation. Furthermore, that unfortunate episode finally made me aware that my mother had inherited Grandma's fiery temper. Also that my status as a young adult and a working girl gave me no immunity from corporal chastisement. Nevertheless, after a few days of icy silence between us, I summoned enough courage to broach the contentious subject once more ...

'Mum, if you let me have ten shillings out of my wages each week — that left about one pound five shillings counting overtime and washing Mr Bull's car — I'll buy my own clothes as well as having my own fare to the pictures and the dance.'

Mum agreed, albeit grudgingly. She soon discovered that it was a better arrangement for the both of us. For me, it was pure heaven to join the gang for a milkshake on Saturday night and a threepenny treat of coffee and biscuits at Con's after work on payday. As to buying my own clothes, situated in Atwell Arcade was a small dress shop called Corot's which was considered to be the fashion centre for smart girls. For a deposit of five shillings and payment of two and sixpence a week, the saleslady would put aside the dress, blouse or skirt of your choice until full price was paid.

Ever since I could remember, Mum was running from one fortune-teller to another. They could be people who foretold the future with the aid of cards, tea-leaves or a crystal ball. When I was an infant, my mother was one of hundreds who flocked to see the famous soothsayer, Argus The Wonder Boy, when he came to WA. Her question which, by the way, she continued to ask many other seers over the years, was: 'Will my daughter have a better life than mine?'

'Yes! Your daughter will have a better life than yours,' replied the wondrous one.

So, when my mother heard that a new fortune-teller had arrived in Fremantle — a Scottish lady who consulted a crystal ball — she made haste to visit the newcomer and ask the inevitable question: 'Will-my-daughter-have-a-better-life-than-mine?' The mysterious newcomer turned out to be a plump, short lady with sandy greying hair and bright blue eyes. She regarded me contemplatively before uncovering her crystal ball and gazing into its depths.

'I see here a cross — no, a crucifix,' said she after a minute or so silence. 'You make obeisance before it. You are a Catholic?' She raised her brows at me and I nodded. 'The crucifix will dominate your life. You are sensitive. You love music and you love to dance. I see you whirling around a dance floor in a yellow ball gown. It has a deep ruffle around the hem — you have such a gown?' I shook my head.

'Fat chance,' I thought. 'I'm lucky to have the one I've got.'

'Nevertheless you will own this gown and you will dance in it. There will be two men in your life. One is fair, the other dark, very dark. He will travel, the dark man, but he will return from across the seas. Beware of the dark man. The crucifix casts a long shadow.'

'I don't know why you bother to consult all these fortune-tellers,' I said to Mum on the way home. 'Even if I could afford a new evening dress I'd never choose yellow. And I will never have a dark boy friend. I don't care for dark chaps.'

Several weeks later, my Aunt Mary and Uncle Curley fled Darwin after the Japanese attack. Aunt Mary called me to her in Grandma's bedroom and opened a large case.

'Here, Pearlie,' she said, handing me a rolled paper object. 'I took this down from outside the picture theatre before I left for the boat.' I unrolled the scroll and gasped with delight to see a coloured poster portrait of Nelson Eddy.

'Here's something else I think you will like. It's too big for me. But it should fit you perfectly.' From the depths of her case she lifted a pretty yellow taffeta ball gown which had a scooped neckline, puffed sleeves and a deep ruffled hem!

The following Monday lunch hour, I was sitting with some of my work mates on the back of Luff's cart (I was deeply enamoured of Luff's carthorse who reciprocated my affection, mainly because I bought him juicy apples for a treat). Magpie joined us and announced that he intended joining the navy. His older brother, he told us, was coming home from Kalgoorlie and was hoping to take his (Magpie's) place at B & D's. He then showed us a head and shoulder portrait of said brother who had, like Magpie, aquiline features and black hair.

'This,' said Magpie, 'is my brother, Jack.'

(From *Outside The Fold*, an autobiographical work-in-progress. To be published in 1997 by Fremantle Arts Centre Press.)

A HURRIED DEPARTURE

I was eighteen and Phil was fifteen. My eldest sister, June, was fourteen and had just left school, working like a Trojan looking after the small children, doing the housework and cooking. It was too much for a girl of her age. Percy, our old man, was still giving orders, but Phil and I helped her in any way we could. In fact we all helped one another and I think we became a very close-knit family because of the fear that Percy had instilled in every one of us.

My expectations of life were not very high, and in fact of late I had become very despondent. I thought of leaving home and weighed the pros and cons. The old man, as far as I was concerned, was unbearable. I could think of nothing I could earn a living at but that didn't daunt me — I would survive somehow — but how would the rest of the family fare without me? I was their main backstop. They depended on me for almost everything, so I decided to stay a bit longer and hope something would change for the better.

The year was 1934, and it was still the aftermath of the Great Depression. Business was in the doldrums and there was no money around. Everywhere seemed to be at a standstill. Lots of people had gone broke just buying enough to eat. There was no work on the wharf in Fremantle, and very little doing in the big wool store. Anyone who had a permanent job was considered a very lucky person.

We had three horses in training, none of them fit enough to win. We were down at Robbs Jetty, Percy, Phil and I, with the three racehorses and the old hack that the old man rode. It was seven o'clock in the morning and lots of other trainers were there too with their horses. It was a good flat beach, and nearly every horse seemed to be doing fast work, galloping. I galloped the first one, handed it over to Phil, took the second horse and did the same thing up and down the beach.

When I pulled up Phil was holding the other two horses and Percy was belting hell of out him. I sung out, 'Let the horses go and run under the jetty,' which he did. Then Percy wheeled on me. He made a grab at my leg which I had just extricated from the stirrup iron. I plonked it straight in the middle of his chest and bounced off the other side and let that horse go too, and took off. It's very hard to run fast in heavy sand, but finally I made it to the road and kept going.

'Don't you be home when I get there or I'll kill you,' I heard him yell, and I thought, 'that's really made my mind up. I haven't got much choice now.' My mind was in a whirl.

I told my sister June what had happened; she was crying and pleaded with me to stay. I couldn't any more but I told her not to worry, I would be in touch with her.

The bus came along before Percy and Phil arrived home, thank goodness. I boarded it with a sugarbag containing a small saddle I owned, an extra singlet, my good suit and an extra pair of working trousers and a shirt. I didn't have any money so I told Peter McLeod, the bus driver who I knew pretty well, that I'd pay him later. He must have noticed I was upset but he didn't say anything. I got off at Douro Road and walked to my Uncle Bill's stables. 'Can I put my bag here for a while?'

'Has he been playing up again?'

I didn't say too much. 'I'm going to the abattoirs to see if I can get a job. I'll pick it up later.'

'Bill,' he said, 'you can sleep here in the chaff house, there's a few spare horse rugs there, as long as he doesn't know you're here. I don't want him coming in and putting on a performance here as well.'

I had to do something and do it quick. I had to eat. My best bet for a job was Gerry Connell, one of the bosses with the Lamb Export Board. I had often told Gerry if I thought one of our horses had a chance of winning when I was loading them for the races. I told him the sad story. He was very sympathetic and told me to come at seven forty-five the next morning. He also lent me five shillings which I gave back out of my first pay, and for the first time in my life I knew the good Lord had put the tongue in my head to use it.

That night I bought two pies, for threepence each, and a twopenny New World chocolate. I ate the chocolate, saved the two pies, went up to the stables and made myself as comfortable as possible on a couple of bales of hay. With two rugs pulled over me I went to sleep. I hadn't been asleep long when something ran over my head. I got up and turned on the light and a couple of the biggest rats imaginable, with their beady eyes, were about a foot away from my pies. I threw a shoe at them and they bolted. The rest of the night I slept on and off propped up against the wall, the light on and the two pies in the bag tucked well and truly under the rugs.

The next morning I was up very early. I didn't feel as if I had been to sleep at all. On the dot of seven forty-five I reported to Gerry. 'Come with me. What have you got there?'

'A pair of working trousers and my dinner.'

'Good on you,' he remarked.

There was no chain system, or production line, in that era. Slaughtermen worked what was known as solo. On the slaughter floor there were about twenty cement chutes, all leading to the blood and bone, or by-products, department. Alongside each chute was a large hook to hang the lamb on while the slaughterman was dressing it. Overhead were the rails to run the lambs along to the cool room. There was a box alongside each chute which held gambles, the curved pieces of steel that went between the lamb's legs to hang them on the hook. Each lamb, as it was killed and dressed, needed a skid to slide it along the rails. It was my job to keep the boxes filled with gambles and enough skids so as not to hold the slaughtermen up at any time. I had one side of the floor and another young bloke did the other side. I would no sooner fix one person up and there would be a call from the other end somewhere. I would have to fly and put them in.

The slaughtermen knocked off at ten o'clock for smoko. The other young bloke showed me the ropes. I went with him into the freezer where the lambs were bagged in stockinet and all the gambles and skids were thrown into big trolleys, so we wheeled a couple of these up ready for the next session. The same thing was repeated at lunchtime. A lovely hot shower after work took the stiffness out of me. I also washed my work shirt and trousers at the same time and hung them out to dry ready for the next day. I was a very tired bloke that walked the couple of miles along the railway track back to South Beach after work. That night I bought two more pies on my way home to the stables. I ate one for my tea, saved the other for lunch next day. Even the rats didn't keep me awake that night.

I had a cup of tea with the boys working for my uncle and I was away to work again next morning. This continued until the end of the week and I made a prisoner of the quid I had left from my first pay.

That weekend I called in to see Sol and Lane, my uncle and aunt. She told me to come for an evening meal. I told her it could cause trouble and I would not do it. She made me promise to come in a couple of times a week and see them, which I did, and I always left with a few rounds of sandwiches and a bag of small cakes. She was very good to me and she knew I appreciated it.

Phil called in one day to see me. Lane had told him where I was living. Phil said Percy had gone very quiet since I had left, so I went out to see the kids on Saturday afternoon while he was at the races. After that I used to go out there often and always kept in touch, even if it meant going to the school when they got out. I worried about them quite a lot and missed them so much.

After about a month the lamb export season petered out and so did my job. I pleaded with Gerry to keep me on.

'There's nothing I can do about it Bill. I'm lucky to have a job myself at present. Things are very bad,' he told me. 'We're thousands of lambs down for the season.'

What to do now? I told old Bill that night and he suggested I look after two of his horses, two top-class sprinters. He said, 'Make a specialty of them and we'll win races and I'll give you a few quid when they win.' I agreed, but I wasn't too keen on this pay-on-results racket. I was a wake-up to it.

I had called into Fred and Flo Fitch's place, halfway to Fremantle, a couple of times. My brother Jack was living with them. She told me to come and live with them too.

Flo hadn't been on speaking terms with Percy for two or three years. She had been looking after Jim, the baby of the family, after my mother died, which was very good of her. One night about twelve months later Percy was drunk, and knocked on their door about eleven o'clock at night. He grabbed the baby out of his cot and abused everyone for no reason at all, only what his own mind had conjured up. Needless to say Aunt Flo was devastated when Percy took Jim home. Jim then was about two years old. Aunt Flo was very good to us all and would go to the school and see the kids or drive out in their Maxwell car when Percy went to the races.

So it was that I moved into Wray Avenue, and slept between sheets for the first time since I was a young lad. It was heavenly.

Jack was working at the wool stores and also studying health inspecting at night school. There was an old broken-down bike at Flo's that I fixed up. I used to ride out early in the morning to Bill's stables. I would stay there all day looking after the two horses, grooming, exercising, feeding and finally rugging them for the night, and then ride home in time for tea. Sometimes, if I was a bit early I would go into Uncle Fred's butcher's shop and help him to clean up. He was battling. I think he was just over sixty at the time. Business was poor but he was scraping along.

After about six weeks, Uncle Bill said, 'I reckon Ganemedes could win that race he's in on Saturday.'

I said, 'He's very fit and he knocked Winged Eagle off in a gallop on Tuesday morning.'

There's a story attached to Ganemedes. Uncle Bill owned a very good horse called Easingwold around about 1921–24. It had won for him the WA Derby, Kalgoorlie Cup and numerous other races, and when taken to Melbourne had run second in the Caulfield Cup. He bought a property in a bit of swamp land at Jandakot and had Easingwold standing at the stud there. I think he put himself into debt to construct the buildings and a small house for the stud master and his family. The idea was superb, only he was in the wrong era. These days he would have made a lot of money but back then, few people who had brood mares could raise the fifty guineas stud fee. Sooner than leave the stallion without any love-life Bill used to suggest that the owners send out the mare and they would take a half interest in the foal. He had to eventually give that idea away because it was costing him a fortune to feed the offspring. Ganemedes was one of those offspring and was part owned by Mrs Reynolds, for whom I had ridden the ponies in the Busselton Show years before.

Chow Read, a jockey of those times, rode the hose and won very easily. That night I said to old Bill, 'All down Ganemedes' neck looks as if he has mosquito bites.'

'Yes,' he said, 'I noticed that. Chow has a sharp fingernail and it scratches.'

Well I might have been a bit dumb at times but not that much. Chow had used a jigger on the horse.

That night Uncle Bill gave me five pounds and said that Mrs Reynolds was coming down on Monday afternoon and she wanted to see me. 'She's got a present for you,' he said. She duly arrived and Bill called me into his office. I said hello to Mrs Reynolds, she was a very nice old lady. She remarked how well I'd looked after the horse, thanked me and gave me an envelope. I opened it when I got inside the horse stall. I was very disappointed — a ten shilling note. That meant five and a half quid for all those weeks work. No future here, I thought.

I did get another three quid from Bill Trewella, the chap that had the ice round in South Fremantle. I told him about the horse and he had a good win. 'I'll be in it again next time too, Bill,' he said. I became pretty good mates with Bill.

That bit of money didn't last long and I couldn't live at Fitchs' all the time under those conditions. A little while later I was stony broke. Someone told me the wool stores were putting on juniors, but only union members were being employed. I borrowed seven and sixpence from Bill Trewella to join the Shop Assistants Union, which covered the wool stores as well.

I went from one wool store to another without success, all

had the same answer, 'We've got our junior team on for the season.' Trewella said he'd talk to the boss at the Western Ice Works where he got his supplies, as he knew him pretty well. The boss said to come down in the morning. I arrived at seven-thirty. He put me to work unloading cases of butter from railway trucks, walking a few yards, putting them on rollers and pushing them in through a small door to a bloke rugged up inside the freezer.

I was still light framed, very skinny and weighed just over nine stone. The fifty-six pound boxes of butter were a piece of cake to lift for the start but by ten o'clock, smoko time, I was like some of those slow horses I knew when they had further than three furlongs to go: looking for somewhere to lie down. Instead of feeling like a half hundredweight they were beginning to feel like a ton. I was struggling along with my knee under the boxes to bunk them up onto the rollers and I had slowed down, to catch a phrase from Damon Runyon, 'more than somewhat'.

The bloke inside the freezer was yelling at me, 'Come on you skinny bastard, push them through.' Little did he know I was flat to the boards. My trousers were worn through at the knees and I felt as though my arse was dragging on the ground. By lunchtime I was settled. I rode my bike home for lunch. When I got on the bike to ride back I had cooled off. I could hardly bend, let alone work any more. The boss looked up from behind his desk and spectacles as I entered the office. 'What's wrong?'

I said, 'That job's a bit heavy for me, have you got anything a bit lighter?'

'No, that's it.'

'I'm afraid I'll have to ask you for the pay for my morning's work, I can't carry on,' I said.

I collected six and ninepence for my trouble — not enough to pay Bill Trewella back — and I had buggered up my working trousers. I was up that well-known creek without a paddle. When I told Fred Fitch, he said, 'Something should be done about things like that, they had a junior doing senior's work.' I vowed that day that I would never belong to another union, and

I never did. I'd had to join the union so I could get the job in the cold store, and then, even though the unions were supposed to look after their members, I was used up just the same. I knew that I would have to look after myself — I couldn't afford to rely on others.

What to do again — the same old story: broke and no job. I was further behind than some of those famous trotters.

'Don't worry,' said my Aunt Flo, 'something will turn up.' Jack paid my week's board. Flo would take ten shillings, nowhere near enough to pay for what I ate. It was only to let me feel independent. She was a darling.

Having sausages and eggs next morning Uncle Fred said, 'Have you decided on anything yet?'

I thought, 'Oh Christ, he's getting sick of me being here.'

It was just the opposite. 'I'll tell you what we'll do, we'll make a job. You know a lot of people around South Beach, go out on your bike this morning and tell anyone you know you're starting a butcher's round and ask them would they give you a turn. Tell them you can guarantee good quality meat and sausages. Put a good spiel on. If you can get twenty customers to start with, I'll give you five shillings to put a deposit on a new bike to take the orders out.'

That night I was elated. I had twenty-five brand new customers with orders to start on the weekend. The following day I walked in to Fremantle to Les and Howard Baldwin's shop opposite the Town Hall and put the five bob down on a new bike, with a contract signed to pay the rest off the cost at two and sixpence a week. I rode the bike home, tied an apron around my waist and prepared to become a butcher.

I became very interested in all aspects of the business. Some of the customers told their neighbours and it wasn't long before my round had doubled in size.

Hygiene wasn't what it is today. Even though Fred was a very good butcher and knew the game backwards he was getting old and slapdash. I couldn't stand the grease and untidiness. I was forever behind him cleaning up or washing down with a bucket of hot water.

I used to dread Tuesdays and Thursdays, sausage-making

days. There were two big round chopping blocks in the shop. Fred would put the mince for the sausages on the spare block, throw the other ingredients in — flour, herbs, salt and pepper — pour a bit of water on and start to mix it up. The water would break through the barrier and he would be flat out trying to mix it all before the water ran down the side of the block. After a while he would realise that there was too much to mix on one block and he'd scoop a couple of armfuls up and heave it over onto the other block. Finally there would be sausage meat everywhere. A customer would come in, Fred would serve them, then there would be sausage meat over the counter, scales, paper — in fact, everywhere. What a job cleaning up!

Months went by and I learned to break up the beef carcases, chop down the lambs and sheep and make sausages. I was a big help to the old fellow, besides delivering the meat. I talked him into buying a tub to mix the sausages in. I couldn't cop that block mixing procedure.

We were both kept fairly busy. He would cut the orders for the first lot of deliveries and I'd take that basketful out and deliver them. By the time I got back he would have the next lot cut, in between serving customers. I would usually finish delivering about twelve o'clock, have lunch and go into the shop and write up the orders for the next day, check the money in to Fred and he'd ring it up on the till. I got to serving the customers, cutting chops, skinning calves. There wasn't much that I couldn't do at the end of twelve months. I was getting ten shillings a week plus my keep and a few other concessions, but most of all I was learning a trade.

The rabbit man used to come every morning with fresh rabbits. We would take about a dozen. He always requested we save the skins for him. I always threw them into the back of his van for him. He never knew how many, so I used to pinch a few each day and peg them out in a shed in the backyard. At the end of the month I would juggle a chaff bag full of rabbit skins down the road on my bike to the nearest wool store. They were worth about ten quid.

I bought a nice new grey suit, tailor-made, and some new shirts and when I stepped out I thought I was the ant's pants. I was a bit sweet with some of the girls. I was always very shy in their company, but that didn't last forever.

I always made a point of going out to see the children, mostly on Saturday afternoon. One day I walked in and who should be there but Percy.

'What do you want?' he said.

'I've come to see the kids, I've got a bit of gear for them.'

Phil was standing there and I handed him a bag with homemade cakes, a few bags of sweets and some fruit. To my surprise Percy called out, 'June, put the kettle on for a cup of tea.'

That broke the ice and from then on I was able to keep an eye on the children whenever I wished.

My Aunt Flo was the one that supplied the bag of goods. I was only the delivery bloke. Percy and she never spoke to one another for the rest of their lives. It wasn't her fault. She was just as generous to his children after the argument as she had been before. She always found a way to get what she wanted out to the kids.

Flo and Fred and their daughter Daphne, who was seven years older than I, were all very kind to Jack and me. We lived with them as part of the family until the war broke out.

(From *The Fall of the Dice*, an autobiography, 1991.)

WHERE THE MUSIC COMES FROM

'Get up to the corner of Mangles and Frankel!'

'What?'

'That's journalism,' explains my Uncle Lubin.

He is harking back to my early wish to join the local paper.

'You can't just write what you fancy: you're there sitting in the office of *Southern Districts Enquirer* when next thing it's GET UP TO THE CORNER OF MANGLES AND FRANKEL: THE DUNNY CART'S TURNED OVER!'

We happen to be on that very corner and as if to jolt the story home, Unc shoots in the clutch with his strong right arm and we fairly catapult over the potholed intersection.

The lawn-mower bumps in the boot.

Unc's Austin is rigged up with a big lever on the right of the steering wheel which works the clutch. Like a motorbike handlebar; also a twistgrip for the accelerator.

Whatever breed of car he has, and Unc has had two or three Fords and Hillmans and so on, there is a family cat continuity about them all: travelling with him always feels the same because he drives them with the alacrity of a mud scrambler down on the Blunders.

Unc's legs are in irons joined to long lace-up boots. When he was just a baby in the bush he got sick. The doctor said it was a chill and to give him castor oil and wrap him up. But it was polio, which that doctor then saw for the first time.

Before he learnt to walk again they gave him a little pedal car, and they also put him in charge of the gramophone. But

Unc doesn't spend all that much time talking about his troubles. You have to find out that sort of thing from Aunt Ettie or the others.

We are safely over Mangles and he gets warmed up:

'Who wants to write up the dunny cart or Mrs Flibbertiejibbs' budgie turning eighty, or how many shorthorns yarded? You might have better stuff to do.'

'Anyway,' I say, 'wouldn't you have said yourself that the dunny cart went arse over tip?'

'That's another thing with the *Southern Districts Enquirer*. Decorum. There's a lot of prunefaces. If you can do it in such a way that you and me and the next bloke can read it and say, Wow, what he really means is that the dunny cart's been and gone arse over tip, then you're firing on all six.'

Description of Unc: round and tanned of face from early wattle & daub schooling and shearers' cook duties in the open. Chucklesome dentures and a characterful wart and/or sun-freckle or two. Fond of scatological epithets and emphases rhetorically prefaced by a clacking tarp, tup or tut of jowelled lips smacked plosively open. The same used in sympathy to another's talk, as if to say, Well I never! As expert at extending hyperbole as local builders are at enclosing verandahs and adding sleep-outs: The Harvey Show was pissweak — Pissfortnight more like!

Sees human endeavour as a series of agitations leading to a culmination or two. Reverses walking-stick for lightning hook at troublesome kids and/or yappy mongrels. Like father, never parks car till shady spot is found. Small businessman. Previously boat hire and cottages at holiday riverside place. Corner grocery shop: melons, magazines: Yessir, we've got all the nudies and rudies here: Pocket Man, Man Junior, Man Senior, Man Old-Age-Pensioner! Agent for Amicable Albion Assurance. Enamel plate on grey weatherboard side of shop says so. Big rolltop desk out the back where he goes through all the dockets spiked week by week — a lot of it Amicable business too, no doubt. If you're good he'll give you kids all those Peters' Ice-cream Bombs that got snaggled when they dropped them down the station.

We are going over to mow Uncle Lubin's and Auntie Ettie's lawn.

The long back lawn stretching down a double block or so and over the fence the trains chant and whistle and rattle by.

Mowing the lawn up and down in big long strips.

Mr Herbert Gates all-hailing from Yorkshire or some other such Pommyshire comes up through the back garden with his Webster Booth records. Been back to the Mother Country and out to Australia twice on the assisted passages, he has, or so the story goes.

Here he comes. I crouch over the mower, bend into the mowing; but no, he's noticed me.

'That's how we got the pigs to make streaky bacon back home, by gum. Ho Ho Ho!'

Always the same joke when he sees the strips of mowed and unmowed grass. As if he'd never told it before — even to himself.

The first time he cracked it, Unc said to me afterwards that here, obviously, was a man who didn't know anything about pigs on farms, since putting them out to graze is tantamount to asking for trouble. They'll grovel out under a fence and wander off, he said, but not before they've rooted up the paddock, so that is why they're penned, and fed and watered by hand.

There is a break for afternoon tea. Scones from Auntie Ettie. She has a habit of starting to disagree or get wound up silently before you finish something, not meant to be unkind, just her. She purses her lips and twitches her head slightly in the run-up as she does now.

Their two girls have brought in a pigeon found in the street and they want to keep it and she can hardly wait to tell them:

'No, they are full of ticks and things and you'll catch something. They are not a Native Bird. They are an Introduced Bird. Now, no, if it was a maggie it would be different ...'

The sweet smell of milk in a billy. Auntie Ett is watching over it on the stove, waiting for it to come to the boil, and she scoots them out, shoos them out with their pigeon ... 'Don't bring that fellow into my kitchen!'

Everything she calls a fellow, like her new electric fridge:

'It's a big fellow with lots of room' and 'I was always having to defrost that old kero fellow.' She and my mother and a lot of others are trying the new copha recipes where you don't have to slave over a hot stove and cook things, you just whack them in the fridge.

It is getting on for teatime. Sometimes Unc will have a crab tea where he sits down near the woodheap — he has two blocks, one for chopping and the other to sit on when he chops. He likes wood that's ready to split.

But I myself can't eat crabs. They make me sick and I see things and puke.

He boils up the crabs which his holiday riverside friends bring round and he cracks them open with a pair of ex-Austin pliers ready to take up to the house.

Mr Herbert Gates is more of a backyard neighbour than a mate and because he does not have a radiogram, he is always bringing up his Webster Booth 78s to see how they sound on Unc's Stromberg-Carlsson model.

Unc and Auntie Ettie are always threatening to go out Sunday night at 6 o'clock and leave Mr Herbert Gates to it with Webster Booth and his 'Take a Pair of Sparkling Eyes'. But they don't have the heart.

This week only they could tell him too, to go up to the city, where according to a tiny ad, hidden and blotchy in the back of the paper, Webster Booth is appearing live in person at a fading night spot called La Tenda.

So, more often than not, Mr and Mrs Gates also, are up there settled in by six.

Evening and Unc will be unlacing his long boots and irons and preparing for bed. Crawling and skidding up the polished lino of the passage on his bum. The radiogram — I think people clubbed in to get it for him — is in the bedroom where he has his usual concert.

With Herbert Gates and Webster Booth there it may be a slightly forced shared concert, because for Unc a little Booth goes a long way, and he would prefer to hear something a bit bushier, Peter Dawson perhaps.

Not hard to imagine the honey and silver voices he and his

folks heard whilst gathered round the wind-her-up gramophone's horn of musical plenty. Not hard at all, because he
plays chiefly those same 78s.

There is an old Caruso record: Handel's Largo: Ombra mai
fu, where he sings in praise of a tree's shade. Maybe Handel
knew about parking a car. On the other side, nothing, not a song
but an etching of an angel on a waterlily.

Dame Nellie, Gladys Moncrieff, old Dawson, Tibbet and
Tauber. They all clomp down at high speed from the stack on
the spindle, slither momentarily, and away they go.

Unc listens as if catching a voice from afar, lifting and
drawing up his face, and at special moments releasing his chops
and going 'Tup'.

'What is it ...?' he asks, 'Where does the music come from?'

The song 'Ah, Sweet Mystery of Life' he calls The Sausage
Song, and as for sweet mysteries of life he says not to worry
about Paris in the Spring and all that because its all going on
here up in the sandhills anyway.

He has Lawrence Tibbet doing The Sausage Song; and on the
other side a flourishy piece: 'Myself When Young' ('... did
eagerly frequent Doctor and Saint and heard great argument').

He's also got Tauber, or is it Crooks? doing Ah Sweet
Mystery, and on the other side ... 'Tup, what is it? ... Song of
Songs, or something.' He likes to turn it up loud.

The walnut cabinet vibrates as if it can barely contain the
strength and sweetness of the long-ago tenor now dead. Are all
the great singers dead?

'Tup,' goes Uncle Lubin and tups his lips again, relishing his
wonder anew. 'Where does it come from, the music ...?'

Reaching the end of the record the grooves click and scratch
and the oblivious noise grows as the needle begins to sway.

It seems the singer singing is balanced on the edge of the
known world. Would he be snatched and thrown off the edge
before the song was done?

Before Unc goes to bed and his radiogram, Herbert and his
Mrs are down in the lounge room, polishing off all the
macaroons and warming themselves in front of the Metters
grate full of banksia logs and going on about bringing up kids.

Very fond of the *Readers' Digest* psychology you can get these days sitting waiting for your haircut or out on the lav, a lot of people are, especially the Mrs.

Auntie Ett might have been telling them about her daughters going on about keeping the pigeon.

'I see in the *Digest*,' says Mrs Gates, 'that the offspring of invalid or chronically ill fathers do have their complexes. It says they see Mum giving so much attention to Dad and they don't want it to be any different for themselves. It said they grow up with an Expectational Cross-Alignment.'

Unc just nods and goes tup, an equable tup as if to say, Well there you are then.

But I want to hit her.

She must have seen my look and then she says something about the *Digest* also saying that kids 'go through a stage' of getting on better with their aunts, uncles and grandparents than with their own parents. She can't remember the term for it, but there is a term.

'Maybe it's something to do with who changes the nappies and fixes the bike punctures,' says Unc.

'No, it's Research,' says Mrs G. 'They've done Research.'

'Tup,' says Unc and he pokes the fire.

When I get back home that evening I say to my father:

'Did you know that Webster Booth is appearing live and in person at the La Tenda?'

'Maybe it's see Perth, sing at La Tenda and die, for Webster Booth,' says my father.

(From a work-in-progress, *Chookwheat*, a novel.)

MY FIRST BABY

I didn't really know what to do with myself, or what I wanted from life. I was just a kid, without that much personal knowledge behind me, and still being formed into my own person. I was drifting, and took what was offered, or what became available in the way of work and other opportunities.

I certainly learned a lot about my fellow human beings and the ways we all lived during these times.

It is incredible that a time of such activity can just happen, and then you move on. There were plenty of adventures during those years for me — running away from home, working, all during those war years. That war made things so different from any other time, with so many men away and more women working than usual.

After I finished at the hospital, I got myself a job looking after a woman and her two sons at Beverley. She was a beautiful and wealthy woman, but a hopeless alcoholic. Her husband was a lovely, caring man, and he employed me to try and keep her away from the booze. No matter how hard I worked to do this and keep her sober, she'd find a way. It was the wiliness of the alcoholic. There was no result, none possible, and I finally left. I was close to eighteen by the time I left. Back to the city, with no qualifications except looking after kids, setting traps, milking cows, pinching sheep, and there was certainly not much call for these skills in Perth.

I stayed a week or two with an aunty who wouldn't let me go out at night, even to the movies in the same street. She told me that if I kissed a boy I would get pregnant, and I suppose I believed her. I'd always thought that babies had something to do with varicose veins, though.

When I applied for a job at the St John of God's Hospital in Belmont, an old people's nursing home, thankfully I got it. I moved into the nursing quarters. It was hard work, and long hours, but I really enjoyed it. It used to make me sad to see all the dear old girls sitting on the verandah day after day, with absolutely nothing to do. On Sundays, they would get us to make them pretty for their visitors, but they only rarely had someone come to see them. They sat with such expectant looks, waiting all day, and then making excuses for their families.

Often those who did make the effort only came for half an hour, and brought a bunch of flowers or a stupid bedjacket that was hell to get on and off a body bent and crippled with arthritis. We tried to make up for these disappointments in our little ways, and I'd make some of them fairly cackle with my jokes and stories.

I remember the first time I was asked to clean the false teeth. The nurse just told me to collect and clean them. I didn't think to get each set and put them in their separate cups — I got a dish and put them all in together. What a time we had trying to find the owners of each set. It took most of the day and many laughs to sort out.

After working there, I always vowed I would never go to one of those homes, and I have told my kids that I will go bush and stay there, wait it out. The loneliness of that place was heart-breaking, and so were many of the stories they had to tell. Talk about birds and animals being kept in cages — this was worse. The authorities would have you in gaol if you did the same to animals.

I started to go out to dances at the Embassy Ballroom, Anzac House, and other ballrooms in Perth, and met many young people, among them my first boyfriend. He had a car and a trade and mobs of money, and the good times just ran on for me. He'd send me corsages, and take me out. We used to go all over the place and have lovely times. I was earning money that I would spend on myself every week — I think I had about twenty-nine pairs of shoes, lovely clothes, and always silk underwear that I bought from a shop in Claremont. I'd had enough of those rough clothes from home.

I was having a good time, and after months of this it was into the cot, and that was that. Devastation. We had held off for a long time before we started having sex together, but not long after we did, I fell pregnant, at less than twenty years of age. Of course, there was no contraceptive pill in those days, and as I remember, it was really big shame to ask for condoms in the chemist shops, and besides, I think you needed a marriage certificate to buy them. And I didn't know which way I was supposed to hold my mouth, or whatever was needed during the act.

This was the first man I'd slept with, and getting pregnant was my greatest fear. I had probably left it for that long because Mum had always expected it of me, and I held off to prove the old girl wrong. When I found out I was pregnant, literally the first thing that came into my mind was, Oh no, what will my mother have to say about this? My other sisters had been forced to marry, or had been chucked out of home, all these trollops she had for daughters. And I was the one she was waiting for to do the wrong thing; she had expected it of me as early as eleven years old.

The good bloke flitted as soon as I told him, of course, so I was really on my own. I was a dumb and foolish girl, I didn't know what to do, I couldn't go home, as I had not really kept in touch with Mum and Dad in all my time away. It wasn't easy then to get an abortion. I must have asked one hundred people where to go for an abortion. At that time in Perth, there were plenty of backyard abortionists, but I only found out later, and couldn't track anyone down at the time.

I did go to a doctor in South Perth who I'd been told would organise an abortion; he gave me pills to make me bleed, so I could be admitted to hospital as an emergency, the only semi-legal way to do it, but the first and second batch didn't work. The third lot did, and I bled everywhere and was put into Royal Perth Hospital, but didn't lose the baby. I woke to find myself hooked up to a transfusion unit, gaining all the blood I'd lost in my bed.

Looking back at this time, I think I was well on the way to becoming a real ratbag, and would have if I hadn't had that baby. Lots of drinking at parties, hanging out. I could have really got the taste for the good life. I spent every cent of my wages on myself. Having that baby was probably the best thing I had ever done.

I had to leave my workplace after a while; the nuns weren't too happy about my predicament, but there was one sister who was good to me. I managed to get a job in Applecross with a lovely family. The mother was pregnant too, and needed help. A small girl and her mum and dad showed me more love and kindness than I had known in my whole life. I looked after the house, and the daughter and the father when the time came for Mum to go to hospital, and stayed for a month after the new baby was born. Then, one night I started labour and was taken to King Edward Memorial Hospital in Subiaco. The year was 1949.

Several hours later my lovely baby girl was born, and I was shifted to a ward with other mothers. When the visitors came, I told them my husband was a shearer up the bush. I didn't realise that two of the girls never had visitors either, and for the same reason as me.

Arrangements were made for the three of us to go to a home for unmarried mothers, and a woman arrived at the hospital to see about adoption of our babies. She worried us every single day, telling us we couldn't possibly keep our babies, that people wouldn't want us, that our families would turn their backs on us, and that we wouldn't be able to find work. The baby born to Marion had a big red birthmark on his face and the understanding, kind, caring welfare woman told her, 'Of course, you know no one will want to adopt a baby like this one.' Marion's reply wasn't fit for printing, and she took her baby and went home to the country with the support of her parents.

So, I was at this Mothercraft home, and was fully intending to adopt this baby out, but I had no idea that every day for three weeks I was going to have to be looking after and feeding her, while she was up for adoption.

And every day, this kind and understanding woman from the

Child Welfare came to badger me into signing papers, as she had this wonderful couple with plenty of money ready to take my baby. This was, of course, after she'd asked about my family: if there were any nitwits or cripples. Eventually, after all that time with my baby, I said no. I was sitting behind a screen one day feeding her — even though it was a Mothercraft home, we had to be modest — and I thought, poor little thing, what am I doing thinking about myself, and not you. And I decided that day to keep the baby.

What an uproar! The woman went crazy, the couple had bought all the baby things and set up the room. I was heartless and selfish, and I would be sorry. They told me I had to go, so I packed my things and left with my baby, not knowing where I was going.

I had only enough money to keep me for a couple of days, and certainly not enough to stay anywhere. I walked to Hyde Park in North Perth when it was dark, and I slept there with my three-week-old baby, cuddled up behind some bushes. Early next morning I walked into Perth and pawned something at a shop near the town hall for the train fare; then to the railway station and I went home to Bruce Rock. I had nowhere else to go.

Mum and Dad knew nothing about the baby; we'd sent each other the occasional Christmas card in my time away, and not had much other contact. When I arrived at that small railway station at four-thirty that afternoon, everyone was in town to meet people and pick up goods. Mouths gaped and fingers pointed at the sight of me, and no one spoke, although I had known these people all my life. This was the first of a number of similar experiences in my life, of being shunned because of my actions.

I walked down the gravel road towards home, the longest road I had ever walked, not knowing the reception awaiting me, but knowing that although my parents would be hurt or disappointed, they wouldn't throw me out.

We all cried together, and I'll never forget the lovely look on my dad's face as he took my baby and held her in his big arms. Mum wasn't real keen, I could see her thinking 'I told you so'.

My brothers and sisters gathered around me, and in a few hours only the memories were terrible, and the little girl was being spoilt by everyone.

(From *First Cuts are the Deepest,* an autobiography, 1993.)

JUSTINA WILLIAMS

THE SORE-FOOTED CITY

Then the sore-footed city
Limped over my days
And the quick stars withdrew
From the neon's bold gaze.

In Perth the plenitude of water is amazing — sprinklers
whirling on lawns miraculously green in summer heat; blazing
zinnia, petunia, phlox, Livingstone daisies incandescent in the
sun; the broad blue expanses of the Swan lapping the city,
exotic palms soaring around its banks. Oh that Kendenup could
share these sudden bursts of summer rain multiplying fantasies
of red, blue and green neon in the river, on wet roads gleaming
under the rushing headlights.

At Kendenup now the tanks will be down to the bottom rung,
dams sliding into mud, water being carted from Lake Matilda.
Every drop is precious, baths are shared, cleanest go first, the
dirty residue poured over geraniums that survive in tins while
the heavy soil outside hardens and the frail flowers wither. The
little Kalgan River will have shrunk to isolated brown pools
where gilgies disappear deep in the mud. Here in Subiaco,
living with Grandma, the night is always lit by the glow trembling above the city on the other side of the banksias and native
shrubs in the soft dark interlude of King's Park. At Kendenup,
such a glow on the horizon would tell of a bushfire raging, the

hush of fear communicated by Muv that it may be sent our way by a changing wind, or menace a neighbour's home.

The shops are fascinating with their arresting window displays — no faded goods or flyspecks here. Elegant dummies, painted wax faces whose eyes stare back with uncomfortable realism, shoe shops an Aladdin's cave of jewelled satin, snake-skin, gleaming black patent, salesmen who will climb the ladder to the topmost box to get your size. So different from Kendenup, where you had to order from catalogues and inquire anxiously day after day at the post office for the parcel that eventually came with a letter 'the design you have chosen is temporarily out of stock so we are sending another line that we hope will be satisfactory'. If the shoes are too small, rather than send them back, you ape Cinderella's ugly sisters, so that you may dance till midnight however painful your feet.

City pavements are also painful as I trudge behind Gwen who trips from one boutique to another on her high heels with marvellous fortitude. The shopping expedition, Grandma puffing along as well, is ostensibly to buy a dress for me. But our role is mainly to exclaim in admiration as Gwen whirls before the mirror like a shaft of sunlight in yellow broderie anglais; or will she choose the sophisticated crepe de chine blouse that enhances her soft full bosom, or the slit black satin that reveals her shapely legs? Hard not to be envious, though I am aware such things wouldn't suit a galumphing country bumpkin. My patience is rewarded with a simple natural tussore dress paid for out of extra money CP has given Gwen — plain enough to be worn to work, yet it has style, Grandma says approvingly. Despite a feeling of guilt, I parade before him that night with a smirk of satisfaction.

It's through Gwen that I come into contact with a union sec-retary, and, very intrigued, start asking questions. Her friend, Doreen Place, is secretary of the Cleaners' and Caretakers' Union. As dark as Gwen is fair, Doreen's wickedly sparkling brown eyes are framed in black kiss-curls. She describes her suitors with devastating wit but doesn't reveal much about the workings of unions, except that she has a grip of iron on the job; and Grandma says it's amazing for a woman to have that position. Not until many years afterwards do I find out that Doreen is a complacent official under the thumb of the Labor right wing, crushing the slightest suggestion of militancy among her members.

How scared and bewildered I was on that first day in Newspaper House! It was the beginning of a heatwave in January 1933. The imposing new building had been opened with a fanfare, the *West Australian* shifted holus bolus from West Australian Chambers to the south side of St George's Terrace after Christmas 1932. Ignoring the temptation to gaze into the arcade shops, I walked timidly through the massive doorway into the foyer gleaming with polished jarrah and plate glass doors, behind one of which sat the staff officer — with the appropriate name, for a newspaper employee, of Shakespeare — who escorted me to the mailroom and gave me into the care of a tall gingery one-armed Frenchman named Gabriel.

As there was an intimidating polished brass sign reading 'Information' above the counter where I would sit, Gabriel thought it wise to brief me on the names and approximate whereabouts of the editorial and reporting staff, his French accent adding to my confusion. 'Already we are good friends.' he said, squeezing my hand. 'You are like ze beautiful young ladies on ze chocolate box.' Walking with a slightly lopsided stoop which I took to be due to the missing arm, he showed me the poky room where the franking machine stood and where I would enter the mail, 'wizout ze blots', in a daybook. In an adjoining cubbyhole brass shells fell with a clatter from overhead chutes, to be redirected to the 'beeg shots' on the mezzanine floor, the sub-editors or the machine room where lesser mortals, the printing staff, worked.

The mercury soon climbed over the Fahrenheit century. Red with sweat and confusion, I misdirected people wildly, figuring that once they got out of sight someone else would put them on the right track. They usually ended up at the desk of kindly, tactful and efficient Alice Biggs, secretary to the editor, a small round deity named H J Lambert who hibernated in his office, only emerging for the daily editorial meeting, and the grey inoffensive Chief of Staff, Charles Frost, knotting pale eyebrows above owlish spectacles as he filled in the duty book with reporters' assignments for the following day. Sub-editors were an aloof race who never looked up or said thank you for anything laid on their desk, leader-writers were stern aristocrats with a human side that forgave the dark-eyed country mouse for giving them somebody else's letters. Each reporter seemed to live in a world of his own. All male, wreathed in clouds of smoke, they clacked away on portable typewriters or rushed away to urgent jobs.

Underneath everybody's politeness, I sensed a wall of reserve, especially in the women's lunch room. 'Because of CP — zey all know you are 'is protege,' Gabriel observed with French candour. 'Perhaps you carry the tales.' But caution was thrown to the winds over his edict on office uniforms: we would all have to wear a heavy natural assam overall with a white blouse. Nobody liked it, criticism raged. 'Don't you tittle-tattle,' I was warned. I didn't, but continued to feel an outsider, not interested in the trivialities discussed: office personalities and feuds over minor things, social chitchat, romances in the making.

An impending staff marriage brought argument — not about the paper's policy of sacking married women if they didn't resign — but religion, the sanctity of church weddings posed against the horrors of the registry office. 'What's it matter?' I said, adding blithely, 'I'm an atheist.' There was no worse way of offending unwritten rules of behaviour in keeping with the social status of *West Australian* employees. We were 'establishment', from the social editor, Dolly Ferguson, stout descendant of an old family, who could spot social climbers a mile away, to the widowed Muriel Chase, thin, white-haired and saintly in her eternal rusty black silk and squashed black straw hat worn at an unexpectedly drunken angle.

These social columnists could make or break the nouveau riche now sprinkling the scene. Noel White, dismissed by Grandma and Gwen as having a face like a horse, was a dedicated journalist in charge of 'Woman's Realm'. Brisk reporter Molly Maginnis breezed through in a mannish suit, the ultimate picture of a career woman, stopping briefly to give the latest news of the Royal family, whom everybody adored right back to Princess Alexandra the First. Ada Doonan, angular and middle-aged senior secretary, had looked after managing directors and boardroom bigwigs so long that she knew all their idiosyncrasies; her companion on the mezzanine floor was Eileen Clinch, whose heavy jowls could even awe tyrannosaurus rex, Sir Walter James.

No doubt behind my back they talked about the way CP would stop his busy stride at the mail room to inquire how I was getting on. The arrival of a plumpish, pasty newcomer to assist Ada Doonan with his typing brought a raising of eyebrows that I didn't understand. Walking lumpishly, eyes downcast, a pale cloud of hair frizzing around her doughy face, she ate her lunch quietly in a corner and only smirked when addressed by her unlikely name — Ramona.

My lowly job of opening all the voluminous mail addressed to the editor and finding the right recipient of personal letters sometimes gave problems. Who, for instance, was J M Harcourt? Inquiries brought only a shrugging of shoulders. A black cloud seemed to hang over his head, people didn't want to admit his existence.

At last, in the prestigious world of leader-writers, who usually continued to gaze thoughtfully into space when you put mail on their desks, I got help from Geoffrey Burgoyne, who put down his pipe and grinned. 'Harcourt — a radical, if you know what that is. Used to be a casual on the "Daily" too. Upset the establishment no end with that novel of his about the pearlers. Supposed to be writing another about Brennan's Emporium. D'you know anything about communists? But of course you wouldn't ...'

'My father says they have a five-year plan that might control markets and prices.'

'Aha! So we have a little bolshie in our midst.'

It just seemed so unfair that farmers couldn't sell their crops when people needed food, I said, telling him about Kendenup. Just as well I wasn't a leader-writer, he said, sucking on his pipe grimly but with a twinkle in his eye.

Brennan's Emporium was the big shop in Murray Street that stocked everything from spades and dunny pans to perfumes and dresses, run by a family about which there was plenty of gossip. J M Harcourt was entrenched in my memory from then on. If I saw his book, I'd buy it even if it meant eating dry bread for lunch for a week!

The family's Sunday drive through the Darling Ranges awakened my interest in another local writer.

Though Harry, with his dark good looks and droll humour was popular socially, he gave up Sundays to drive us all in the A-model Ford Grandma had given him for his eighteenth birthday, on an excursion to the hills. Grandma, ensconced in the back seat, looked forward to the drive all week, annoying Harry with constant inquiries on whether he'd checked the water, tyres or other things mechanical of which she was totally ignorant. Ascending Greenmount's steep stretch, the radiator fulfilled all her fears by boiling over.

The car stopped at the junction of Old York Road — the original route to the Eastern Goldfields — and Great Eastern Highway, almost at the gate of a small wooden cottage half hidden by pale blue plumbago and tangled grape vines. A red witch lived there, Grandma said, named Mrs Throssell. 'One of those red-raggers?' Harry asked, aware of her liking for supernatural tags and heavy-handed jokes.

'She's quite a famous writer, anyway — married our first Victoria Cross winner, Captain Hugo Throssell. I remember when his father was Premier. An awful scandal about her book, all about white men up North and their black velvet.'

'What's black velvet?' I asked, sure by now that books that caused scandal usually exposed some hidden truth.

'That's what they call Aboriginal girls used for sex.'

'She writes under her maiden name — Katharine Susannah Prichard,' Gwen said. 'CP said he wouldn't give me a book like that to review.'

My desire to meet her stirred. Perhaps one day I might interview her and find out how you started writing a novel! By studying great literature, accumulating experience of the world, or by using events from your own life? Who could know of the great tragedy stalking her, the suicide of her husband? The house was empty. Harry got some water somewhere else and we moved on.

At the *West Australian* office, CP initiated shorthand lessons for cadets and would-be journalists like myself. Reporters needed shorthand, just as the sporting staff needed to know all about baseball, which CP was enthusiastically establishing here, pressuring comp room men to take it up, coached by a much-disliked American bully boy whom he'd imported into a cooked-up job out back. But who was I to criticise when the managing editor ostentatiously paid for me to be taught Pitman's by a married couple who conducted a private business college? As well as struggling with outlines and contractions, I had to fend off the wandering hands of the teacher, whose colourless wife turned a blind eye.

Pete Thomas, an outrageously witty cadet, breezed along in the shorthand lessons to win the prize for reaching 180 words per minute. Pimply and gauche compared to the suave older men to whom Gwen and CP had introduced me, Pete romped around in an uninhibited way that was quite innocent and appealing. I hoped he didn't know of the family scandal, the double life I led as a youthful chaperone.

Sundown excursions to a shady pool in the Swan River near Guildford, well away from prying eyes, were supposed to be a closely guarded secret. The portly managing director, white skinned and freckled as a shark, frolicked in the clear green current with his love, slim and graceful as a water nymph, while I floated in the shallows. Gwen would have liked to be seen in public with him — an acknowledgement of her position — but he wanted to preserve his marriage with the long-suffering wife, perhaps to protect his daughter, a blossoming socialite, and reporter son. Afternoon dances at the Embassy Ballroom with a discreet party in a curtained loge were considered safe, as were asparagus and champagne suppers with trusted business associates at the exclusive Esplanade Hotel.

But now he exacted tribute for paying for the shorthand lessons, calling me during my lunch hour to his imposing office on the mezzanine floor — embarrassing occasions supposed to be secret, though a coolness from his secretaries told me otherwise. Fearful of his authority at home and in the office, plagued with conflicting loyalties, I would walk in like a marionette for the kissing session. As his heavy jowls came closer, gingery eyebrows arched over small shrewd eyes, thick chin divided by a deep cleft, receding reddish hair above a hawkish nose, I felt I was paying a heavy price for my indebtedness.

It was a shock to find these fatherly old men so eager to put their hands down the front of my dress, desisting only when I looked at Gwen with mute appeal and CP shook his head. Clothed in a superbly cut grey suit and the awesome power of Collins Street, Melbourne, millionaire W S Robinson always occupied the boardroom when he visited the West. Impressed by his commanding presence (he was over 180 centimetres tall) his urbanity and his age (more than three times my own) I was flattered by the invitation to make a foursome with him, CP and Gwen at a quiet restaurant in the hills. In the back of the Nash driving up Greenmount Hill, I squirmed and struggled silently under his roving hands. There was further ignominy when he sent via CP an envelope containing a twenty-pound note.

'Should I give it back?' I asked Grandma and Gwen, who had received a similar envelope.

'Certainly not!' Grandma said stoutly, to my relief, for I'd never had a twenty-pound note before.

Then Harry came in, asking with awful implication, 'What's SHE doing with twenty pounds?' Grandma assured him it was all right, defending my virtue.

Banking the money, I felt horribly uneasy. Was this the first step on the downward path? What would my parents think? And Harry's suspicions rankled. Naturally enough he was jealous of my privileged position, sharing the affection of his mother, and the generosity of his sister. Nominally the male head of the house since Grandfather's death, he looked after the garden, paid full board from his clerical job in the Electricity and Gas Department, and didn't really approve of our 'goings-on' as they were called.

On the days when he visited Gwen after work, CP would give me a lift home. One day he took a new route, driving under the subway to a lonely patch of bush near the Claremont Asylum, where he turned off the engine and put his hand up my skirt. 'I'll tell Gwen!' I threatened, at which he started the engine and drove back down Onslow Road. Seeing us arrive from a westerly direction, Harry was immediately suspicious, looking at me with contempt. Gwen believed in CP so implicitly that I could never have actually told her of his peccadilloes.

With a distaste for older men building up, I allowed the rich Hale School push to take me partying in their fathers' cars, the boys in dinner suits, the girls in long evening dresses. We had no difficulty in getting served with cocktails in the opulent lounge of the Palace Hotel. We left one of these parties crowded into the car, streetlights long since out, the boys half drunk. At an intersection, we hit an obstacle amid the sound of smashing glass, the whinny of a horse and the owner of an overturned milk cart yelling abuse. Our driver put his foot on the accelerator, shouting: 'All keep your mouths shut and we'll be okay.'

Although haunted by the thought of the poor milko, his living ruined by hit-run upper-crust vandals, I kept quiet, trembling when I saw a policeman. There was no prosecution.

Refusing to have any more truck with the Hale School bunch, I enrolled for the Leaving Certificate at Perth Technical School, a two-year course crammed into one year. Economics was taught by Dr H C Coombs, eventually to become Governor of the Commonwealth Bank. 'Nugget' always rushed into class with his bedraggled black university gown flying behind him. Considered a left-winger, he was easily sidetracked into discussions of Marxism by students bored with the theory of marginal utility.

The 'Leaving' was the minimum educational requirement of the Australian Journalists' Association. I scraped through, and as soon as the union's strict ratio of young newshounds to graded staff permitted, obtained the coveted cadetship, dreaming that work on the women's section would one day lead to general reporting.

There was no thrill to be compared to the rumble of the great Crabtree press coming to life several floors below. The underground monster shook the whole building as the *Western Mail* ran through its weekly printing, followed by the *Broadcaster* for radio fans; and six days a week the midnight roar as the *West* rolled out to be loaded into Bays' vans waiting in the lane with engines idling, ready for the dash to the suburbs and country towns.

Noel White, a true professional, allocated our reporting tasks. Her father worked in the composing room, his name mentioned in whispers because of his association with a certain Rosie of dubious reputation — Noel's mother was divorcing him. Still fond of him, Noel took me to meet him out back, a fascinating, noisy place, the proofreaders' droning voices flowing from one corner, linotypes clanking as fast-fingered operators pulled the lever that turned out shining lead slugs of type from the pot of molten metal bubbling at the side of the machine; the comps locking still-hot silvery columns into formes for the pages. The workmen liked to show me all the fascinating intricate processes of printing, including the old handset tall wooden type font for billboards that might have come straight down from Gutenberg.

The views of management were often aired by CP, who always blamed agitators for any unrest. Process and manual workers seemed to be a race apart from journalists and 'were always causing trouble'. When machinists and compositors went on strike, CP strode about the Onslow Road kitchen boasting of how he stalked into the composing room and sacked one of the agitators as a lesson to the rest. I believed Noel's father was one of them — she'd said he was a good unionist. Gwen's tender heart was shocked.

Poor Gwen, so beautiful and talented, so sweet-natured. Surely, I thought, she deserved happiness, not this bitter relationship with an old, though certainly virile love whose family hated her. Spending her days waiting for the nights when they could go off to their hideaway in the bush at Mount Claremont; trying to keep herself eternally young with expensive unguents, wheedling favours for her family; during the day keeping boredom at bay practising her songs; accompanying herself on the piano, Grandma throwing in advice about proper breathing as they hummed up and down the scales. Her bad days every month, lying on her bed in torment, dulling savage menstrual pains with gin.

Naively pinning her hopes of happiness on what Grandma saw in the cards each morning, dreaming of the baby she'd have one day, Gwen was unaware of the cruel twist of fate in store. Coming home mad with frustration after useless arguments with CP about divorce, she would grab plates off the table and hurl them to the floor; or lock herself away when Mrs Smith came to the gate screaming abuse for all the street to hear.

Poor Grandma! Burdened with her daughter's woes and a prickly grandchild, in her widowhood she tried to make ends meet on the rent from the other house, music teaching, Harry's board, a small contribution from my meagre pay, while relying on Gwen for the phone, or new curtains. Her own needs were simple — cigarettes, Danish blue cheese or garlic sausage from Boans, a glass of stout and jellied trotters for supper after Saturday night at the trots, where she put small bets on the tote. She dreamed about Biddie returning to the stage, and worried about some danger she saw in the crystal ball for my father ever since we told her of the immense treacherous rock formations of the south coast where he went fishing.

Grandma never complained about my sending a small sum each week to Muv, to salve my conscience for deserting those six brothers and only sister. The family were now camping in the ghostly Kendenup dehydrator among the big iron troughs and slatted wooden benches of the drying rooms, festooned with cobwebs, cold vast spaces that kept everybody around the open fire; except Muv, cooking on the primus stove that she always feared would explode.

In letters it was hard to tell how much I missed the quirky humour of our family life, the interplay of so many different personalities, each with their own special talents and niche in our affection. Better not to tell Muv that Grandma still blamed her for each new baby, while recounting her own horrific toll of miscarriages.

Her Fred could do no wrong. I'd never thought of criticising him either, respecting his code of honour, knowledge of science and literature, his singing and music. He always sent a telegram on Grandma's birthday — easy enough to remember, St Valentine's Day. At least she was pleased that her grandson Geoffrey had been born so close to it, on 15 February 1924, given Samuel as his second name after Grandfather Allen. She'd admired Anthony, a beautiful sweet-tempered child who had arrived in 1926; who sang 'Santa Lucia' as sweetly as she could wish, grey eyes sparkling under long dark lashes, and Donald, the baby who came after I left Albany High, now becoming a wiry observant youngster. But Jack, still victimised, she thought, for his devilry, was her favourite.

Gwen had at last attained one of her dearest ambitions. Based on her empathy with children, she persuaded CP to let her secretly become Aunt Mary of the *Western Mail* children's page. I would be the front — a deception that I loathed, though I didn't mind handing her the thirty shillings a week that I collected.

Unable to tell the Kendenupites the whole story, I concentrated in my letters home on matters more enhancing to my reputation. A Perth miniaturist, Margaret Johnson, asked me to sit for a portrait. Axel Poignant took studio photos of me looking very smug in a white rabbit-fur jacket, donated by Gwen because the fur fell out on the black dinner jacket of one's escort.

Going to balls to report on what the socialites wore, I was surprised by their eagerness to get their names in the paper. I wrote of reading the news summary on 6IX, the *West*'s radio station, of the way cadets were trained by throwing them into the deep water, and reporting the seamy side of life in the local courts, interviewing joyful Golden Casket winners and bereaved mothers.

I described the newspaper men they knew of through their by-lines: small rotund Ivor Birtwistle, editor of the *Western Mail*, darting about like a balding kiwi; 'Hooky' Davies, the short stooping finance editor, his aquiline nose pointing to the floor as if following the trail of alluvial gold; the perky grey cameraman Fred Flood whose offsider Doug Burton photographed me with a bunch of realistic woollen wildflowers for a pic-story. Big-boned horsewoman Emily Pelloe cantered into the office with her column. My parents had met her in 1921, when she visited Kendenup, climbed Mount Mondurup in the Stirling Ranges; and presented them with her book on the orchids of Western Australia, published by C J de Garis. The Women Writers' Society met at her home, the verandahed colonial building on the corner of King's Park Road and Thomas Street.

I felt no need to mention the pain and fright of being called into the sub-editors' room for a curt rebuke and the fear of a libel suit on the paper from one's careless mistake. No need to tell them of my escapes from a fate worse than death: the Italian doctor who took me home from one of CP's discreet parties and offered to show me his surgery — where he dashed a large bottle on the floor. The sweet odour of chloroform wafted up from the broken glass — no good when it's old, he said, but I hadn't waited to find out.

And I avoided mentioning the attentions of Stan Rosier, brassy deputy chief of staff, CP's loud-mouthed but likeable sycophant. Cultivating the Hollywood image of a newspaper man, he had an enormous knowledge of films and their distribution — advertising them ran to many profitable pages of the broadsheet *West*, in exchange for laudatory reviews. A cosy relationship with the managers of Perth cinemas led to heavy promotion of the annual Movie Ball, usually fancy dress. Gwen enthused CP about a Mary Pickford set — she did have a resemblance to the queen of the silent screen and the same indefinable charm. A pretty young dressmaker, Ethel Boom, fiancee of my uncle Harry, would make the six white organdie crinolines adorned with lace and roses that would be worn by Gwen, her actress friends Renee and Kath Esler, Ethel, Mrs Rosier and myself. At the ball, while Stan was big-noting himself with the committee, Mrs Rosier confided to me that her period was late and she feared pregnancy. So much for his story of marriage in name only — how lucky that our association had never gone beyond kisses and cuddles!

On St Valentine's Day, 1936, a telegram reached 72 Onslow Road saying that Muv was in Mount Barker Hospital with a premature baby, another Frederick (Bob's second name was

Frederick). Grandma said: 'Good God, that makes nine! How I wish Marj wouldn't be so careless.' Although I was concerned for my mother, it was hard to work up enthusiasm for another baby, beyond sending down nappies and nighties because there was no layette. And how would my sister Lauri feel — the younger ones were never told about pregnancies that Muv concealed with a big bony frame and clever dressmaking.

When they brought the baby to Perth, his tiny head encased in a warm bonnet, layers of blankets keeping him at womb heat, there was no rush of sisterly love; until, left to mind the tiny, struggling scrap of life, I was won over, and sobbed with homesickness as Der revved the ute for the long drive back to Kendenup.

But the city had claimed me. Homesickness soon became a thing of the past in the teenage struggle for identity, belief in a cause, and political commitment even though voting at twenty-one was a long way off. Noble aims, however, conflicted with social climbing to shed the stigma of Gwen's liaison. Pete Thomas, now a constant companion, urged me to join the elite King's Park Tennis Club. With a Peppermint Grove address, he had no trouble but friends of the Smiths opposed my nomination. Eventually accepted, I won some minor tournament. The prize was a book token.

This small event had an immense influence, because at Foy and Gibson's I found Sholokov's *And Quiet Flows the Don*, Bocaccio's *Decameron*, then banned, and Katharine Susannah Prichard's *Coonardoo*. Sholokov opened vividly the proscribed struggle of socialism to defeat the invading armies of the West; Katharine Susannah portrayed the Aborigines as thinking suffering human beings, not the pathetic hawkers of clothes props we saw in the suburbs; Bocaccio's droll stories confirmed that my revolt against religious hypocrisy was soundly based, and also that censorship was an unjust political stricture of freedom to read world classics. *Ulysses* by James Joyce was also banned, but I managed to get hold of it.

In journalism, unspoken rules were becoming clear, rules that couldn't be broken without risk to your job. 'All the news that's fit to print' excluded a vast area that you got to know by experience. We were our own censors. I soon found out how this operated. A lot of newspaper stories were gathered from the great ocean liners that arrived weekly at Fremantle, first port of call for ships coming from Europe via the Suez Canal, then the main means of travel. We would wait for our turn up the gangway after customs, shipping agents and waterside workers with vicious-looking hooks in their belts. On board we'd dash to the purser's office to scan the passenger list for famous or infamous people — the newspapers got cables only about the most important. On an Orient liner I interviewed a local wool buyer and his wife who had been to the Soviet Union. The Prevosts gave an interesting and favourable account of the USSR — a real scoop, I thought, certain the *West* had never published such material. The story hit the subs' wastepaper basket.

Another experience that made a deep impression was in 1934, when the *Strathaird* berthed with Egon Kisch among its thousand-odd passengers. The male journalists said he was a Czechoslovak writer going to a peace conference in Melbourne for the world committee of the Movement Against War and Fascism. They already knew or guessed he wasn't going to be allowed to land. Federal Attorney-General R G Menzies had denounced the Melbourne congress as a front for communist propaganda. The word went around that Kisch was giving an interview in the smokeroom on board the ship. Sitting on the outskirts (the men did all the big stories), we heard him protest against the baggage search that had taken place in his cabin — not for prohibited imports but for political books or pamphlets — and a ban on getting off the ship.

Could this small greyish cultured man speaking in fluent English about peace and the need to oppose fascism really be so dangerous that Australians should be prevented from hearing him? It was said he spoke twelve languages, so it seemed the usual dictation test would be useless. I followed subsequent events with interest: how he jumped from the ship's deck to the wharf in Melbourne, breaking his leg; that Katharine Susannah Prichard and a young doctor, Alec Jolly, had been on the committee waiting to receive him before he failed a dictation test in Scottish Gaelic, and the High Court ruling against his deportation. And I eagerly read what was published of the views he espoused.

Although female journalists got the same pay as males — barmaids being the only other women in Western Australia so privileged at the time — I was abysmally ignorant about the role of the Australian Journalists Association. Pete explained the campaign to lessen the spread of hours worked, with a reasonable time for rest, so that after finishing a job late at night, you couldn't be put on early next day. This made sense as I often slept through the jangle of the alarm after reporting a ball for the social pages.

Pete and our irrepressible fellow cadet, Doug Watt, keeper of the salacious wall paste-up — shockers that had gone into print — undertook my education in union matters. If the AJA got us a wage rise, we wouldn't have to go for 'conts.', the extra contributions that were paid by the line, or in the case of a regular extra like the role of 'Aunt Mary', by a specified modest amount. This role had finally been ceded to me by Gwen when, sick of the deceit, I proposed that I would do all the work but hand her the money. Seemingly a fair deal, it was cruel to deprive her of a task performed with love, whereas for me it was only extra work and made me the butt of jokes.

I learnt all about the file-room 'morgue'. On the death of celebrities, the obituary was ready to hit the front page long before they died. In the case of royalty, whole pages were made up ready to go. In the love affair of Edward VIII, it wasn't easy to predict the outcome: there were two sets of headlines ready: the abdication or continued kingship. To give up a throne for the sake of love pleased Grandma and Gwen. The royalists of 'Woman's Realm' were pleased for a different reason — a twice-divorced woman couldn't be Queen of England!

Afterwards, with a bit more space for other events, the *West* settled down. Cadets were to be given time off for lectures in the Diploma of Journalism at the University of Western Australia. Most of the senior literary staff believed that reporters were made in practice, not by having university degrees. Once again I studied economics under 'Nugget' Coombs, often being late because of the slow progress of the tram screeching around the curves of Mounts Bay Road. After the first term history exam, Professor Fred Alexander, raising bushy grey eyebrows at my paper, patiently explained that technical school attitudes to the glorious British Empire wouldn't wash at university.

As external students rushing back to work after lectures, cadets weren't absorbed into student life. We relished the story of Griff Richards and Jim McCartney, and their legendary 'rustication' (a kind of temporary expulsion) from the institution for editing what was then considered a particularly pornographic edition of the student paper.

At home, Pete Thomas was accepted as my boyfriend, liked for his wicked humour and sense of the ridiculous. A wide grin revealing perfect teeth made up for a certain unevenness of feature, turned-up nose and high forehead. When he was born, his mother — a woman of strong opinion — had decided that the name Harvey Alfred would look well on a doctor's brass plate. But his father, carrying out the registration, had wilfully tacked on Pete, without the 'r'. On his father's early death, the family was hard up, and his mother contemplated selling the family home. Pete, instead of studying medicine, became a lowly cadet journalist on the strength of his high marks at Perth Modern School, while his brother Jack continued his engineering course at university.

The 1930s were good soil for socialist ferment and questioning, beginning with the slide into the Great Depression, and the rise of fascism and Nazism. So many political events on which one had to take a stand on one side or the other! There had always been political discussion at 72 Onslow Road, ranging from Grandma's staunch Labor views, Harry's brief delving into Douglas Social Credit, my own search for economic justice and the path to peace, hopes pinned on the League of Nations as Mussolini invaded Abyssinia and Australia joined Britain in applying sanctions. Now there was more argument than discussion, especially when Biddie came on a visit from Sydney, loud in her support of the New South Wales Premier J T Lang and her condemnation of his contentious sacking.

Biddie approved without taking an active part in the 'Lang is Right' movement, maintaining that the Lang Plan would have pulled the State out of its economic woes. She was indignant about Captain de Groot's sensational dash on horseback, during the opening of the Sydney Harbour Bridge, to cut the ribbon with his sword in defiance of the official party. A member of the rabidly anti-communist New Guard, formed by big business, he was demonstrating its power to smash the Lang Government, Biddie said.

Priding herself on her wide reading of political and economic theories, Biddie nevertheless kept a foot in both camps, the rich and the exploited, although more firmly based in the world of business, and Uncle Reg Randall's profitable land sales, from which she derived her opulent lifestyle. Eventually she persuaded Grandma to abandon her Labor views and, possibly out of contrariness, began to champion the rising dictators.

CP listened tolerantly to arguments coming from a beautiful and enchanting woman. She wasn't moved by the misery of millions of hungry unemployed, and the destruction of stockpiles of food that couldn't be sold because people had no money to buy it.

When Biddie had gone, Grandma and Gwen bore the brunt of teenage rebelliousness that in the usual course of things would have been directed at my parents. How could they ignore the horrors of the Spanish Civil War, the overthrow of an elected government, the intervention of Hitler and Mussolini? Completely wrapped in Gwen's troubles, they spent hours with the tarot pack laid out on the lounge-room carpet, my aunt growing more and more enraged and frustrated by CP's refusal to be seen at public functions with her. Anonymous letters were coming more often, accusing her of being a home wrecker. Usually she ignored them, but one was so specific that she went to the address at the time the letter said she would see CP with another mistress.

When she saw him met at the gate by the dowdy little typist Ramona nursing a red-haired child, she was face to face with the brutal reality of her situation. Her anguish, tears alternating with terrible rages, shook the house for weeks until we all feared for her sanity. The arrival in her life of a tall dark man, as predicted by the cards, helped give her the courage to send CP packing.

Urbane, cadaverous, hair thin on top, eyes recessed behind heavy library lenses, Gordon Johnstone had been a funeral director before becoming the licensee of the Hotel Metropole in central Hay Street. After a low-key courtship and marriage, he installed Gwen in the spacious apartment on the first floor with a new baby grand piano as a wedding gift. Soon left alone, she practised her songs, her favourite 'Villanelle', 'O follow the swallow' echoing through the empty rooms; and tended the flowers in window boxes on the balcony overlooking the busy city, baiting traps with carnation buds to catch the rats that scurried from one building to another.

I began to blame Grandma for Gwen's fate — her ambition to relive her own career through her daughter — and forgot her kindness, and her unselfish kitchen slavery, in my desire to escape from the oppressive atmosphere, my search for freedom to live my own life, and a clean start in a new atmosphere free from scandal. Pete, with some self interest, urged me on.

I rented a cheap flatette in Parliament Place, West Perth, with a gas stove in a lean-to balcony and use of a communal bathroom. Within walking distance of Newspaper House, it was conveniently close to Parliament, with Pete working in the press gallery learning the ropes from Griff Richards. The parliamentary library, Pete said, wouldn't miss the heavily bound copy of Karl Marx's *Capital* that he stole for us to study, certain that no Member would ever read it. Skimping on food to buy curtains and saucepans, fighting loneliness, longing for the Kendenup family, I was somewhat comforted by the thought that the move had established an impeccable reputation for me, until I heard the current rumour: CP was paying the rent, and I was now one of his mistresses.

(From *Anger and Love*, an autobiography, 1993.)

EMMA CICCOTOSTO &
MICHAL BOSWORTH

PETER AND ME

Peter Ciccotosto was born at Vasto in the Abruzzi in 1920. He was the second of five children, two boys and three girls. Vasto is on the coast and fishing there is an important industry, but fishing never pays very much money, or it didn't in those days. Peter's father left home to work before he came to Australia. He had emigrated to Buenos Aires after his first child, a daughter, was born. After four years away he returned with a little money, bought some land and built a house with mud bricks. There, he and his wife had another four children, but he decided that he could not support his family living in Italy and so he emigrated to Australia around the same time as my father. He shared my father's experiences of living hand-to-mouth in the bush with only a tent as shelter. He could send very little money back to his wife because of the bad conditions in Australia, so she had to work hard to support the children. She was a big woman, nearly 1.8 metres tall, and she took all sorts of work, including labouring in the fields, to keep them going. After her husband had been away for nine or ten months he wrote to her asking her to send Peter out to work with him, but she replied that either they all came or nobody would, and so they emigrated together as a family. But like my family they left one behind. Teresa, Peter's eldest sister, was already married when the family decided to go and she stayed on in Vasto where she was beginning her family of five children. I met her many years later when I visited Italy on holiday.

Peter was clever at school and because of this his mother

managed to keep him at the Scuola Marittima until he was eighteen. He topped his year, and if he had not then had to emigrate, his career might have taken quite a different path. They came to Australia in 1937 on the *Esquilino*. They enjoyed their trip and they liked what they saw when they first reached Fremantle and Perth, but when they got to Hamel, near Waroona, where there was a rented house waiting for them, they received a shock. To reach it they had to walk across a paddock and under a barbed wire fence, for there was no proper track to it. They had to make one themselves. It was an old, abandoned weatherboard house in the middle of nowhere, and they did not like it at all. During those first days if they could have caught a boat back to Vasto they would have. When we arrived a couple of years later Mrs Ciccotosto came up the hill to see my mother. She told her about her first impressions and then said, 'Now it's better. I'm happy now. There are other families living here and we get together sometimes, and pass our time like we did back home.' When my mother heard that, she cheered up too. She felt better after that visit.

Peter's father had been happy to see his family again and he immediately took his sons with him to dig potatoes; they also grew some of their own. Because they were good workers, they had a bit of luck that first year and made enough money to buy ten hectares of irrigated land at Hamel, where they built a new house. Peter's family grew vegetables, potatoes, pumpkins, peas and beans for the Perth market.

Hamel, as Peter's mother had said, had a few Italian families. They kept themselves to themselves, mainly because they couldn't speak English very well and they knew that their Australian neighbours expected them to be able to speak English almost straightaway. The older people found it very difficult to pick up the new language — my mother never managed to do so — but the young ones picked it up quickly enough. It's easy to say, 'You come to this country, you learn to speak our language,' but for the older people that was the hardest thing. They could not change the language they had spoken since they were babies without a lot of effort. The younger children went to school where they soon learned

English as I did, and Peter picked it up from reading newspapers. He also acquired a bilingual girlfriend, which was a help.

Peter was one of those people who always had friends. If there was anything going on everyone made sure that Peter would be there. I remember him telling me how he and his friends would sometimes stay up all night, talking and laughing. The next morning he would be still sleeping when he was supposed to be up and his mother would find it hard to wake him. She did not believe him when he told her what he had been doing; she thought he had been with a girl because girls fell over themselves to be noticed by him, he was so good-looking. He liked girls all his life, for he was attractive and happy-go-lucky. Peter's mother didn't like the idea that he was chasing girls, for in Australia the girls were much freer than they had been back in Vasto. She soon found that girls called on the house to see if Peter was home. She said to Peter, 'You tell them not to come.' But Peter laughed. She insisted, 'You have to go to work. You must not worry about girls so much.' Peter hated trouble, so he met the girls in town, but his mother knew, and from then on her favourite son was Caesario. Everyone liked Peter; he never gossiped or had a bad word for anyone. He was a gentleman.

After he had walked out of the army he began to visit our farm more regularly, and my brother, who was only a year older than him, enjoyed these visits very much. They played cards together and when they went out they went around with other young men their age. There was a group of four or five of them and they spent a lot of their spare time together. Eventually Domenico noticed how much I admired Peter and he grew jealous, partly because he was very careful of my reputation and he cared for me a lot, but also because he didn't want Peter to waste any time with me. My brother at this time had just got married by proxy to a girl he had known in Italy. Because of the war it was to be many years before he saw his wife and he must have been lonely for a companion. He kept reminding me that Peter had a girlfriend and could not possibly be interested in me. I knew that! There was nothing between Peter and me; I just liked looking at him because he was so nice. I knew about him and the girls he had chasing him, so I didn't really think it would be possible to be his girlfriend. I was six years younger than him and more than thirty centimetres shorter, but you can't stop girls from dreaming ...

As we settled into our new life we got to know the other Italian families in the district and we sometimes had parties in our sitting room when we would dance to the sound of an old wind-up record-player. They were evenings we all enjoyed; evenings that took the chill from being strangers in a strange land. I loved dancing and I could go on for ever. We danced old favourites like the tarantella, and we danced the 'broom dance'. It was a bit like musical chairs. One of the men had to dance in the centre with a broom as his partner. When the music stopped he had to grab a new partner as we changed, and the one who was not quick enough was left with the broom in the middle. I loved dancing, and I still do, and so did Peter. He danced with everyone, me included. Nevertheless I was surprised when one day Peter followed me as I was cycling home from town on the sandy track. 'What do you want?' I asked him. 'You don't want to talk to me. You have a girlfriend already, I know.'

'No,' he said. 'That is all finished. I like you. I want you to be my girlfriend because I want my girlfriend to be mine only. I finished with her because I caught her with someone else. I loved her so much, but she should not have done that to me. I want you to be my girlfriend now.'

I was happy. I stopped, and he came close. I was scared; I did not know what to say to him; I didn't really believe him. He was so good-looking he could have had any girl around. I said, 'My brother won't let me go anywhere with you.'

'Never mind him,' said Peter. 'We will meet somehow.' The next time they had pictures in Waroona I desperately wanted to go because I thought I would see Peter there. My parents did not seem to mind whether I went or not; it was my brother who said no. So I stayed at home and cried all evening. My brother was back by eleven thirty and was soon asleep, but I remained wakeful. I was wondering whether Peter would come up to the house. I went to my window and there he was, standing in the yard. 'He loves me, he really loves me,' I said to myself, and I pushed up the window and got out of the house without anyone hearing me. 'How did you know I was here,' he asked. I had to tell him that I had hoped he would come and I had had a feeling that he might. He told me he loved me and that one day he would marry me. I was very happy.

We saw each other at the pictures from time to time, for in Waroona films were shown once a week and my brother did not always insist that I stay at home. Sometimes I went to his house to see his sisters or they came to my place and he came to get them, but no one knew about us. I didn't tell anyone. Each time I saw him I had butterflies in my stomach. My mother told me that Peter had too many girlfriends and wouldn't be marrying me, but she didn't know that I was meeting him secretly each week, crawling out of my bedroom window late at night to see him in the back shed. We would stay together for about two or three hours kissing and cuddling. I was scared all the time in case my mother or my brother found us out. I even worried about his mother discovering us. We talked about ordinary things we were doing. He was digging potatoes then and they were paid by the number of bags they filled each day. Peter was proud that he could fill more bags than the others. He was strong, but being so tall it was hard work for him at the end of the day to bend down and put the potatoes into bags. They had to fork them out, sort them and bag them, and to do fifty bags a day was a lot of work. But everyone then was working hard to put away a bit of money.

At this time — I was sixteen — I was completely ignorant about the facts of life. My first period had come as a complete surprise to me. I was a late developer and my mother had told me nothing. When I first found blood in my pants I thought I had injured myself and I went to her and said, 'Look, there's this blood.' She looked and said sharply, 'You're grown-up now,' and left me to figure it out.

I already thought I was grown-up, so this did not tell me anything, but I gathered some rags of an old sheet and used them as pads. When I changed them I did not know what to do with them. I was too embarrassed to ask anyone, so I threw the old ones under the bed. I told myself I would wait until the house was empty and then I would wash them, and so I did, but the whole process and what it meant remained a mystery to me. As I was very irregular it never occurred to me that its absence would indicate a disturbance of any kind. I did not know that bleeding stopped during pregnancy because I did not know anything like that about my body.

Peter must have known that he was dealing with an innocent girl, for he was not an innocent. Indeed, I later learned that he had come to me after being with other girls in the town first. But one cold night as we lay wrapped together under a long army overcoat, without me realising what was going on, he briefly penetrated me. I did not feel a thing, but afterwards I noticed blood and I thought I was having a period. It didn't turn out that way. This is probably difficult for people to believe, but you must remember that we kissed and cuddled in the dark and he was by this time quite experienced sexually, while for my part I was, as I have said, completely ignorant. We saw each other about twice a week, but neither of us mentioned this particular experience to the other. We talked instead of other things. I worried that his mother didn't like me, whereas he felt that everything would be all right when the time came. I don't think he meant to do what he did, because he didn't do it again, but the damage was done.

Anyway, about two months after this time I began to feel peculiar in the mornings, and once I vomited in front of my mother who looked at me and said casually, 'You look just like a pregnant woman.' I gasped. She had said it in all innocence, but for me the penny dropped. Perhaps I was pregnant. I would have to tell Peter at once.

'You must see a doctor,' he said once I had told him.

'What?' I was scandalised at the thought. I was terrified. How could I go into town and see a doctor for that reason?

'It's the only way you'll find out for sure,' he said, and I knew he was right.

I was so worried that I decided I had to do it, so I cycled in the next day to see the local doctor. On my way I noticed two army cars and my stomach began to churn for another reason. What if they had finally come for Peter? But once I was in

Waroona my first worry returned. I was only seventeen and it was a big thing for me to have to ask a doctor the question I needed to know the answer to.

'Can you tell me if I'm pregnant, doctor?' I heard myself ask it, but I wasn't prepared for the internal examination which was necessary to find the answer. I was terribly embarrassed.

When he had finished he asked me, 'How old are you?' I told him.

'You are too young,' he said severely. 'Yes, you are pregnant.'

I felt sick. I didn't know what to say. I just got up and walked out of the surgery and then I began to cry. I wanted very badly to go back and tell him to do something for me, but I was too scared to see him again, and anyway it was 1943, and those days were not like today. He probably would not have helped me the way I wanted.

My one thought was to tell Peter, but he was now in trouble for another reason. The army cars were nowhere to be seen when I came out of the doctor's surgery, but my fear had been right. They had come for Peter and that very day he was taken off to Fremantle Prison. My brother told me that night, and a couple of days later I got a letter from Peter himself telling me what had happened. The letter also contained the news that he had to do one year in prison for absconding from the army. When I read this you can imagine how I felt. If he had to spend a whole year in prison this baby would be born during it and would be illegitimate because we would not be married. I felt desperate. I did not know what to do. Should I write back and tell him, or should I wait a few days and tell my mother? I waited, but day went after day, and I found I could not tell my mother.

I now had a really bad two weeks. I had no friends I could talk to and ask for comfort and advice. The other Italian girls in Hamel would have been very jealous if they had known about Peter and me and so I couldn't tell any of them now. It would just cause a scandal. It seemed to me that my family could never be told. In those days unmarried mothers were an unheard-of disgrace, especially in the Italian community. I knew my brother, and probably my father too, would be very upset. I clung to the hope I could see Peter and tell him what the doctor had said and hoped that he would still want to marry me.

My mother went to Perth each month to visit a specialist for her health, and after two weeks it was time for another visit. I went with her. When we arrived at the boarding house in North Perth, I told her we had to go to Fremantle Prison at once to see Peter. 'What for?' she asked, reasonably enough. 'You can wait to see him.'

But I couldn't. The more I insisted, the more anxious I became, the more my mother understood. She was so angry and upset. 'You're pregnant,' she cried.

Defiantly I agreed. I knew I had disgraced the family and behaved badly, but somehow I hoped through all my mother's tears and reproaches that once I had seen Peter it would all be put to rights.

So my mother and I caught the train to Fremantle. My mother was so upset she didn't stop growling at me all the way, and because she didn't speak English this was in Italian. I felt even worse because people looked at us when they heard her. When we got to Fremantle we didn't know where to go so I had to ask someone where the prison was. Following directions, we found our way to a big door on the side of the prison walls. The guard asked who did we want to see and I told him 'Peter Ciccotosto.' At my side my mother was still growling on, and I was trying to hush her. '*Stai zit,*' I said, 'keep quiet,' but she wouldn't.

They let us into a big room where there were other visitors sitting and waiting and soon they marched in the soldiers. Peter was in uniform and looked very smart.

I was so nervous at having to tell him what had happened, but he knew as soon as he looked at me. My mother was so angry with him. She wanted to blame him for everything that had happened to me. I wanted to say so many things to Peter but I couldn't get them out. He was quite calm.

'It's all right,' he said. 'We'll get married, but as I've a year's prison sentence from the army you'll have to see my Commanding Officer and get his permission.'

That started my mother off again, the thought of me having to see an army officer, but there was no other way to arrange it. For my own part I was relieved that Peter had stayed so calm and had wanted to marry me. 'Everything will be all right,' he assured me, as he told me where I had to go in Perth to see the right officer.

I was nervous about the thought of seeing an army officer, but I did not have to go far to find him. The army headquarters was in Francis Street, not too distant from the boarding house where my mother and I were staying. I left my mother there and walked to the barracks by myself because I knew that as my mother didn't speak English she couldn't help me with this interview. I was a bit worried about my own English. In those days I was not as fluent as I have since become, and I was scared I would forget the words for what I had to say. As I walked along Francis Street I decided the only way to approach the officer was to tell him exactly why I had to get married. I could not see any other way of making him give Peter permission. But to see the right officer, a Major Harvey, I had to pass three other officers, each of them wanting to know exactly why I had to see the Major and no one else, and to each of them I had to say, 'I've got to get married and my boyfriend's in gaol.'

Major Harvey made no difficulties. He telephoned the prison to see if Peter confirmed my story and when he did he gave Peter leave to get married outside the prison, provided he was back inside the prison by six o'clock the same night. I was so happy that we were given permission to marry, but I cried all the way back to the boarding house because I knew we now would have a lot of trouble to get everything arranged.

We got a lot of opposition from people who knew us. Peter's mother was furious. She did not want her son to marry me and she wrote to him every day he was in prison, telling him not to. I knew she didn't like me, but when Peter showed me her letters even I was surprised at what she said. Just as it had with my first communion the Church once again stood in my way but this time there was no easy way out. I had to find a priest, and the one I found told me I was under-age and I needed a letter of permission before he could marry me; furthermore it would take six weeks to publish the banns. I didn't want to get a letter from my father and I didn't want to wait for six weeks, so I looked for another way. At the boarding house they told me of something called a 'special licence', so I went back to the priest, and he said it would cost us ten pounds. I had no money and when I saw Peter in prison he had none either. I asked him to write to his mother to see if she would lend it to us, but she refused. I said to Peter then that the only thing I wanted from his mother was her permission to let her daughter Lucy come to Perth to be my bridesmaid. I was friendly with Lucy and I wanted her there, so Peter wrote, but his mother said Lucy was not allowed to come to Perth, and no one from the family would be coming. Peter was as upset as I was at all these unhelpful developments. He wanted to get married because he didn't want me to have the baby as a single mother and he didn't even mind having to go straight back to prison after the ceremony.

My mother went back to Waroona, leaving me to sort all of these problems out. She could not stay away from my father and the farm for too long, but I knew that she would return for the wedding if it ever took place. I took my courage in my hands and went back to the priest again. I said, 'We don't have the ten pounds, but we have to get married. If we don't get married this baby is going to be illegitimate.' So the priest agreed to find the money somewhere and get the licence for us. Luckily for me in those days I found a friend called Lucia who helped me along. She was a friend of Anna who had come out on the *Remo* with us. She had come to Australia a couple of years before me and she and her husband were really good to me. I moved out of the boarding house and stayed with them while all of this was going on. I talked over all my problems with them. They wanted me to stay with them after I got married, and at that time I felt they were the only people in the world who wanted to know me.

I bought myself a wedding dress with the little money I had left from what my mother had given me. It was cream, with puff sleeves and a heart-shaped bodice, and I found it in a shop in Perth. I even had to buy myself a wedding ring. I didn't have enough money to buy one for Peter and he never had one. We got married on Sunday 2 October 1943 by special licence in St Brigid's, West Perth. The priest was an Irishman, Patrick Kelliher. My brother and my mother came from Waroona to be there, and so did some of my friends from the boarding house. Domenico was Peter's best man, and a nice married lady from the boarding house was my bridesmaid. We couldn't afford a photographer and so I have no pictures of my wedding to show my children. Peter was released for four hours, from two o'clock to six, under escort, but when he got to the boarding house where I was waiting for him, the soldier with him left and said he would pick him up later. Peter was in uniform and he looked good to me. He looked at me and smiled. The church was not far from the boarding house and so we walked there. After we were married and had come out of the church I was surprised to see a lot of people had gathered to watch and I began to cry as they congratulated us. I was happy because we were married, but so many things were going through my mind. Not one member of Peter's family had come to the wedding. Peter told me not to cry. 'We'll be all right. I love you and that's what matters.'

The owner of the boarding house had offered to do us a small celebration in her dining room before Peter was picked up and taken back to Fremantle Prison. When we got back from the church I looked at the table she had made ready for us. It was beautiful. She had put on a white cloth and there was a big vase of fresh roses. Again I wanted to cry, but I made myself look happy and thanked her so much.

Getting married in this way, facing all the difficulties that I had to, taught me a lot. I came through this experience a lot more confident about the world. I felt I could face anything.

(From *Emma: A Recipe for Life*, an autobiography/recipe book, 1995.)

BURNING OFF

Vic and Angela lived right in the town, down by the river. Wes and I lived out a bit, under the hill. As the summer came we spent a lot of evenings sitting out on Vic and Angela's front verandah.

Up at our place, the first that Wes and I had ever shared alone, the darkness seemed to lap around our ankles. The town sprawled out below us, a faraway marquee of lights. But here with Vic and Angela we were deep within a community of sounds. Frogs croaked in the still air by the river, Angela's little sprinkler whip-whipped by the gate. Half a block away Poddy Stratton's TV droned under its giant antenna. The girls in the schoolteachers' house behind us sent scraps of laughter echoing across the town.

'I thought they were having a night off,' Angela said. 'The big blonde one told me they all wanted to wash their hair.' A few cars went by. Most were turning up to the schoolteachers' house. The teachers were said to be a 'good crowd' this year. They joined in, they were having a ball.

No doubt we were being observed too, sitting there like a flashback in the light of a kerosene lamp hung by the door. There was a campfire smell from the mosquito coils that Angela had lit for each of us. Vic's was too close, he knocked it over reaching for a can. Angela relit it. While Wes kept playing, discreet runs that went nowhere, as if to himself.

Poddy Stratton liked to surprise us. Prowl up the verge so as not to crunch the gravel. 'Hod enough for you?' He'd pause by the gate as if he'd just seen us. Vic raised a can to him, Wes put down his guitar. They worked in Poddy's garage when it was busy. Angela pulled out a spare chair. She'd been in the town almost a year now and no longer asked 'Where's Maxine?' Everybody knew that by this time of the night Maxine Stratton would be under the weather. Poddy went everywhere alone.

Poddy sat forward, legs apart, and fitted his stubby finger through the ring of a can. His pull was vicious, froth ran onto the floor. 'Cheers,' said Poddy. We all sat forward a little, in his honour, our visitor.

'Ye-es,' said Poddy, as if continuing a conversation, which in a way he was. 'It's gunna be a record summer.' His voice was pitched to reach the end of the verandah. He scanned us with his dark, ringed eyes. Poddy after hours, shaved jowls and sports shirt sleeves ironed out in right angles above his biceps, had a headmasterly air about him, a self-appointed distance. 'Useta think about putting in air-conditioning.' He wiped his long upper lip. 'That was before your friend Goof took charge of course.' He had assumed from the start where our sympathies would lie. 'I tell you what, everyone's gunna feel the pinch this Christmas. All your university types, your bra-burners, unionists and what have you. They aren't gunna like it any more than we do.'

He waved his hand at us, our bare feet, the ragged deckchairs, the cockeyed flywire door. Which side did he put us on now? We sagged back. Once I had taken him on, look there's a world recession, think what's been done for the etc, but I'd lost energy in the end, retreated — well anyway, it all boils down to, maybe it's just a temperamental, it's not that I'm really into ... (Wes, where are you? ...)

'I hope he doesn't stay long,' Angela said in the kitchen. She was trying to light her little camper stove to make a cup of tea. 'He'll wake up Nat the way he carries on.'

'I hate it when we all just sit and take it,' I said. 'Pod's pet hippies.' I muttered like this sometimes to Angela, when we were alone. Angela never seemed to hear. She was always doing something, providing something. I hovered behind her with the vague reflex feeling that I ought 'to help'. I tried to wash out some cups in the sink but it was full of drowning nappies.

There was a cough from the bedroom, and a long surprised wail.

'There!' said Angela. She paused on her way out. 'It's all Gough's fault of course.'

I was left, free to prowl. Since Poddy had come, you could disappear behind that beaded curtain in the country, 'women's work'. You only had to turn up with the tea. The flame beneath the kettle flickered near to extinction. Angela must be running out of gas.

Angela's kitchen was a lean-to, tacked on to the back wall of the cottage. The city owners asked no rent on the understanding that Vic would build a proper kitchen. He had laid the concrete slab for the floor. The dark end of the room still held the cement-mixer and a jumble of tools. Into the weatherboard wall, between the louvres, Angela had knocked a dartboard of nails. Here hung her pots, her mugs and nappy pins, her dusty bunches of drying rosemary and everlastings. Postcards from friends in New Zealand and Bali and Nepal were wedged in between the boards.

From the doorway I could see onto the verandah. Vic now held his son, loosely, high up on his chest, his dark face blank as it to say 'this makes no difference to me'. Poddy was still talking. I thought how people in middle-age seemed to occupy their own features, they seemed overdrawn, stamped with use. Like babies, they were a different species.

I remembered how my own parents used to entertain on summer evenings. They called it 'having a few couples over'. For this my mother would sweep the porch and sponge down the leaves of her pot-plants, wearing a snail curl crisscrossed with bobby pins over each cheek. She would put out guest towels and at the last moment, as the bell rang, shed her shorts and tread into a skirt. Fussed. For a handful of heads on a lit porch — sniper-like my sister and I knelt and picked out favourites — the anecdotal growl of the men's voices, some woman's helpless nervous trill-like punctuation, echoing out into the suburb. The vast starry night was undisturbed.

It was in the kitchen, if you padded out in your shortie pajamas, where the women got the supper, heads bent over the

144

hissing kettle, that the evening's true exchange seemed to be taking place.

Were we after all so very different?

And, spying like this, would I have picked out Wes to like, to watch, *mine*, as he yawned, as his bare satiny shoulders curved guard again over his guitar?

The first thing we had done when we came to the farmhouse was to set up the stereo on its packing-case frame in the empty living room. At last, full volume. The wet paddocks, the stolid hill received Zappa, Jeff Beck, the Allman Brothers. This was the environment we were used to.

'10, 9, 8, 7, 6 ...' shouted Pod on our doorstep one knife-cold night. 'When the hell is blast-off?'

Wes started putting on more and more country blues. Even if we were talking, after a while Wes's eyes slid sideways as his head chased up a beat. Those nostalgic voices were stronger than our own. In the mornings I would know that he had gone by the absence of music. These days he was leaving earlier and earlier for the garage.

I could not train myself to become a morning person. I had counted on this just happening in the country. Change of regime = change of person. Was this part of my work-ethic upbringing or was it really profoundly Zen? Funny how much they all seemed to be linking up: Bad Karma = Reap as Ye Shall Sow etc ... I lay on the mattress on the floor and tried to think about this. The sun slanted in through the broken venetian blinds.

The Inner Light grows in Silence and Concentration. I had to shut my eyes not to read this on the sun-slashed wall, not to see myself, felt pen in hand, on our first night here. My own uneven letters mocked me like graffiti. Yet still I did not try to remove them, or even cover them up.

In the city, in the big house where I had met Wes, the walls carried signs like a political meeting place. Indian gods behind the kitchen door. Over the stove, a newspaper cutting of Whitlam and Barnard waving after they had announced the conscription amnesty. A big mandala above the fireplace in what had come to be called the meditation room.

145

I'd thought then it would be easier to meditate in the country, to get up, work in the vegetable garden ...

The vegetable garden was no more. Such as it was, some lettuce-pale silver beet coiled up like flags and other, unidentified fronds, had disappeared entirely one weekend when we were in Perth. Tours of inspection now included not only the pen where we *could* have chooks, but the vegetable garden's graveyard, its frail wire netting looping among the grass, its scarecrow climbing canes.

Anyway, why were vegetables such an index of virtue? The eating of them, their growing, the disposal of them back to the earth?

... *In Silence and Concentration* ... The 'S' was oversize, it seemed to leer at me ...

The house was not silent. It was a hollow contained within a sleeve of animal life. In the ceilings and walls, under the floor, rats, cats, possums were they? skittered and thundered on ceaseless missions. The sleeve had holes. At night they gambolled in the passageways with the whispery abandon of out-of-hours children. Now the house itself creaked hospitably as its joints expanded in the heat of the sun. Crows bleated out in the paddocks. The day was cranking open before me.

Some time before we came here, this house had been dispossessed of its land and left to perch as a rental proposition on the crossroads between the town and the hill. A previous owner had tried to turn in into a city house, *à la mode*. You cleaned your teeth over a water-buckled vanity bench. The toilet had just made it inside, wedged in, not quite square, home-tiled next to the shower. (While the old dunny lurked outside among the grasses, its round white pedestal crouching in intimate darkness, its door forever on the point of being closed.)

A breakfast bar butted across the kitchen on spindly legs where a big wooden table should have been. The fireplace had been boarded up. On the sink a single cup trailed the tail of a tea bag. The guitar sat in the one comfortable chair.

There was only the country women's programme on the radio. It was like being home, sick, in the suburbs at midday, part of a community of grandmothers and invalids waiting behind lowered blinds. The heat here islanded you to the shelter of your own roof.

Outside the kitchen window the long yellow grasses marched up from the paddocks, consumed the fences, halted at the edge of the firebreak beside the straight gravel road. Although the day was still they shimmered and rocked, an imported pastoral ideal. I grabbed my shoulder-bag and shut the front door behind me with a bang that sent Wes' Javanese windchimes into brief, oriental applause.

It seemed quieter out on the road. Just the regular swish-swish of my thongs on gravel, throwing up little ankle wings of dust, and a great airy stillness around me. Crows rose and fell in the distance. The sun swamped everything. The drab homespun belly of the hill was exposed, too close behind me. I walked fast towards the haze over the town. I became an engine pumping up heat. I was haloed an inch over with my own heat. I thought about Coca Cola in thick glass bottles. I thought of shopping centres, as of great humming cathedrals. I thought of pine trees and of wading into the cold oil of the sea on a hot day. Although I had never been to a dinner party, I thought about soft lights and crystal glasses, and the fine picking up of lines of thought. Cheeses and wines, meat in cream, all that refined acid food that made you aggressive and decadent. And interesting. I trod out my own stale band of thoughts, oblivious to the landscape. While my higher mind slumbered, unsummoned for yet another day.

There was always a moment, as Angela and I turned into the main street, that I saw the town as distanced, through a lens, and our approach to it as something slow and heroic, a response to a sudden call for 'Action' ... The two women trudge on, faces to the sun, their long skirts blowing against their bodies ... The pusher rattled a pony-cart accompaniment, a flimsy candy-striped city job that jolted poor Nat sideways, his towelling hat across his eyes, his fat fists clenched on either knee.

'Whoa there boy,' sang out Angela, swooping down and straightening him, her long hair still damp from the paddling pool where I had found her, balancing Nat on her naked brown stomach. She and Nat smelled of talcum powder.

The main street narrowed down to vanishing point before us as it sped on into the wheatbelt. The shopfronts rose into turrets and mouldings, the clock in the Town Hall struck midday against the white-blue sky. But as we entered the town, past the dusty Municipal rose garden, the wide street swallowed us, and the shops broke into their familiar sequence, the Co-op, McIntyre's Newsagency, 'Verna' Hair Salon, the Post Office, Kevin Scragg's, The Bright Spot.

Why was shopping so consoling? A relief from the daily round of giving out, these small smooth purchases bumping against you, a newspaper, stamps, a bucket and spade for Nat, fresh bread, the first watermelon! It was like nourishment ... especially with Angela who did not worry about confusing wants and needs, who rummaged and fingered passionately while the Co-op girls, school-leavers with engagement rings, clustered around the pusher. 'Isn't he *gor*-geous!' they cried.

The pusher rolled on, Nat unblinking, wedged among the parcels.

'Just a minute,' Angela said, when we had nearly passed the butcher's. 'I've got to get a chop for Vic.' Vic was an unrepentant meat eater. He added a chop or some polony to Angela's wok vegetables and united them with tomato sauce.

'I'll wait outside with Nat,' I said. I did not even like to catch Kevin Scragg's eye as we walked past, his knowing salute, chopper in hand. He liked to ask you how you were finding life in the country, and to read your T-shirt, eyes lingering, for the benefit of the other customers. You knew, by the little silence as you made your way to the door, that you were going to be talked about as soon as the bell rang your exit.

I pushed the legitimising pusher back and forward under the window. At the kerb a girl in high-heeled sandals was stowing groceries and a baby into the back of her car. She gave me a quick church-porch smile across the pavement. Loretta Wells — one of the Wells. Did she see me as a sort of poor-white, a younger version of Mrs Boon, who shuffled into town with a shopping trolley from out near the drive-in?

Through the window I saw Angela's bangles shiver down her

arm as she took her tiny white parcel from Kevin Scragg's outstretched hand. The hand held, for a moment the parcel was a
tug-of-war with Angela laughing and shaking her head.

'Let's go,' she muttered as she joined me, her escape
jangling behind her. 'I'm not going in there if he's on his own
again.'

Poddy's garage was a block further down the road. Out in the
yard Wes' ute and Vic's Kombi were nosed up next to one
another.

'Vic!' called Angela. We stood at the top of the driveway
leading down to the black mouth of the workshop. A transistor
was playing loudly in its depths. We waited. Vic came out
slowly, paused at the door, took out his tobacco.

'Want to come to the Bright Spot with us?'

'Na — got a job on.' He squinted up at us over the paper
bandaided across his bottom lip. He clicked his tongue at Nat. I
cleared my throat.

'Is Wes about?' I hardly ever spoke to Vic. He wore footy
shorts and workman's boots; he propped one shapely leg across
the other, leaning on the workshop door. You could glimpse an
earring through his tangled hair. 'Wes!' he called out over his
shoulder.

Poddy's red beanie shadowed Wes at the entrance. Wes was
carrying a coil of rope and the transistor. They were moving
towards the yard.

'Any chance of a lift home?' I said.

'No way.' Pod answered for him. 'He's gotta follow me in
the truck.' Wes lifted his shoulders above his armful and gave
an idiot-grin. He called himself a grease monkey these days. He
marched off, Pod right behind him. With his ponytail and his
big boots he looked like the garage mascot.

'Wait at our place.' Vic gave a nod in the direction of the
river. 'Have a sewing circle or something.' He breathed out
smoke and smiled broadly at us, conscious that he might have
gone too far.

'Do you see yourself living here always?'

'Always?' Angela frowned as if it was a word she didn't know.

I knew it was a low-consciousness sort of question. All because I couldn't bring myself to ask: Are you happy? I drew up hard on my strawberry milkshake. There was a lot of it, it tasted of crushed chewing gum, I felt it flooding through every cell of my body. *Daily renewed sense-yearnings sap your inner peace* ...

We were sitting at one of the laminex tables in the Bright Spot, the traditional end to our shopping trips. There had been times, when Vic and Wes were with us, playing the pinball machines amongst the town's milling adolescents, that we had recognised the Bright Spot's fly-spotted nostalgic charm. Today we were the only customers. Most of the chairs were stacked on the tables up near the kitchen. A whirring fan bowed to us from the counter.

'Actually,' Angela said, 'Vic's talking about moving on. He'd quite like to try opal mining up at Coober Pedy.'

The plastic streamers in the doorway swayed and kicked in a gust of afternoon wind, straight from the desert. A jumpy brightness was suddenly flung across the table.

'Do you want to go?'

'I don't know.' Angela pushed back her fringe and for a moment her small forehead stared out, white, next to her hand. 'I don't mind I guess.' She looked past me towards the door.

We looped our bags over our shoulders and prepared for that moment of darkness through the plastic streamers. There seemed to be a new silence between us as we set off again, into the glare of the long afternoon.

My parents had come to visit Wes and me. This time Evvie, my sister, was with them. It seemed crowded in the kitchen round the breakfast bar. Outside the whole country spread, bland in the late afternoon sun. But for all of us the world had shrunk, temporarily, back to this, wary faces across a shadowed table. Between us was the cake tin with the Highland Tartan border. We ate the cake from it over our crossed knees. Christmas cake, my mother's year-round speciality. Before she left I would give her back the tin, empty. It would come back full again.

Evvie didn't eat the cake. She filled in time examining the

kitchen. She was seventeen now; all at once she had very long legs in very tight jeans. Her blouse, satin with little ragged caps of sleeves, was the sort of thing you find by a dedicated haunting of the op-shops. Her blank survey of my kitchen said *Not for me.*

'You've been making jam!' my mother said, smiling.

'Mm. Fig.' She would never know how I had flung the figs, my only crop, into Angela's big pot, bored, martyred, mad with itching ... 'You can take some home with you if you like.' With any luck my mother would forget. Though out of desperation for some proof of this lifestyle, fruits at last, she would probably persist in pushing the tarry substance across her morning toast ...

'Still no job turned up for you?' my mother asked me. 'You'll be getting broody if you hang around too much.' Her laugh turned uncertain. She had to go on. 'I'm too young to be a grandmother!'

My father stirred. His big form was hunched up in one of our frail chairs. I hoped she wouldn't go further. I hoped she wouldn't say: 'Mind you, there's a lot less hypocrisy about the young people of today.' But she turned and looked out the window. 'Oh this poor dry countryside,' she said. She sighed.

I knew how to look out that window, to see, defined against her, the grasses moving for a moment across that other landscape, *the country*, luminous in fading light, waiting for us.

'How's the guitar going, Wes? Do you get enough time to practise?' My mother had turned to Wes.

Wes looked up. 'Oh I get around to it now and ... haven't had a really good session for a ... '

'He's been working really hard at the garage,' I said.

My mother smiled at him, nodding. 'It's a wonderful chance to learn a trade.'

Then my father did something surprising. He uncoiled his hand from his elbow where it had seemed to be holding him contained. He stretched it across the table, his red, whorl-jointed hand, part of my former life, and picked up Wes' restless fingers.

'These aren't mechanic's hands,' he said. He put Wes' hand

151

down gently. He didn't look at anybody. He cleared his throat in a business-like way.

I was sitting, crease-eyed from a heavy siesta, on the front steps of the farmhouse. From time to time I ducked in through the open front door to put the needle back on to my favourite sides of Wes' records. This was something that I was too shy to do when he was home. I felt I probably liked them for the wrong, unmusical reasons, for the feelings they gave me, their melancholy landscapes: I waited for certain songs, to retaste that sensation of the right chord struck, again and again ... Bonnie Raitt singing 'Guilty' and 'I Thought I Was a Child', Linda Ronstadt's 'I Never Will Marry', Randy Newman's 'Louisiana' ...

> *They're tryin' to wash us away,*
> *They're tryin' to wash us away,*

I droned, private, flat, stamping empty time on the step below me, calling up something to happen.

The step was still warm from the day, but the glare was gone. Lights began to trace the streets of the town. Dogs barked.

A pair of headlights was advancing up the road with the darkness. I heard the homecoming changing of gears. The ute.

'Did you listen to the news tonight?' Wes called as he came towards me up the path. 'Have you heard?'

'What?'

He stood before me on the steps. 'Gough's been sacked. Kerr's sacked Whitlam!' He wore the half-smile of the newsbringer.

'When?' I stood up too.

'This morning. It came through about midday. Fraser's forming a government.' He was edging past me up the steps. 'Pod's been at the pub all afternoon,' he called on the way down the hall. 'It's pretty wild down there. You'd think they'd won a war or something.'

He came out again with his guitar.

'Where are you going?'

'They want some live music.'

'You're going back there? Now?'

Wes gave a swift loop of the ute keys over his fingers. His eyes flickered. I felt the wordless authority of his feeling, that chose when he came forward, or kept back.

'I'm going to play,' he said.

The fire when it came was swift and stealthy.

On a day when the sun hung venomous, whitening, striking a sharp light off leaves, I heard a distant crackling like a friendly winter hearth. I looked out the window and saw a low line of flames snake across the paddock as if it rode along a fuse.

From the verandah, down the hill, a truck was crawling up the road, the fire's keeper. I could just make out the figures of some men by the fence, and then they were lost in billowing smoke.

I thought: Do they know I am here?

The fire took over. The house was darkened. I ran from room to room shutting the windows. A roar seemed to run under the roof. I heard the windchimes' futile alarm.

I stood by the kitchen window and watched the flames pass the house in vast erratic tacks across the grass.

(From *Sister Ships,* short fiction, 1986.)

MILLIE AND STAN

Jack Appleyard left England for Australia in 1924. He was twenty-seven years old. He stayed for a short time with Aunt Martha and Uncle Henry in Adelaide. It was different from being at the house at Ackton.

Martha was very different from Emma, Jack's mother. At Aunt Martha's home it was impossible to relax. Every room was filled with an air of importance. You had to watch what you said and did, and how you acted. It was difficult to hold in one's mind the fact that Martha as a little girl had lived at 26 Good Hope Row, that she played diabolo on the Common, and that she had gone to the little school on the edge of the recreation ground. Martha was now beautiful, elegant, and very self-assured. She chaired important church meetings, and she hosted gatherings of influential people. She still looked exquisitely feminine and fragile. She was sagacious. Her determination not to look back, not to be held back even by family connections, was as inflexible as ever it had been. She was held back by the reins of her time. All of this she knew, and resented, charmingly. She did her best to make her Yorkshire nephew welcome. She did her best.

Jack moved from Adelaide to a farm at Port Broughton on the eastern side of Spencer Gulf. The farm was a few miles inland. Life was hard. Yet when Jack looked at the Australian blue skies and, on his half-day off, swam in the cold waters of Spencer Gulf or went with friends to the rifle range at Port Broughton, he had no hankering to go back to the coalmines of Yorkshire.

On Sundays he went to the Methodist Church. His church

was as necessary to Jack as breathing and eating. He became a member of the Masonic Lodge and expanded his thinking to take in Masonic philosophy and wisdom.

But he was lonely. The loneliness and his sense of being isolated from the family permeated every letter he wrote home.

His mother worried. She pictured Jack out there in far-off Australia. She looked at the map and saw the name Port Broughton. Right down there, almost at the bottom of every-where. Percy, she remembered, had been alone at Archangel, at the end of the earth. It was not what she had planned for her sons. It was not how it was meant to be.

Emma was just as determined as Martha. Within her mind she had a blueprint for her children's lives. Emma, no doubt influenced by the fact that she lived at the Great Hall, had raised her lads so that when they were able to lift themselves out of the coalmines they would feel at home, living as gentlemen, anywhere.

All four girls had been brought up to clean their brothers' shoes, to thread their brothers' ties through the stiffly starched white collars men had to endure. Clean handkerchiefs had to be put into the lads' pockets. Their Sunday suits had to be got out, brushed and pressed ready for Sunday church, and for the Sunday afternoon walk. The girls had to stand in the hall, near the front door, three of them each holding a bowler hat and a walking-stick; as if the girls were servants and the boys the young lords of the manor. It was how Emma saw the roles of men and women. Women were created to wait on and to care for their men: fathers, brothers, husbands.

Emma had not come to this way of thinking by herself. Her mother, Alice, had drummed it into her, and into all of her children: men were all-important. Women would live happier lives if they accepted the fact.

'I think,' Emma said one day when all four of her daughters were home, 'one of you girls should go to Australia to look after our Jack.'

All four girls were full of consternation.

'I can't!' Nan said. 'What would Lady Clarke do? I'm her personal maid. She depends on me.'

'I'm too young,' Madge said. 'I couldn't go out there.'

'I can't!' Alice said. 'I'm married. I have a family of my own!'

'I won't go,' Millie said. 'I won't go! I won't!'

'I'll write to our Jack,' Emma said. 'We'll see what he thinks.'

Emma's letter took more than six weeks to reach Port Broughton. Jack's reply took another seven weeks to get back to Ackton. Millie cried and raged all the time.

'I won't go! I'm twenty-four years old! I don't want to go to Australia. I won't go!'

'Our Jack thinks it's a champion solution. How it should be. So one of you must go,' Emma said.

Everyone looked at Millie.

'What about me?' Millie cried. 'What about my life?'

She pleaded. She cried. She reasoned; but Emma had made up her mind.

'You must do as you're told,' she told Millie. 'You are to go to Australia to look after your brother Jack.'

The arrangements were made.

Percy accompanied Millie from Normanton to London. Percy had spent so many months in an army hospital in London that Emma considered he should know his way around. Millie was to sail from Tilbury on the SS *Orbita* on 28 April 1928. She left Normanton feeling as hopeless and as condemned as the convicts who had been sent to Australia a century before. How could she survive away from her family, and away from Yorkshire?

In London Millie and Percy were met by a friend who, all the time Percy was in Finsbury Square Hospital, had visited him and when he was well enough had wheeled him around the hospital grounds. The three talked sadly about Millie's being sent out to Australia. They all saw it the same way: Millie was being despatched to a distant land with no say in what others had ordained for her.

She had in her luggage a half-dozen silver teaspoons which had belonged to her grandmother, Alice Booth. And she had the two-spouted teapot. These things the family had given her to sustain her in her new life.

Millie, Percy and their friend stood on the London station looking at the boat-train which was to take Millie to Tilbury.

'Go with her to Tilbury,' the friend said to Percy.

'It's only for people who are sailing.'

'Look, Percy Appleyard, you get on that train and go with her.'

Percy got on the boat-train. Percy and Millie waved as the train pulled out from the station. The ticket inspector on the train, after he had heard Percy's explanation, scribbled out a ticket for him.

Millie looked out of the train window. It was a beautiful April day. The green grass in the English fields shone palely as the breeze rippled through it. Roofs displayed their full colours. Chimneys smoked thinly. The grey-blue mist of smoke drifted into the blue summer's sky.

At Tilbury Millie said goodbye to Percy. She was never to see him again.

Millie left Tilbury docks with other passengers in a small boat which took them out to deep waters where the SS *Orbita* was anchored. She found her way to the four-berth cabin which was to be her home for the next six weeks.

Millie sat on her bunk. She was small, fair-headed, and very Yorkshire. She was also very much a Booth. From now on, she determined, she would take charge of her own life.

In her cabin was a girl called Kathleen with whom Millie was to form a friendship which would last a lifetime. Kathleen was going out to Melbourne to marry her fiance, Fred, who was a tool maker working at Ford's in Geelong.

To Millie the whole journey was invigorating and exciting. She made new friends. She looked forward to arriving and exploring every port at which they called. She pushed her loneliness aside by remembering happy events.

She told Kathleen about everything.

'We'd walk to Mill Farm through the woods to my Uncle Charlie's and Aunt Lizzie's ...

'My father was born at Foxbridge Row. That was just one street behind Good Hope Row. My mother and father went to the same school. Around the Common everyone knew everyone ...

'We used to put one halfpenny in the collection at Chapel when we were little. All those halfpennies ...

'In 1911 King George and Queen Mary had their coronation. That was when Aunt Martha and Uncle Henry came to England with their son, Willie ...

'Funny things you remember ... like washing days. The peggy stick and rubbing boards ... The brass copper. We kept it as polished as the kettles in the kitchen ...

'Making bread, and yeast buns, and tea buns ... Making soap ...

'What will I do in Australia? What does anyone do in Australia?'

When the ship arrived at Fremantle Millie was met by my mother and Jessie. Millie brought presents from Yorkshire. She brought me a little wooden jewel box her father, George, had made.

At Adelaide Millie was met by Aunt Martha and Uncle Henry. She stayed with them for a month before she wrote to her brother Jack at Port Broughton telling him she was ready to be picked up.

She saw very little of Aunt Martha who was busy with parish work. Uncle Henry tried to make her feel at home, but she could not relax. She could not take part in the social life of the church where Martha was so much at home.

'I'll go to our Jack at Port Broughton,' she said one day. 'It's why I had to come.'

On a Sunday morning in July 1928, Jack drove his old Ford car from Port Broughton to Adelaide. It was a cold winter's morning. Millie had arrived in Australia to be greeted by cold winds and heavy winter rains. She had left all of her winter clothing in England.

'Everyone told me it was sunshine all day and every day. I was a raw Yorkshire lass. Quite daft, thinking Australia had no winters. Well, I learnt, didn't I?

'Jack took me back to Port Broughton. The farm was a few miles inland. Jack had his own little house. I had to look after Jack's house and help in the farmhouse, and with the farmer's children. I used to separate the milk in the dairy, clean the separator and do all the jobs the farmer's wife asked me to do.

'We went into the port on a Saturday. While the men went to the rifle range we women looked around the town or took the children down to the beach. The beach in winter! All that sand blowing! We used to worry about getting back to milk the cows. When the men arrived back in town from the rifle range they'd shove us women and children into the car as if we were blocks of wood. We were always an hour late starting the milking.

'The sand! It was just sand. We never dusted. The sand was always too thick over everything. We used a little hand brush and dustpan. We swept dressing-tables and sideboards. When we made the beds we used to throw an old sheet over them to keep the sand out. When you went to bed you'd gently pull the sheet off. Setting the table for a meal ... You'd throw a sheet over it to keep the sand off everything. They say everyone eats a peck or two of dirt in their time; I reckon I had someone else's share as well.

'It was a typical Australian farmhouse, with a verandah all around. I used to try to sweep it clean. You just about needed an earth mover. Goannas would come up onto the verandah. Sometimes they'd even get inside. You'd step off the verandah and there'd be goannas and lizards everywhere. You couldn't touch a fence post or a gate post. There'd be a lizard under your hand. They were the same colour as whatever they were on. If they were on brown they looked brown. If they were on grey, they looked grey ...'

The change of worlds from the soft Yorkshire moors and dales, and from the city of Leeds with its tramcars and bustle of people and traffic, was too great a shock for Millie.

This same Australian scene thrilled many an Australian by its stark, clean beauty. Even the flying, whistling sand created a music which they knew and understood. The amazing frill-necked lizards from which Millie ran in dismay filled Australian hearts with pride. This was Australia. These creatures were Australian. The sky, the trees, the land, all so alien to Millie, were built into an Australian's blood and sinews.

A picture of gentle Yorkshire fields and rich greens was fixed in Millie's mind. It was right. This out here was not to be trusted.

Millie's unhappiness, loneliness and homesickness increased. Only Sundays gave her a sense of belonging. She went with Jack, and the farm owner, his wife and family to attend the Methodist Chapel at Port Broughton. The parents of the farmer's wife lived at Port Broughton. They regularly welcomed Jack and Millie to Sunday afternoons in their home. The Sunday dinner was as fine a meal as any Millie had seen in Yorkshire. The afternoon tea and Sunday tea were as well-prepared and as generous as any Millie's mother and sisters had served at Ackton. But out on the farm Millie's sense of isolation deepened. She saw the farm as a sandy waste set on the edge of the Never-Never.

Millie found some relief in the letters she wrote to Kathleen, who was now married to Fred. They lived in Geelong. Millie's outpourings to Kathleen revealed everything she felt. Trapped. Was this to be her life? Was she to care for her brother for evermore? Was this to be all? This emptiness? This loneliness? This sand? She had no thought of finding romance among the men of the district. The men who came to the farm to buy bags of chaff or other farm produce seemed to Millie like fiction figures from the Wild West. They were unshaven, with heavy moustaches. Their hair was uncut. 'They were all like Rasputin,' Millie says as she remembers them. 'All hairy, and black with the sun and not shaving.'

One Friday in November a telegram from Fred arrived at the farm at Port Broughton: 'Meet you in Geelong on Monday.'

Everyone in Port Broughton knew the contents of Millie's telegram before she did. The post office operated from a little sweet and confectioner's shop. The postmistress had said to everyone who went in 'Miss Appleyard's going to leave us. She's going to Geelong.'

The postmistress rang the telegram through to the farm. The message was received by the farmer's wife who, hurt by what she saw as contrived deceit on Millie's part, relayed Fred's telegram to her.

'I knew nothing about it,' Millie told everyone. 'I'm as surprised as you are. I didn't plan it at all.'

No one, including her brother Jack, believed her.

'It was all connived,' Jack said.

'It wasn't! It really wasn't!'

'Anyhow, it makes no difference. You're staying here.'

Now, for the first time, Millie took charge of her life.

'I'm going to Geelong, Jack.'

'You're not. I won't take you to Adelaide.'

'That doesn't matter. I'll go by train.'

'Only one train a year comes through here. And that's a goods train to take the harvest.'

'I'll walk it.'

'You going to take a drum of water on a wheelbarrow, or are you going to take a very long drink before you set off? Do you know how far it is?'

'I'll walk, if I have to.'

'In summer?'

'I'll walk.'

Millie telephoned Aunt Martha in Adelaide and asked her to book a seat on a train to Melbourne on the following Monday.

Jack, realising Millie would not change her mind, agreed to take her to Adelaide. They left Port Broughton at four o'clock on Sunday morning. No one said a word all the way.

Often during the many years until Jack died, aged eighty-seven years, Millie tried to tell him that Fred's telegram had come as a surprise. He had never believed her.

Aunt Martha had prepared Sunday dinner. There was very little conversation during the meal. Immediately after the meal Jack got up and went out to his car. He neither looked at Millie nor said goodbye to her.

Millie stayed at Geelong with Kathleen and Fred for a month. Her small savings, put together shilling by shilling, were dwindling fast.

'I have to find work,' she said to Kathleen and Fred.

'Things are getting tight.'

'I know; but I'll find something.'

An advertisement in the newspaper for a housemaid at Methodist Ladies College, Kew, provided the answer. A telegram from the college asked her to go immediately.

It was, Millie says, 'a lovely job.' She and another girl,

Mary, looked after the college dining room.

As Australia and the beauty of the city of Melbourne became more familiar to Millie she began to love it. Her yearning to go back to Yorkshire lessened.

During one of the long summer holidays Millie worked on a sheep station at Glenorchy, near Horsham. It was, Millie says, 'away from the world.' While she was working at the sheep station Millie met Stan Hitchen. Stan had come from Yorkshire to Melbourne in September 1928. He was by trade a tool maker. By the end of 1928 the first chill of the coming Depression years was already being felt in the manufacturing industry. Stan, after months of being unemployed, considered he was lucky to get the job of under-gardener on the large sheep station. He and Millie met at a station dance.

'Stanley being from Yorkshire,' Millie says, 'there was a kinship between us. He was very shy. When I came down from the country I went to stay a short time with Kath and Fred. Fred was still a tool maker at Ford's in Geelong, so when Fred told me to write to Stan because he, Fred, would get a job for Stan in his own trade, I did. Stan came at once and Fred got him a job at Ford's. It was the beginning of the Depression. The two foremen at Geelong — the day foreman and the night foreman — didn't like each other. The night foreman, the one who had put Stan on, was an Englishman. The day foreman was an Australian. He didn't like Englishmen being given jobs. When the night foreman went on annual leave, the day foreman put Stan off. They said he was the last man on, so he had to be the first man off. That was the last of Stan having a job for three and a half years.'

Millie left the Methodist Ladies College where she was being paid twenty-five shillings a week to take a position with a well-known and wealthy family where she would be paid thirty shillings a week. She became cook-housekeeper.

'It was something like being back home,' Millie says, 'with everyone coming and going at all hours. Dinner started at six o'clock at night and went on until eight-thirty. Everyone who came to the front door was invited to dinner. They'd ring through to the kitchen for another dinner to be made. Supper trays began later. Even at eleven o'clock at night there would be requests for trays for four or six people. They had two Rolls Royces and two chauffeurs. Six in the kitchen staff. Seven in front of house. They were lovely people in themselves; but they had no idea of how to conduct staff. No one would have the stamina to remain as cook-housekeeper for very long. Breakfasts served at seven in the morning and suppers until after midnight! Trays collected and washing-up done!'

Millie prudently left this household when the family moved to a new area. She found work at Royal Melbourne Hospital as third cook. The Depression now had a stranglehold throughout Australia. Millie lived through it on two levels. She was secure in her own work where she was very capable and hard-working. She suffered with Stan, sharing his hardship, trying to alleviate his loneliness and hopelessness.

Stan left Geelong and travelled to Melbourne.

'He got a room in East Melbourne at eleven shillings a week. Just the room. No meals. He rang me at the hospital and asked me to meet him. So I met Stan in front of the Royal Melbourne Hospital. Poor Stan. He had no home, no job, no family, and very little money. I met him every night for three and a half years. We walked around Melbourne. On my day off we walked to Brighton and Hampton and back again. Every night we walked around the King's Domain and the Botanical Gardens. We saw the workmen dig the foundations for the new Shrine. We watched that Shrine being built.

'There was no work. No work. No work. Everything got worse. The Depression got worse and worse and worse. There was only the unemployed. Everyone was unemployed. There was no unemployment pay in those days. Nothing. Nothing of any kind. Stanley tried to make his little bit of money last; but it didn't last, of course. Three and a half years is a terrible time to live without a wage. I was getting thirty shillings a week as cook at the hospital. I used to give Stan one pound of my wages. Sometimes I'd give him twenty-five shillings. All he ate every day were two yeast buns.

'I was nothing but a friend to Stan then. We weren't even considering walking out together as sweethearts. We were just two people from Yorkshire together in Melbourne. In that Depression. He was a kinsman from Yorkshire ...

'Lots of people told me it wouldn't be their affair, but it was mine. Some folk thought it was awful Stan taking one pound or twenty-five shillings from me every week. He didn't take it. I gave it. What could men like Stan do? There was nothing. No one. After he'd paid eleven shillings a week for his room, what was left? Not much. None of the people who criticised him and me thought about that. I told them all, it was just between Stan and me.

'Stan really went "down the Nick". He tried his best to live on that money. He had to pay one shilling and sixpence a week Union fees, just in case any job came up. Without belonging to the Union he knew he wouldn't stand a chance. He had to pay one shilling and sixpence to the Druids, in case he got sick. He could at least have a doctor free. So that was fourteen shillings gone. Sometimes he had only six shillings on which to live. Sometimes he had eleven. Poor Stanley. He didn't have a square meal in over three years. He became as thin as a lath, and weak and sick.

'When the Depression was getting over, Stan got a job at the munitions factory at Footscray. It was night shift. When he came out of work in the morning he went to the railway cafe. The food there was as much as he could afford. Stan wouldn't go into the cafe in his work overalls. He first went to his room in East Melbourne, got washed and changed, then went back to the city for breakfast. At night he had his dinner at seven o'clock, before we started walking around the King's Domain, and the Shrine. He would leave to go back to Footscray at eleven o'clock at night.

'Stan was far from well. He'd had no proper food for years. The food at the railway cafe was a lot better than the two yeast buns a day Stan had survived on all that time; but he needed extra care. He was tired out and weak from having to walk up and down, round and round. There was never enough money for tram fares.

'One night I said: "Stan, I think we'd better get married, then I can look after you properly."

'Well, I didn't have to say that twice. We had been walking around together for years, as friends; but we weren't really in love, then. We were married on 25 November 1933 at the Wesley Church in Lonsdale Street. Lady Clarke, back in England, sent me a pair of pillowslips she had worked in blue embroidery. Nan, my sister, sent me a matching pair. It was nice thinking of Lady Clarke and our Nan sitting by the fire making pillowslips for me.

'Stan and I went to live in a half-house with a Mrs Voce. She was an English lady. She was seventy-six. We had all the upstairs of the two-storey house in Albert Street, East Melbourne. We had a kitchen, a bedroom, a lounge/diningroom and a bathroom. We stayed there for three and a half years.

'I never went to work from the day I was married. Stan didn't believe in married women going to work. He used to say: "If you want to get married, well your place is in the home. If you don't want to stay home, then don't get married." I could have earned good money; but Stan wouldn't have it.

'We had five pounds between us the day we were married. But even on that little money Stan wouldn't let me go to work. I used to do a lot of work downstairs for Mrs Voce, unpaid, of course. When I had a baking day I baked enough for Mrs Voce for a week. She said she couldn't ever have got anybody better than we were.

'We heard about the little house in Richmond. Two sisters who were great Methodists owned it. It was next to their big house. There was the big house and our little house and two gardens, all on one block. We got that little house for one pound a week. We had been paying twenty-five shillings a week at Mrs Voce's. We were sad to leave Mrs Voce. She was a dear, dear soul. But Stanley's wage was only three pounds five shillings.

'Stanley had walked around for practically four years in just one suit he had brought from England. He needed some clothes. Five shillings a week was a lot of money.

'Stan was gradually getting better in health. I gave him delicate, invalid food for many, many weeks, until a day came when he could eat a proper dinner and proper meals. We built up his wardrobe, and he began to feel respectable again. After all that, we began to put one shilling and sixpence into a box every week for the bank. When it got to be one pound I would take it to the bank.

'Stan was now working in Richmond, day shift, so he was able to walk to work.

'Our little house was in a back street. It was no use thinking of where we would like to be. Stan and I made a lovely garden.

'For ten years neither Stan nor I went on a tram or a train. On Sundays we went for a walk through the Botanical Gardens. That was us. We loved gardens. We never had a holiday for thirty years. We saved and saved. Stanley never spent one penny on himself. He didn't drink, and he didn't smoke. When you have lived in great poverty and near starvation you can't forget. Many people of our generation were marked by the Depression. It goes so deep you can't shake it off.

'Right from the first week's pay after we were married Stanley brought his wage packet home and handed it to me untouched. He did that until the last pay-packet when he retired. I admit, I did save pennies.

'We had saved five hundred pounds when my poor Stanley became very ill and needed an operation. He couldn't get into a public hospital. We didn't know anyone who could help. He was too ill to go to work. He was home for a month, with no wages coming in. In those days if you took time off for being sick you didn't get paid. We had to pull money out from the bank book. Stanley wanted to go on waiting for a bed in the public hospital; but the doctor said Stanley couldn't wait any longer. The operation in the private hospital, and another two months off while Stanley recuperated, cost us every penny of the five hundred pounds we had saved.

'We began again. We saved and saved.

'When Stan became very ill a second time we did manage to get him into a public hospital. But he was off work for three months, without wages. Today if you aren't working you're looked after. In our day there was nothing but what you'd saved yourself. And they call them "the good old days".

'When Stan went back to work we began to save again.

Sometimes, when we treated ourselves to going to the pictures, we walked into the city on a Saturday afternoon. It was one shilling and a penny each for the afternoon session. The next seats were one shilling and ninepence. If we missed out on the one shilling and a penny seats we walked home again. We walked back along the Yarra bank to Richmond.

'When wages went up a little bit we were able to save a little more.

'A friend of ours had a house to sell for six hundred pounds. I wanted Stan to let us put a deposit on it. He said: "No. I saw too many people in the Depression lose their homes. If we put all we've saved on that house, and anything happens to me, you couldn't pay the house off. You'd have to sell it and you probably wouldn't have enough to take you back to England. When we buy a house we'll pay cash for it and it will be ours."

'The two sisters who owned our little house died. The two houses had to be sold. We would have liked to buy the little house; but as both houses were on the one deed they had to be sold together. So we had to look around.

'We now had enough money to buy a house. We had saved the money shilling by shilling, pound by pound. We could pay cash. We wanted a house near Richmond so that Stan could get to work. Eventually we saw a house advertised in the *Herald*. It sounded just what we wanted. It was in Box Hill North. One or two men who worked with Stan came from around there, so we didn't have to worry about Stan getting to work. We read the advertisement on Friday night. The house was brand new. Stanley went around to the public telephone booth and rang the builder. The builder told us exactly where the house was.

'On Saturday morning we got on the train, went to Box Hill and found the street. The house was only a shell. The plan of the house was nice, and the rooms were big, with high ceilings. We'd expected to be able to move in straightaway; but all the finishing had to be done. All the light fittings and plumbing, and painting. There were no paths or fences. Stanley thought it was a bit big; but I said: "That doesn't matter. There's a bus at the bottom of the street that will take you right to where you work."

'As we were looking around the agent came to see us. Stan

was still worried about the house being too big.

'"Look," I said, "you're always talking about if you died you'd want to leave me all right. Well, if we bought this house with three bedrooms we could always sell it."

'The agent, a young man, went home with us to Richmond. At that time, in 1962, when we bought our house, nobody had any money, and the banks weren't lending. The young man said, "We could probably get private finance for you."

'Stanley's Yorkshire came out, proud and independent. "We don't need financial help, thank you. We can buy the house. We can pay for it."

'The agent couldn't believe us. Here we were in that little house in a back street! Stan and the agent talked in the little sitting room while I made the lunch. They still talked. I left them together. I made the afternoon tea. They still talked. My shy Stanley! You see what having something to be proud of can do?

'I made the tea and went in and told them tea was ready. It was one o'clock on Sunday morning when the young man left. I don't know what they had been talking about, but they must have found something to say to each other.

'The next morning Stan and I went to the bank and got a cheque for one thousand pounds as a deposit on the house. We had to wait a month for the house to be finished. During that month and for a year afterwards Stan and I spent every spare minute we had buying all sorts of things, from soap dishes to curtains and floor coverings. Every Saturday morning we went around the shops. How we spent money! After save, save, save for thirty years it was suddenly spend! Spend!

'We were so happy.

'Stan left the house at six-twenty every morning to catch the first bus at the bottom of the street at six-thirty. Stanley was always at his lathe, with his overalls on and his tools in his hand, when the whistle blew. The average workers were just running through the doors, but not Stanley.

'Time hadn't moved on very far when Stanley got sick again. He insisted on going to work for two years when he should have been at home. That was Stanley. He finally gave up the

168

engineering job because the accuracy with which he had to cut the tools was too much strain. He had cancer. His health was in a very bad state. I said, "Stay home."

'He stayed home for about six weeks. He was sixty years old. He was worried about being too young to get the pension.

'One day he went out and wandered around the city. When he came home he said, "I wonder if there's anything in the Public Service? Any jobs?"

'Later on that night he said, "I'll go and see."

'He went to the Public Service the next day and came home with all sorts of forms to fill in. There were forms for chauffeurs, for parliamentarians, art gallery attendants; all sorts. Stan filled in a form to be a tipstaff in the courts. He got the job. For the last five years of his working life he was a tipstaff for Judge Gowan. Stanley liked the job. The Judge thought a lot about Stanley. When the Judge went on a country circuit, Bendigo, Ballarat and Mildura, Stanley went with him in his car.

'Stanley's health got worse. He was turning sixty-five on 28 April. That Christmas in 1969, I said to him, "You're not going back to work any more. Give your notice in and say you're not coming back after Christmas ... "

'Stanley loved being home. He loved not having to go to work. He had a beautiful garden. We never stinted on what he wanted or needed for the garden. His delphiniums were over five feet tall.

'Despite everything, despite all the loving care, Stan's health got worse and worse. In February 1975 he died. He was seventy years old.'

It was forty-seven years since Millie's mother had sent her out to Australia to look after her older brother, Jack. Somewhere along the track of those years Millie had become an Australian. The big gold, brown, red and green land, with its faraway open skies, had become home. She was in tune with it now; nevertheless she began to think of visiting Yorkshire. In the beginning, when she had yearned to go back, she could not afford the fare. After she married Stanley, and their savings would have allowed them to go back, Stanley would not take the time off work. 'After that Depression,' Millie said, 'no man who had suffered like Stan ever took time off for pleasure.' Millie would not go without Stan.

One day in June 1975 Millie left Tullamarine Airport for England. A small crowd of people went to the airport to see her off.

'I knew,' she says, 'that in England all the Yorkshire folk, all the old ones who were still living, and all the new ones born in the last forty-seven years, would be waiting.'

(From *Against Time and Place,* an autobiography/family history, 1990.)

BATTLES

We heard the roar of the motorised convoy moving out in the early hours one bleak July morning, leaving under cover of darkness, as they had come. For almost a week, the white gum ridge beyond the homestead had concealed the tents of a battalion. Out in the open paddock, trucks, utilities and gun carriers were camouflaged with nets and bushes to look like trees and shrubs. Bly, riding out around the sheep early in the morning, had been mystified, thinking they were trees that had suddenly sprung up — until he had a closer look.

Rumour had it that a large contingent was soon to embark for an overseas offensive, and an unknown destination. It was said to be a survival exercise, and all week long small parties of khaki-clad men straggled around the district trying to live off the land. They were hungry and everything was grist to their mill. They made strange figures as they lumbered away with shirt fronts or greatcoat pockets bulging with oranges (a long way from ripe), while garden vegetables were consumed on the spot. When fresh-laid eggs ran out, they accepted 'keep eggs' with equal relish, but even those failed to reach camp as was evident by the pile of eggshells behind the trees outside the orchard fence. The rabbits were also temporarily eradicated, leaving paddocks looking as though a major battle had already taken place where the warrens had been ripped open with shovels and bare hands.

One particular group of men seemed to have adopted us, and I even broached our emergency ration cupboard, telling myself they could have been my own brothers. One day I was standing there trying to convince a small group of soldiers that there was nothing edible left, when a number of gawky young cockerels sauntered enquiringly by. Quickly the little Scottish sergeant asked, 'Will y' sell us a chicken then?' 'You can have that lot,' I said, figuring they had slender chance of catching even one, but I underestimated army organisation. 'Right men,' ordered Scotty, 'Six t' the left, six t' the right, and the rest forrad.' In about three strides they fell on the surprised birds and carried them off, leaving not one for procreation! About an hour later the whole clan returned licking their lips, to report that: 'The cockerels were so good we even ate their crow.'

The last time I saw them, they came stumbling up the path like a bunch of weary schoolboys in khaki shirts and baggy shorts, their thick woollen socks hanging over heavy army boot tops. They followed Scotty, who was being towed along at a rather undignified rate by a big yellow dog on a length of frayed binder twine. As they scuffled into a semicircle around the basket of wet clothes I was pegging on the line, Scotty said 'We've come to say goodbye t' ya. An' me and the lads thought we'd like to show our appreciation of your generosity by offering you our mascot.'

I looked at the dog, a handsome, noble-looking creature, but I said, 'It's a sheepdog we need.' 'Tut, tut,' said Scotty. 'Not too loud, or he'll bring all the ruddy sheep in the district, and we'll be had for sheep stealing.' 'What's his name?' I asked, trying to ignore his tomfoolery. 'Teddy,' they chorused, but the dog was too absorbed in the activities of some hens scratching under a carob bean tree to recognise his name. 'He doesn't look much like a sheepdog to me,' I observed. 'Well lady,' said Scotty, 'ye could set the dog t' mind the bairn and bring in the sheep y'se'l.' He carried on for a while about how good the dog was at minding his sister's children. 'Why,' he said, 'if the baby drops its dummy, he'll pick it up — and always by the string!'

There was a shuffling of boots, so Scotty said, 'Well chaps, it looks like the firing squad for our faithful friend.' 'You mean shoot him?' I asked, thinking to myself he might be just what Bly needed to bring the cow home at milking time, as she was one of those exasperating animals that seemed to have to graze all the way home.

The clan was beginning to break up, so Scotty said, 'I'll tell y' what, lady. We'll leave the dog with y' until y' good man gets in, and we'll come back tonight and see what *he* sez.' I brought the collar and chain from our last beloved sheepdog, and Scotty fastened the collar around Teddy's neck, leaving him chained to an old fig tree near the back door.

When Bly rode in that evening, I heard him snorting as he dismounted. 'What the devil is this! Who does it belong to?' 'He's supposed to be good with sheep,' I said lamely. 'Looks more like a blasted Alsatian to me,' he scoffed.

I recounted the story briefly as Bly handed the bridle reins to me and walked towards the dog. But the dog wrinkled his nose, showing strong, white teeth and looking very ugly. We offered him food and water but he ignored it. I told Bly the soldiers were coming back at night to see whether or not we wanted the dog, but he scoffed 'That's what YOU think.'

At the end of the second day the dog still refused to eat. As it seemed there was no getting near him, Bly said, 'We can't keep the poor brute chained up forever. We'll have to think of something.' A little later he came from the house carrying the rifle. I first thought he meant to shoot the dog, but he cocked the rifle and handed it to me, saying, 'Now I'm going to walk straight up to the hound and let him loose. He can go to Timbuktu as far as I'm concerned, but if he turns on me, let him have a bullet anywhere you can ... I'll finish him off.'

It wasn't easy to keep the rifle steady, even though I rested it against the verandah post. Bly walked matter-of-factly to the dog, who had his eye on me. He dropped the chain from the collar and the dog bounded over to me! We fondled him and called him a good dog, then he want careering around in circles and back to us again and again. Bly emptied the bullet from the rifle saying 'He's all right. It was only fear.' He put the gun away and I continued with preparations for tea, while the dog went scampering around the orchard.

When the dog returned a few minutes later, he dropped one of my best laying hens at Bly's feet, but before Bly could get angry, a handy hint came to mind ... one we had been storing for just such an occasion. Taking the dead bird by the legs and the dog by the collar, Bly administered a token beating. Feathers went in all directions, while the dog yelped and writhed, then capitulated with his four feet in the air.

Teddy proved to be utterly useless with sheep, and despite Bly's painstaking attempts at training him to bring home the cow, he would desert and make for the house.

Early one morning Bly came to the bedroom searching for bullets in the drawer. 'I'm going to give that mongrel hound a lesson in obedience,' he said. 'I'll shout, "Come behind," and if he doesn't, I'll fire a shot into the dirt just ahead of him. Don't look so worried, I couldn't hit a moving object if I tried.' I must have dozed off, for presently there was a lot of scratching and scrambling on the polished lino in the passage. The next instant a whimpering hundred pounds of dog landed on top of me, flapping his ears and spraying blood everywhere, trying to get under the covers. I was still trying to get him off the bed without waking the baby, when Bly strode in demanding, 'Where's that fool of a dog?' 'I think you've killed him,' I wailed. 'Nonsense,' he declared, 'I merely did as I said I would.' Then, when he took a look at the dog, lying as still as death at my back with his head on the pillow, he went quiet.

We got the flaccid body onto the bedside mat and dragged him out into the daylight. 'He's still breathing,' Bly said. Then we started to search for the wound, surprised to find that all that blood had come from a minute hole in the tip of one ear. Bly insisted it could only have been made by a grain of sand sprayed up by the bullet.

As soon as Bly's back was turned, Teddy came to life. He wasn't even a good watchdog, but he certainly was loyal and very ornamental, and he never even looked sideways at another fowl.

(From *The Way it Was,* an autobiography, 1993.)

FAYE   DAVIS

TO WHOM IT MAY CONCERN

The cart, the colour of dirt, came up the hard gravel drive. Everything upon it had taken on the colour of dirt and dried, weathered wood. None of the tools or utensils on it lent any colour, nor did the men who rode upon it. The men, too, were the same colour, their faces barely definable from the grey of their work clothes. The cart came close to the house, which seemed to vibrate with its noise, then went down towards the shed. Soon the men would be in. Mary poked the fire to hurry its response to the kettle, pushed the two small doors together to prevent the heat wasting into the kitchen, and heard Albert cursing at his horse as he released it from the cart. She knew well that this alone did not release Albert's frustration.

She prepared sandwiches and placed them upon the table, added some fruit buns from the large glass jar that stood on top of the safe, and placed these on another plate. She took down five large cups and saucers and prepared them for the tea which she would not make until she heard the men walking up the drive. She heard a raised voice, heard the tools being unladen, and sent the younger children out to play.

Mary heard the boots on the drive, the empty billies and pannikins rattling too, and poured the steaming water into the large teapot. They would not all come in after work. Mick would go straight home to his own family, but the other workmen, Mate and Tom, would have tea before they went. She heard them at the door, but did not greet them then. There was a ritual: they washed at the trough in the washhouse first. Albert washed his face and his hands for a long time under the flowing water, but Mary knew the tiredness would not be washed from

175

him. The men came into the kitchen, and she and Albert acknowledged one another then, but silently, he tired, she apprehensive. Tom invariably nodded, but Mate always smiled at her and spoke a greeting.

Hello, Missus. Nice day.

They drank their tea thankfully. Their eldest boy always had tea with the men. She did not sit down with them, but drank hers apart, always ready to serve them, anxious to avoid any undue tension.

Mary hated the tension. However hard she tried she could not avoid the tension. The land did something strange to men. She remembered Albert had been different. It seemed a long time since anyone had been sensitive or interested in her. The land was demanding, had taken Albert from her, she thought with resentment, had put a harsh barrier between them. She, too, had now withdrawn into her own isolation.

Mary was slightly built, but certainly larger than when she and Albert had been married on the Goldfields. She brushed at a strand of hair and caught it in place in the knot at the nape of her neck. Her face carried an expression of tension and disillusionment now. She could not remember when she had been carefree. Perhaps it was before she left Bendigo, before her mother or her father died, before she had to join her married brother in Menzies over here in the West. She stood near the fire now, though it was warm in the late afternoon, and added more hot water to the teapot and refilled the large teacups. It was not necessary to ask them if they would drink another cup. They always did.

The men talked intermittently about the day's work, of the progress made on the drains and the fences. Mary had once gone with Albert out to the paddocks and seen the fences they erected and the drains they dug to make it better for the winter months. Albert told the men now what they would do the next day. Mary relaxed a little now the men had had their tea and some food. Tom and Mate would go home soon and Albert would go outside to attend to other work. They rose and Mate thanked her for the tea. Mate always did that and Tom nodded as he left. She had liked Mate, if for no other reason than he acknowledged her. But the children told her they had seen him beat his dog recently as if he had lost his senses. She worried about this and thought it was not good for him that he lived alone.

The children came back into the kitchen when the men had gone, but Mary sent them to do their jobs, to feed the fowls, collect the eggs, and fill the box at the back door from the woodpile. The girl would help her bring the clothes from the line. She restored some order in the kitchen then cleared the table, washed the tea things, and knew she must soon prepare the evening meal.

Albert was a good man. Mary knew that deep inside him he still had feelings, but she rarely saw them displayed. Occasionally he would touch the long, fair hair of their girl, or take her with him on some short errand, but with herself and the boys he was always stern. She heard the wood being dropped into the box at the back door and knew that job had been done. The boys never dared not do their jobs properly. One of the children brought in the eggs and she went to help wash them. It was time then to help with the clothes and talk awhile with her daughter. Mary was aware of her own disillusionment and hoped for a happier existence for this child, hoped she would not live out her life on the land if it meant such loneliness and need of companionship.

From time to time Mary saw the other women in the neighbourhood, but that was not what she missed. Most of all she grieved for the companionship she had expected from marriage and did not find. She did resent the land, felt it had devoured Albert, and the resulting loneliness had devoured her. From the clothes line she looked across to the home paddocks and saw the earth in freshly turned furrows. Nothing had yet flawed their perfection. She saw the cows make their way to the milking shed and knew they were well cared for. She had to acknowledge Albert was a good man, but he was not her companion any more. She was as trapped by the land as he was, caught up in the everyday cycle of serving it.

The younger boys quarrelled and she sent them off to weed the vegetable garden, and she and her daughter brought in the

177

clothes. The child related an incident that happened at school earlier in the day, and Mary enjoyed sharing these moments with her. Another hour and the sun would go down over the horizon, its redness disappearing over the far paddock. Albert often worked until it was too dark to see, then came in more tired and distant, often angry.

She thought briefly of Mrs Kitsen who had come visiting, actually collecting for the church, and how she had overheard Albert's profanities. She knew Mrs Kitsen would talk about Albert's ungodly ways to the neighbours, knew it would be a long time before Mrs Kitsen dared to come near him again. But Albert would not be worried.

When they left the Goldfields to settle in the Swan Valley, Mary expected it would be different. She was proud of Albert's prospecting ability, knew he was highly thought of on the mines. It was hot and conditions harsh up there, but there had been time for leisure. Albert's father was a sea captain, and alcoholic, so Albert had left school when still a boy, and been lured by the excitement of mine sites from Bendigo to Menzies. He had been more successful than most, had eventually come to manage one of the mines, but decided then to buy up land and leave the mines behind. Only today when tidying some papers she had seen the letters again, the character references, the papers marked: To Whom It May Concern. She had read again the one from the Minister of Mines, others from mine managers. It concerned her, she thought bitterly, yet it was not addressed for her concern, she knew. The letters had all spoken of the same qualities: his excellent character, his honesty and straightforwardness, his diligence, his ability to handle men. She opened the oven door and hot air thrust at her face. She removed the vegetables from the baking dish, lifted the roasted meat and set it aside, poured the hot fat from the dish in readiness to make gravy. When she had made it it was put to the side of the stove to keep hot.

She lit the lamps now, and set the table. Albert would be in any moment. The younger children bathed before the evening meal, and she prompted them to finish before their father came in. Her eldest son had already come in earlier from the milking.

Heavy footsteps were at the back door now, and she knew Albert was at the bathroom. She heard his boots, in turn, drop heavily on the floor at the bathroom door. He would bathe before he came in, for his ritual was never broken, and she never tried to break it. Too much indifference existed between them now for her to do anything spontaneous or act voluntarily toward him.

Mary served the evening meal and during it the children attempted to share an incident with their parents. Albert was distracted, did not encourage the conversation, so the attempt at family communication ended abruptly. With the meal over, the table cleared, and the dishes and milk things washed and put away, Mary prepared the cribs for the next day. She filled the large kettles and set them back on the stove ready for the morning, put another piece of wood upon the fire, and closed the doors. Then she placed Albert's work pants and his flannel on the guard where he would expect them to be in the morning.

When she came from the kitchen Mary saw Albert had already gone to bed, but she had expected it. He retired early, rose early. She prepared for bed too, changed silently so she would not disturb him. She heard his heavy breathing become more even, more rested. She lay between the sheets next to him. Their bodies were close in bed, yet their minds were now those of strangers. It was a long time before she began to drift off to sleep, her comfort. Before her eyes she kept seeing the words: To Whom It May Concern ... To Whom It May Concern ... To Whom It May Concern ...

(From *Paisley Print,* short fiction, 1984.)

SALLY MORGAN
& JACK MCPHEE

I'M A WHITEMAN NOW!

Susie and I settled back into Marble Bar, it was good to be home again and to be close to my family and friends. I went down to the Comet mine and fortunately for me they were shorthanded so I got my job back straightaway.

I still felt uneasy about the Citizenship thing, I was worried that they might not approve of us. I knew we both had our Exemptions so I was hoping that might help.

Gordon Marshall was still the policeman there and he helped me fill out the forms and recommended us as being proper people. We had to be examined by a doctor who swore we were free of certain diseases, like leprosy and diphtheria. There were the same conditions about not mixing with Aborigines or supplying them with grog. It was also like the Exemption Certificate in that if you didn't live up to your side of the bargain, you could lose it.

It had never occurred to be before that I might not be an Australian citizen. I thought everyone born here was Australian. My mother had been here before any white people, so I'd never thought we might be considered strangers in our own country. Gordon explained to me that unless you got this new Citizenship you weren't really an Australian at all.

'Well what are you then?' I asked him.

'I dunno.'

'Are you as good as a migrant?'

'Not really, because migrants become citizens.'

'So a Mulba who doesn't go for this is nothing then?'

'Well yes, I suppose in the eyes of the law he is nothing.'

It all seemed bloody silly to me, it made you wonder what kind of people were running the country.

Anyway, our applications were sent to Perth. They were signed there and then returned to Marble Bar. A time was arranged for Susie and me to go before a magistrate so he could decide whether we could have it or not.

In the meantime I had to organise witnesses who would stand up for us in court and say that they should grant our application because we were living up to the whiteman's standard.

We were very nervous the day we went to court. Even though we felt we had a good chance because of our Exemption Certificates we were still scared they might not grant us Citizenship. I wore my best clothes and so did Susie and we tried to speak in the proper way and so on.

The magistrate asked my name and where I was working. He had it all on the form in front of him but he asked anyway. Then he said, 'Do you live like white people, you and your wife?'

'Yes Sir.'

'Do you get drunk?'

'I have done one or two times with my friends.'

'Will you supply liquor to natives if you're granted this?'

'No Sir.'

'Describe to me how you live.'

I did that and then he said, 'Well, you seem all right to me, I think we'll pass you.'

And that was that.

We used to joke about the whole thing amongst ourselves, we could see it was silly, but not many other people thought so. We'd say things to each other like, 'You eating with a knife and fork, is your plate china and not enamel, you better get it right or they might take your Citizenship away!'

Others would say, 'Hey Jack, why do you need that Dog Licence? You walk on two legs not four!' And so it went on, we all called our papers a Dog Licence, we thought that was a better name for it than Citizenship.

I remember when a friend of mine got his papers. He was a bit of a character and he came running down the main street of

Marble Bar from the courthouse shouting, 'I'm a whiteman, I'm a whiteman, I just left my black skin at the courthouse!' By gee, he was funny, I laughed and laughed.

Then he said to me, 'Hullo whitefella, you got your whiteskin on?'

'Ooh yes,' I said, 'can't you see I've changed colour?'

'Courthouse got your old skin too eh? I hope you've got a silver knife, no more tin for you. No more enamel mugs, we got to have bone china now.'

By gee he was silly, he made a big joke of the whole thing and I really enjoyed it.

Of course there was a lot of conflict between those who had their Citizenship and those who didn't. Some people who could have gone for it refused to on principle; ngayarda banujuthas (people with entirely Aboriginal ancestry) never went for it because they knew they wouldn't get it and felt it was of little use anyway. Those of us who went for it were hoping for something better for ourselves and our families, that was our main reason. The Mulbas who decided against it thought we were too flash for them. They thought we were putting ourselves above our own people. They were real sarcastic buggers. You'd walk down the street and they'd call out, 'Hey whitefella!' or 'Don't get too close whitefella, our black might rub off on you!' And they were your friends!

There was a big problem with the grog too. We used to come under all kinds of pressure to buy grog, it was terrible. Mulbas are very good at making you feel awful, especially when they're related to you. You had to be really strong to hold out because supplying liquor was a very serious offence and a very quick way to lose your Citizenship. I was caught this way once myself.

It was Christmas time and Dougall came up to see me. He was loaded up with goodies for his family, and he said, 'Look Jack, you can see how loaded up I am, I can't manage a case of wine as well, here's the money, can you buy one for me and I'll pick it up later on. Take a bottle out for yourself as well.'

He was that casual about it that I assumed he had his rights. I took the money and bought the wine and Dougall picked it up late in the afternoon.

The next day Gordon Marshall came down and asked me if I'd bought wine for Dougall. I told him I had, that I'd taken one bottle for myself and that Dougall had taken the rest home.

'Never mind about home, Jack,' said Gordon, 'he took the case down to the reserve, they all got drunk and had a hell of a big fight down there. The gaol's nearly full! Did you know Dougall hasn't got any rights?'

'No, I thought he had them.'

'This is serious Jack, you know how the Aborigines Department feels about this sort of thing.'

'Well he was that casual about it I just thought he must have rights.'

'You better not do any more assuming, make sure first. I'll put in a good word for you because I wouldn't like to see you lose your rights, but I can't promise anything. The judge will have to decide when you go to court.'

'I'd appreciate that, thank you.'

'Look Jack, I know it's hard for you, but I have to give you a warning about something else as well. I can't help noticing that you've always got a few natives and half-castes round your place. I know they haven't got any rights and you're supposed to be living like a whiteman and not mixing with them. Now, it's my job to keep an eye out for these things and to report to the Aborigines Department, I can't keep turning a blind eye. I have to tell you that by consorting with natives you're in danger of losing your Citizenship. I've warned you, so it's up to you what you do about it.'

What was I supposed to do? They were my friends and relations. Mulbas aren't like white people when it comes to their relations, it's very hard to cut them off. You always have obligations to relations, even if you don't like them. None of them were troublemakers, we just enjoyed mixing up together.

I went to court not long after and breathed a sigh of relief when I was only fined twenty quid. That was the only time I was ever caught for supplying liquor, there were other times when I gave my mates a drink, but I made sure everyone kept it quiet so there was no trouble.

About a month after I'd been to court Gordon Marshall got a

letter from the Aborigines Department saying that they'd noticed that I had been convicted for supplying liquor to natives and according to the Natives Citizenship Act of 1944 I could lose my Citizenship on any of three grounds.

'You better listen, Jack,' Gordon said, 'because these are the grounds. First, if you fail to adopt the manner and habits of civilised life. Second, if you get convicted of the same offence twice or are drunk a lot. Third, if you come down with leprosy, yaws, syphilis or granuloma. Now, I've done my duty and read that to you. Now, they want me to reply saying whether I think they should take your rights away from you or not. I want you to know I'm telling them I don't think it's necessary, but I'm telling you all this so you can see that it's very serious and so you'll be careful about the way you live in the future.'

I thanked him for supporting me. I knew it was hard for him because he had a job to do and if I wasn't very careful he might not have any choice but to recommend that I lose my rights.

The year that I was granted my Citizenship was the same year of the now famous Pilbara strike by Aboriginal station workers. I was kept well informed about the goings on of the strikers because one of the leaders was Clancy McKenna and he used to tell me what they were fighting for.

Even though Clancy was a mardamarda (a person of mixed Aboriginal-European ancestry) like me he was one of the ones that didn't agree with either the Exemption or the Citizenship. He was a big, clever man and he could turn his hand to anything. He was also more of a thinker than I was, and he felt a deep responsibility to his mother's people. While I had been mainly brought up by whites, he'd spent more time with blacks. They'd gotten into his head and heart and it was impossible for him to pull away from them. I could understand this and at the same time he could understand me, so even though we had different views, we were still close to one another.

The other difference between me and Clancy was that he was fearless and I wasn't. He faced trouble head on, even encouraged it if he felt it was right. I tried to live a quiet life and avoid fights with the police and the Aborigines Department. I couldn't help admiring Clancy because he was so game. He'd walk into a pub knowing he had no rights and demand a drink. He'd answer squatters back and disagree with their views. He was a fighter.

(From *Wanamurraganya: The Story of Jack McPhee,* a biography, 1989.)

VASSO KALAMARAS

THE SHOT

Night has fallen at last.

Beniamino was lying down in his clothes, loosening his belt. His bed was made of old planks resting on four rickety wooden boxes. He had made the mattress himself, stitched the hessian bags, and filled them with hay. For a pillow he had a thick Tasmanian overcoat, carefully folded in two, and on top of this a dirty towel. His blankets, originally colourful, now resembled discarded hides.

Beniamino closed his eyes, exhausted from the day's hard work. He started thinking. To the left of him lay Bridgetown, to the right, Pemberton. His thick fingers, like overstuffed sausages, fumbled blindly over his chest, unbuttoning the rough flannel vest with difficulty. He belched, stretched out, and farted loudly with satisfaction, then spoke quietly to himself in his own tongue.

'Yes, left Bridgitowni, right Pembertoni, in the middle Manjimupa.' He wanted to write to his son in Italy. Salvatore was a novice studying in a Catholic monastery. In his last letter, written in a round, clear hand, he had asked, 'Father, just where do you live out there? They are teaching us Australian geography at school right now — Salvatore.'

Beniamino was already snoring. His lips, so thick they looked swollen, were vibrating. They were like a garnish on the round fat cheeks that looked like over-risen unbaked cottage loaves.

Outside the hut the frogs made a deafening noise in the swamps around the edges of the paddock he was clearing. Some charcoal was still burning from the firewood, turning to ash in the wood stove, which was made of corrugated iron, long, narrow and low, daubed with grease. On it stood a blackened frypan with leftover food.

He had built the humpy himself. Two strides in width and two strides in length, the ceiling so low you had to stoop to go inside. It was made of unplaned off-cuts, which the mill threw away. He had picked them up here and there, nailed them together and hung sugarbags for a door. As if he needed to lock up his wealth and possessions! Doors and keys are for those who need them.

The only precious things there were a radio from a second-hand dealer, the stove, the kerosene lamp and his suit which he wore for special occasions. He did not bother to light the lamp when he was alone, but lit the place with a little oil lamp. He had forgotten to blow it out, so it was still burning, the flame flickering in the air.

He kept his food in a wooden vegetable crate. Nestles milk, sugar, coffee, matches, methylated spirits, salami, Kraft cheese, macaroni. There was always bread. Above his head, hanging from a beam, were half-a-dozen sausages and a plait of garlic. In a corner on the earth floor were a heap of onions and a half-full sack of dried red beans.

He was snoring with gusto.

Before we arrived at the door this sound could be heard from a distance.

Leon called out, 'Hey, anybody in?'

We had left the car lower down. It was a bad track, full of soft earth. We did not want to be bogged at night.

We were walking and calling.

'Beniaminooo, Beniamino, is anyone there?'

With his short hair standing up straight around his head, Beniamino appeared in the opening looking surprised.

'Oh, come in, plissa come inside.'

He put two wooden boxes on end for us to sit on. Hurriedly he pulled another pair of trousers over the ones he was wearing, and buttoned only the waistband; unbuttoned in front, the other pair showed through. Both were roughly patched with unmatching pieces of cloth and thread. All this stood out distinctly in the half light.

He started to light the kerosene lamp whose glass edges were chipped and black from smoke and lack of washing.

'Don't bother with the lights Beniamino, we've only come for a moment.'

We sat down and he offered us his homemade wine in two teacups, one without a handle. As he offered them to us I thought his hands trembled; those puffy hands, that looked swollen, with their short stubby fingers.

Was he pleased or annoyed by our unexpected visit?

Was I afraid or too embarrassed to look at him?

I glanced out of the corner of my eye at the shape of his head, like a round, rough stone. His hair was cut like a convict's, and this evening he was unshaven.

'Scusa me,' he said, as if reading my mind. 'I no manage to shave today. I find too much work in the paddock. I'm clearing it plant olive trees.'

We told him about our cow. He listened carefully, then spoke slowly, trying to make us understand him. Like us, his English was not good.

'Everything is monee monee, we do everything for monee. I know this very well.'

Then referring to the sick cow: 'The cow need a gun. Why you keep her? These vets, they take all your money. Not man not beast feela sorry for them. Monee, monee, monita, all they want is your money.'

Leonidas explained to him, he could not shoot it. Not after the way the cow had looked into his eyes.

Beniamino laughed heartily, his short, heavy, fat frame was shaking, while a row of large, white, strong teeth made his fleshy lips beautiful, though his nose was short and fat, as was his whole appearance.

'Ha ha ha,' he stirred the air with his two hands, the fingers spread like a strange prehistoric reptile.

'Me, Leonardo, I don't look at their eyes; only the girls, I look in their eyes and at their bottoms.' He made a sly gesture to convey the shape of a woman's backside.

He called Leonidas, Leonardo.

We explained to him. 'Tomorrow we are leaving at dawn for Perth at four o'clock.'

'Eh, so letsa go.'

He stood up first. There was a hoarfrost; the temperature dropped quickly in the evenings at this time of year; by morning everything would be frozen. The paddocks looked like glass, with a dull gleam. The ice on the new grass crumbled like crystal in your hand.

He picked up the short overcoat from his pillow and put it on, puffing.

His fatness and obstinate energy fought each other noisily.

He left everything as it was, the little oil lamp shining, the kerosene lamp alight.

He turned back and blew out the flame of the lamp noisily, saying, 'Eh my friends, oil is very 'spensive these days.'

We got into the car, he sat in front. We stank of dung and dogs, he of moist earth, kerosene and dirt. He was chatting as if he had not just woken up, his two hands were holding the gun by the barrel, the butt between his legs. He held it like a living creature in his embrace.

He read my mind.

'Missis, I have fight many years in the mountains of my country.'

'Do you want to go back there Beniamino?' I asked him stupidly.

'Me Missis, me Missis?'

He was disturbed, the colour rose in his face, as he spoke, first one then the other hand left the gun, spreading out and expressing more than his words.

Now the prehistoric reptile, with the strange lively wings, groped in the darkness in front of him, digging for beloved faces that he entertained only in his dreams.

'Missis, my wife no want to come here. You see she a very religious woman, she loves very much the priests. She do only what the priests tell her. The boy he's a good boy. His momma give him to the school. He study to be a priest. My son, he'sa called Salvatore.'

'Bravo, bravo, Beniamino, everything is for the best.'

'Leonardo!' He expressed his disappointment as if he wanted to say, 'Where do you see all this good?'

Then again, after a silence:

'Eh, my friends, you must understand, because you are my friends. You're Greek, not like the bloody Aussies.'

'Bah!' I said.

'Yes Missis, they're not all bad, we have some good and some bad in Italy.'

'It's the same here Beniamino,' I replied, 'Australia has good and bad.'

'Um!' he nodded his heavy round head bitterly. 'They don't want us.'

'Huh, what of it? They'll want us in time. They'll understand Beniamino, don't let it get you down,' I said, without believing it myself.

We arrived at our own farm. The three of us got out. The cold stung us and we huddled in our clothes. I think we were shivering. I was wearing a white fringed scarf with an old brown beanie on top, trousers under a loose, check shirt, and a fifteen-year-old shaggy woollen jacket. I felt uncomfortable with Beniamino, I was trying to forget why we had brought him here.

He turned to me earnestly, pointing to the house.

'You better go, Missis. Thisa man's job.'

I did not look at them, an unimaginable weariness and sadness clutched at me.

'Goodnight,' then in Greek, *'Thee mou!* (My God!)'

I went through the small porch in the yard towards the house. Leonidas was talking. The two of them walked towards the hay shed where we had fixed up a place for the cow that had not been able to get up for two weeks. One of them stopped, then both stopped. Leonidas held a torch, switching it on and off so that the beam spread and dissolved in the thick darkness.

I heard Beniamino's voice again, it was strong, with a strange resonance like an echo coming from that spot.

'Leonardo, I know this very well, when my time comes, I will go to die in Italy, there in my own village, I want to die with dignity. My friend, you can live and work like an animal, but when you die, this must happen as it should for a human being. Here I'm an animal.'

His laughter, bitter as bile, sounded strange, resounding like the groaning of a wild beast in a cage.

I turned to look at them; Beniamino was pointing to himself with one hand, and with the other he was waving his gun in the air threateningly.

'Leonardo, you see me, here me, Beniamino, I'm worth nothing to nobody. I not even worth a bullet. They wouldn't even give that to get rid of me from this country. My friend, I want to die over there,' he pointed with his thick finger. His hand appeared more swollen in the darkness, becoming to my eyes, a special force, a living black bird caught by the foot.

The gun gleamed in the torchlight.

'I go there to die. There I make my bed as I want, my friend. My size. I go when I want, you understand? Italy is the country of Beniamino.'

Now his laughter sounded more bitter, stronger, it turned into a cough.

The sound of their steps began again. He coughed and laughed. They turned at the first tobacco kilns.

Silence.

A bleak silence. It was unbearably cold. Winter in the depth of the bush, covered with fog like a dark cheesecloth, a veil, hiding all the various parts of the landscape. Some poor chilly wandering stars bathed in an atmosphere of milky fumes. The black trees stood out here and there, fantastic mythical silhouettes of Gods.

The gunshot shattered the frozen silence.

The noise startled the frogs and my heart.

Our dogs began to bark angrily, then to howl horribly.

I covered my ears.

Holy Mother, what a terrible waste. Her eyes were still before me, they looked at me speechlessly with a moist human pleading. Life! Big brown eyes with an infinite sweet sadness.

Leonidas had said, 'I can't do it. She looks into my eyes.'

Translated by Vasso Kalamaras and June Kingdon.
(From *The Same Light,* short fiction, 1989.)

T A G HUNGERFORD

THAT TIME OF LIFE

Finally I had to shoot one of the crows. I didn't particularly want to do it, but while they were around, peering down, none of the other birds would come in for their handout; or if one were to, it was in a state of nervous tension which must have shot its digestion to hell, squinting over its shoulders, leaping inches in the air at every sound or movement.

Only the doves seemed unconcerned — which from my own observation of them is perfectly in character. To get more than a fair share of the wheat I throw them, the big trample on the smaller, the smaller on the smallest. They stop feeding only to fight or to make love, which they seem to be able to manage several times during a meal, *and* on a full crop. By and large they're the most unlovable of all the birds who come to the bun rush, and it's beyond me how they ever qualified to feature on just about every 'holy picture' ever given to me by the nuns at my first school — sixty-five years ago, now.

The lone crow hung around for a few days, heartachingly crying out its loss. It made me feel like a murderer, which I suppose I was. Then it drifted off for good.

Otherwise life moves on, Canning Vale style. The chestnut filly in the big paddock across the road from my place grows so beautifully that it almost stops my heart just to see her galloping in the sunshine. My roses are a living testimonial to the excellence of the product of the old black cow, who continues to deliver two or three Coles plastic carry bags of the good stuff every day. I call her Old One-four-two, for the tin sale tag still dangling in one ear — nobody has ever thought to remove it.

I pick up her offering when I take the dogs for their walk in the evening. I've got nearly four acres on this side of the road, but once a day — more often if they can pressure me into it — they've got to get over there for a while. They come and smile at me at about four o'clock, no matter where I am or what I'm doing, wag their tails ingratiatingly, and smile, and tell me I'm a good bloke, and smile. I've this endearing mental picture of them watching me from somewhere higher up in the garden, or from the verandah. They consult their omens, and one says to the other: *Okay! Time for the walk. Let's go and give Fatso the business!* If I don't respond immediately, by dropping every-thing and taking off with them, one of them will wander off — oh, so *casually* — and will return with a stick. *It means absolutely nothing*, they assure me, *I just happened to pick it up*. If that fails to galvanise me, the stick is brushed against my legs — again, quite by mistake. Only as a last resort does anyone bark. Always Billie — of course, the lady. The affection I can give them, and that which they give back to me, the care I take of them and the company and entertainment which they repay me, make life a lot more pleasant than it might otherwise be.

It all points up the sheer inhumanity of rules forbidding lonely old people in retirement villages from keeping pets. One has seen enough research into the matter to expect that the authorities would say: *Sure! Dogs, cats, budgies, hamsters, goddam wildebeests, if you want to! Bring 'em all along!* I know people in retirement villages, and it is touching to see how they entice animals who live around-and-about, and secretly feed them and love them — all, of course, in fear of being unmasked to The Office. Comfort and Bingo are not enough.

My Sam is ten years old, so that if you go along with the belief that one year in a dog's life is equal to seven in a man's he's now as old as I am — that skinny little black pup who used to curl up inside my shirt, or sit on the back of my neck while I was driving: or, when I was sitting in front of the fire at night, reading, would climb laboriously into my lap — meanwhile stu-diously pretending that he was doing nothing of the kind, that *really* he was still lying on the rug at my feet. He still tries it on sometimes even now, big-and-all as he is. I let him get away with it, for old-times' sake.

At one time, over in the paddock, he chased sticks and I chased him. Now we walk around quietly together, as a couple of friendly old blokes should, looking in the trees for birds' nests, keeping a weather-eye out for snakes, talking to old Snow in the next paddock. He's an ex-racehorse, however, and a bit snooty. He stands staring out across the paddocks into some old dream of his own, maybe hearing once again the roar of the crowds on the lawns, as in his dreams he turns into the straight, well clear of the pack.

Sam and I leave stick-chasing to Billie. She's much younger than we are — and sillier. She came into the family on the morning of the 1982 Federal election — a tiny, scraggy, famished, terrified little black bitch puppy, about as pretty as the south end of a north-bound camel. She'd been dumped, at the bottom of my drive, because it was time for needles and other fairly costly adjustments to her persona; and, probably, the kids had got tired of her anyway. There's a specially deep and dreadful level of hell yawning for the reptile who dumped her — although as it turned out he did me a favour. I'd hoped that Bill Hayden would win that election, and to celebrate his anticipated victory I called her after him — and, of course, it was on him that the honour was conferred.

Following the long-ago advice of a vet I decided to let her have one litter before I had her spayed. Sam didn't object, and in time she produced nine pups. With unusual luck I'd calculated the day correctly, and was on hand for the *accouchement*. I'd decided not to keep any females, and had a bucket of warm water ready for the murder. I wonder now how I managed to do it, how I could snuff out those exquisite little creatures so long and so miraculously put together by clever little Billie. I'd psyched myself by recalling previous episodes of traumas with lady dogs, and also had convinced myself that the newborn pups would find little difference between one lot of warm water and another. There were four girls, I immersed them as they arrived, put them into the bucket and held them down with sheets of newspaper, put them all into a hole which I'd already dug and planted over them a fern which I had standing by in a pot. When I'd finished I went back to the house and threw up all over the laundry floor.

The pups were so beautiful, and so puzzling. There were four distinct families. Of the five I saved one was an exact replica of Sam, one was a perfect little red cocker, two were perfect little cream Labradors, and one was a perfect little mixture of Billie and Sam — her colouring and his shape. I'd been told years before — but had never quite believed it — that a bitch can conceive to more than one dog in a single pregnancy. When I took the family to the vet for their needles, etc., (I'm still recovering financially) I asked him if it was so. 'She can conceive to ten dogs if she'll stand still long enough!' he said, matter-of-factly. It was a very lonely house for a while after they'd all departed.

I could rationalise the red cocker strain. Billie had a great liking for one which used to join us for our afternoon walk and manure-getting in the paddock over the road: I knew where he lived, in a house cater-corner from mine across the paddock. When Sam alerted me to an interesting new plateau in his Billie's development I used to chase the cocker away, much to his puzzlement. When we disappeared up our drive he'd sit forlornly at the bottom of it and gaze after us with what I imagined was a plea to be allowed to come in and play. As it turned out he was plotting how to get past me to Billie, which with her eager connivance he did very successfully. When it became obvious that he had achieved his ambition — although Sam still exercised the *droit de seigneur* — I permitted visiting rights: rather than having her cross the road to visit him, which she'd taken to doing whenever I turned my back.

The cream Labrador strain remained a puzzle for a long time, however. I'd never seen a Lab anywhere near my place, and knew nobody who owned one. The mystery was solved a couple of months later after the pups had all gone to their new homes and when, no doubt, former lovers might have been thinking it was time to call around again. One midday I heard Billie carrying on from the bottom of the drive, where there's a little swamp, and conceived the dreadful suspicion that what I'd always feared had happened — that she'd bailed up a snake. There were a lot of them around Canning Vale at that time, so much so that a carter I'd engaged to bring me a load of wood refused to get out of his truck. 'Not on your life!' he protested, when I asked him why he insisted on staying wedged tightly behind the wheel. 'This joint's lousy with snakes!' When later on I'd enticed him out of the cabin he told me that usually when he had a late afternoon delivery, which that one was, his missus liked to come with him for the ride. 'Not today, though!' he said. 'She reckoned she wasn't coming to Canning Vale to be bitten to death by bloody snakes!' For the record, I hadn't seen one for a long time until last summer when one — a tiger — wriggled amiably across the carport as I stepped out at the back door.

It was no snake which had aroused Billie's rage, however. When I walked quietly and carefully down to investigate, dead scared that if I were to distract her attention from the snake it would get her, I discovered her in what is now called eyeball-to-eyeball confrontation with two cream Labradors. One was an old, ponderous boulevardier, broad across the beam and a little worn here and there, obviously a veteran of myriads of such romantic forays. His companion was a brisk and smiling youngster, just as obviously a tyro in the business; a son or nephew or neighbour to whom the old bloke had decided to reveal the existence of this scented garden of dalliance in Amherst Road. Billie was absolutely raving, her bared fangs only inches from their surprised faces. *You've got your damn nerve!* she was screaming. *Look what happened last time — nine bloody pups, and me left to cope with them! Get your ass off this property — and take that young lout with you!* The old fellow took off, followed by his young friend, and they've never been back.

I often wonder if Billie has forgotten those heady days, although I don't know why she should have. I haven't forgotten mine, and they're a lot more distant than hers. She will still chase sticks until I'm too tired to throw them ... and then, when we get home, she flops onto a mat and says as plainly as ever my own mother did when she came in from a walk: *Glory be!*

My feet are killing *me!* She's probably one of the best two dogs in the world. Still — whose dogs aren't?

Fred and his missus and his mate usually drop by most evenings, particularly during the summer when the swamp dries up and the couple of little ponds in my garden offer a haven for their lot. Fred first showed up about four years ago, by himself, prancing about on my kitchen windowsill. He'd probably rationalised that where there was light there would be moths, a most handsome green-and-gold bloke, slender and angular, enormous come-to-bed eyes, and quite a Baryshnikov. After a while he was joined by his missus, an exquisite little bit of jade not half his size with eyes like chips of gold and a bone structure quite as beautiful as Marlene Dietrich's. Last of all to appear was Fred's mate. He's not quite as handsome as Fred, nor as big. He's a little inclined to let himself be pushed into the background, and to shrug his shoulders as if he didn't care, when obviously he does.

Almost every evening, soon after I turn on the kitchen light, the three of them arrive for a bit of moth hunting. If I'm at the sink at the right moment, the first I see of them is a pair of delicate front paws and two bulging golden eyes rising above the edge of the sill. They prop there while the owner cases the joint, for all the world like that peripatetic fellow Foo, who used to decorate the walls of public lavatories. One spends far too much precious time watching them, but it can't be helped. Among the attractions of the Festival of Perth they'd be a riot with their graceful, angular moth-catching pavane. They can leap practically the full height of the windowpane, and hang against the glass by the tiny suction cups at the ends of their fingers, displaying the smooth pale-green ovals of their bellies and the entrancing Elizabethan-farthingale effect where their abdomens join their thighs. When one of them open that cavernous mouth to engulf a moth, it is a flash of geranium pink, and he stays as still as a frog of alabaster while those gold damask wings fold, slowly, like a tiny fan. Until suddenly — plop! — it's gone. They all miss occasionally, and when that happens, whoever's goofed lies sprawled for minutes at a time just where he landed, obviously feeling very foolish. You can imagine — one does, anyway — that he is drumming his fingers in exasperation, just as Oliver Hardy used to do when *he* took a pratfall.

Their performance has such an hypnotic quality — like running water, or playing children — that you can watch them forever: although for some time I've suspected that they come up to the house to watch me and my friends. I like to think of Fred, down in the pool at dusk, saying to his missus: *Let's go and have a look at the people!* And then: *Coming mate?* Why not? I know from years of watching the maggies that they talk to each other — so why not frogs? We've got to get over that hubristic idea that we're the only ones who're capable of doing it, but we're fighting an awfully grim rearguard action!

The first time I became aware of maggie-speak was one day seven or eight years ago when I was feeding them on their customary spot on the driveway under the rose she-oak. I'd hardly begun when one of them let go with the tuc-tuc-tuc-*tuck!* which I now recognise as their top-priority warning to get the hell out of it. They all took off immediately, but also in a very unusual fashion. They flew only a couple of inches above the ground until they reached the shelter of the big paperbark at the bottom of the drive, and then did an abrupt right-angle vertical turn to end up in the shelter of its branches. While I was still wondering what had upset them, I became aware that there was no sound and no movement at all on the block. Willies, peewits, maggies, honeyeaters, doves and butcherbirds had all gone to cover. Even the wattlers, and anything that buttons up the bill of a wattler must be something indeed!

It was something. A moment later the biggest hawk I've ever seen around here hove into sight on the far side of the paddock across the road. He flew across my garden — it seemed to take him half-an-hour — and disappeared towards Kwinana. It was only then that the first of the maggies came back, very tentatively, to the feeding station. The other birds took up their interrupted gossiping, and you could tell by the very sound of it they were discussing the hawk. *Just let him poke his bill down here, and see what happens!*

Also I'm learning basic Twenty-eight Parrot. Every year they take every one of my almonds — the trees have been bearing for five or six years and I've never harvested so much as one nut. They take about a third of my nectarines, a good swag of my grapes and — apparently when things are tough — far too many of the soft young red shoots of my roses.

Four years ago I bought a gun, and for most of one summer I shot them. I couldn't make myself go on with it. You can buy nectarines and almonds, but you can't buy those lovely thieves, that mindbending comet of green and blue and gold as they flash among the trees of the garden. On destruction bent, no doubt, but ... okay. When I hear them whistling all about the house at this time of year I know I'm certainly not hearing just random noise. What I'm hearing, from one flock to another, is a joyous cry: *Hey! C'mon over here! Fatso's nectarines are ripe!* I should do something about it, but I've arrived at that time of life — some, but not I, would say 'that psychological plateau' — at which to share seems the proper thing to do.

That time of life. This time of life, this *now*. Sometimes I wonder, as I guess all of us do, how long it will last. After all that has passed, the surprisingly fleeting seventy-odd years of work and war and worry, of love and joy and triumph and travel, and sins and shames and subterfuges, how long it will be before I'm carted down my driveway in a box, past the strelitzias and the azaleas and the gerberas, the roses and poinsettias and the lovely camphor laurel at the gate, the maggies probably casting inquisitive glances from the rose she-oak or one of the lemon-scented gums as I go by.

I look back on it all, even the worst of it, with pleasure, with a friendly sort of understanding and affection for the stumbling erk who enjoyed the good bits, and somehow navigated through the minefields. I was about to suggest that he had found it fun, but that is to belittle the whole magnificent shebang. Fun is for fools, the least of all the myriad threads in the magic carpet we fly on between wherever we came from and wherever we're going to.

I keep a fairly open mind on the nature of that destination. Maybe it's a black velvet curtain we slip behind, and simply disappear. Maybe it's like when you climb up through the portico of the Acropolis, thinking to yourself: *This* must *be the peak!* and then see rearing up before you what stands on the top of the rock. Despite all that has been said and written and proclaimed as gospel, nobody since the beginning of the world has ever known the truth of it, and not one of us ever will know until he finds out for himself.

I'm looking forward to the finding out, whichever way it goes. Either I'll know nothing — no great change, some would say — or I'll know the lot: how many universes there *really* are, how many angels *can* dance on the head of a pin, did we *really* start off with a Big Bang, as some suggest, and if we *did*, who caused *that?* All the mighty matters men mull over in their minds. It's a stunning prospect. I might even learn a cure for the common cold, which so often stops so many minds from mulling.

In the meantime, I can hear the cockies at my nectarine trees. I'd better go out and try to impress on them that I have at least a share in the crop.

(From 'And Now...', *Red Rover All Over,* autobiographical stories, 1986.)

ELIZABETH JOLLEY

THE NEIGHBOUR WOMAN

The neighbour woman, I always think of her as I walk up this side of the orchard, on the neighbour woman's side. The neighbour woman, who was always watching to see what I was doing, told me to burn out the broken handle of the mattock.

'Throw it on the fire and burn it out,' she said. I would never have thought of doing this and would have worked a long time at the split wood trying to cut it out. She always used to appear at the fence. She was already sick then. As she became more seriously ill her face, normally gaunt, looked round. This roundness made me see something of the child she must have been. To be reminded that there was once a child, with all the shy hopes of childhood, and who is still a part of the adult, is sad.

All I can think of just here, by the fence, is that when the neighbour woman's husband told me that she had died he could hardly speak for his grief. His eyes were red and swollen with weeping and I understood that I was face to face with someone who really loved the neighbour woman and that he would never get over something which is brushed aside in the word bereavement. Sometimes now, after all this time, he speaks about his wife and the tears well up in his innocent elderly eyes and it is as if she has just died all over again and left him alone in his paddocks here at the edge of the bush for ever. Because of this it is possible to know that love exists where the idea of it may be overlooked ...

GREAT BRANCHES FALL

And what of the dead
We shall see and more probably we shall not see
A life open to death
Annihilation
Even so the annihilated built the cottage and made
The path from the township slowly
Cleared the land and for some reason was it weakness
or reverence? left here the old trees which from
Other slopes have gone beyond imagination.
Some sat in this place feeling the winter sun fade
And staring up through pointed leaves trembling
Saw the sky
The trees the birds the quiet wild things
Indifferent yet caring perhaps serving
The wind moves the trees great branches fall
In the wind or in the stillness
A few feet nearer and I should have been crushed
Into the greater stillness.
If we love what does not yet love us
Can we not give it love
The dead, whether annihilated or surviving, the trees
The high up eagles as they look into the sun
Together can we not wait serenely for whatever
Awaits us.

(From *Diary of a Weekend Farmer*, 1993.)

CONTRIBUTORS NOTES

Elizabeth Backhouse was born in Northam, Western Australia. She has had novels published in Australia and the United Kingdom. She has also written for radio and television, as well as stage plays and a scenario for a ballet. Her family history, *Against Time And Place*, was published by Fremantle Arts Centre Press in 1990.

Michal Bosworth was born in New Zealand in 1944 and moved to Brisbane in 1952. She has worked as a historical researcher and writer. She has published books for school children and articles about women and is co-author, with Emma Ciccotosto, of *Emma: A Translated Life* and *Emma: A Recipe For Life*, published by Fremantle Arts Centre Press.

Emma Ciccotosto was born in Italy in 1926 and migrated to Western Australia with her parents in 1939. Since her retirement she has been actively involved in community work, and has published books, *Emma: A Translated Life* which was re-issued in a substantially revised edition as *Emma: A Recipe For Life*, written with Michal Bosworth.

Ron Davidson was born into a Perth newspaper family in Perth, Western Australia, in 1936. He worked as a journalist in Australia and overseas and currently lectures in psychology at The University of Western Australia. His first book, *The Divided Kingdom* (with Connie Ellement), was published in 1987. A second book, *High Jinks At The Hot Pool*, was published in 1994.

Faye Davis was born in Perth, Western Australia, and spent her childhood in the grape-growing Swan Valley. She has published widely in literary journals and anthologies and has received numerous awards for her writing. She has published one collection of short fiction, *Paisley Print*, with Fremantle Arts Centre Press in 1984.

Connie Ellement was born near Boulder, Western Australia, in 1912 and spent most of her childhood in orphanages. She became interested in writing while translating books into Braille and her first book, *The Divided Kingdom* (with Ron Davidson), was published thirty-five years after she began writing it. Connie Ellement died in 1992.

A B Facey was born in 1894 and grew up on the Kalgoorlie Goldfields and in the Wheatbelt of Western Australia. He went out to work when he was eight years old, and droving in the North-West at fourteen. He had no formal education and originally wrote his acclaimed autobiography, *A Fortunate Life*, for his family. A B Facey died in 1982.

Kenneth Gasmier was born in Western Australia in 1949, where he spent his early years in the Wheatbelt and other country areas. He currently works as Librarian at The Western Australian Academy of Performing Arts and also writes as music and arts reviewer for the *Sunday Times*, Perth, and the *Western Mail*. He has published short fiction in Australian literary journals, newspapers and anthologies, and his first collection, *Stars In Nights To Come*, was published in 1990. He was awarded an Australian Council Fellowship in 1995.

T A G Hungerford was born in Perth, Western Australia, in 1915. He served with the Australian Army during World War II and has worked as a journalist in Canberra, Hong Kong, New York and Perth. He has been widely published in journals, newspapers and anthologies and has published a large number of fiction, autobiographical and general non-fiction titles, including six with Fremantle Arts Centre Press.

Elizabeth Jolley was born in the industrial Midlands of England and came to Western Australia in 1959 with her husband. She has had fiction, plays and poetry published in Australian literary journals and anthologies, and has broadcast on British and Australian radio. Elizabeth has published seventeen books, the most recent is a novel, *The Orchard Thieves*.

Gail Jones was born in Harvey, Western Australia. She graduated in English from The University of Western Australia and now teaches there. Her first collection of short fiction, *The House of Breathing,* which has won numerous literary awards, was published in 1992.

Vasso Kalamaras was born in Athens, Greece, and came to Western Australia in 1950. She publishes in both Greek and English. She has published short fiction and poetry, and has had a number of plays produced for the stage. Vasso has received numerous literary awards in Greece and Australia. She has published two collections of short stories with Fremantle Arts Centre Press, *Other Earth* and *The Same Light*. *The Same Light* won the 1990 Western Australian Premier's Award for Fiction and the 1992 Hellenism Award.

John Lane was born in England in 1922 and was placed into an orphanage in 1924 before being sent to the Kingsley Fairbridge Farm School in Western Australia in 1933. He served with the Australian Army during World War II and was a prisoner of war for three and a half years. John has published two volumes of autobiography with Fremantle Arts Centre Press, *Summer Will Come Again* and *Fairbridge Kid.*

Simone Lazaroo was born in Singapore in 1961 and migrated to Perth with her family in 1963. Her novel, *The World Waiting To Be Made*, won the 1993 TAG Hungerford Award for Fiction and was published in 1994. It also won the Western Australian Premier's Award for Fiction and was shortlisted in the Nita B Kibble Award.

Joan London was born in Perth in 1948. She has published in journals and anthologies and has published two collections of short fiction with Fremantle Arts Centre Press, *Sister Ships* (which won the *Age* Book of the Year Award in 1986), and *Letter To Constantine*.

Pat Malcolm was born at Bruce Rock, Western Australia, and left home and school aged fourteen. She has had a number of different jobs in the North-West of Western Australia, and published her autobiography, *First Cuts Are Deepest*, with Fremantle Arts Centre Press in 1993.

Bill Marks was born in Fremantle, Western Australia, in 1916 and has had a varied career, mostly as a butcher and in the racing industry. He served in the Middle East and New Guinea during World War II. Bill published his autobiography, *The Fall Of The Dice*, in 1991. A second book will be published in 1997.

John A McKenzie was born in Boulder, Western Australia, in 1916. He graduated from The University of Western Australia with an Honours degree in History in 1936. He was a foundation member of the Secondary Teachers' College and first head of the Social Sciences Department. He published his autobiography, *Challenging Faith*, in 1993.

Jack McPhee was born in about 1905 in the North-West of Western Australia, of tribal Aboriginal parents. He has published two books, including *Wanamurraganya: The Story Of Jack McPhee*, with Sally Morgan. Jack McPhee is Sally's grandfather through Aboriginal kinship.

Connie Miller was born in Cheshire, England, in 1904 and came to Western Australia in 1912. After studying at night school she attended The University of Western Australia where she gained a Master of Arts degree. She has had three volumes of autobiography published by Fremantle Arts Centre Press — *After Summer Merrily, A Season of Learning* and *Memory Be Green.*

Sally Morgan was born in Perth, Western Australia, in 1951. She has published books for both adults and children, including her acclaimed autobiography, *My Place.* She has also established a national reputation as an artist and has works in many private and public collections.

Kim Scott was born in Perth, Western Australia, in 1957. He graduated from Murdoch University and currently lectures at Curtin University. He has had poetry and fiction published in anthologies and literary journals, and his first novel, *True Country,* was published in 1993.

Joyce Shiner was born in Katanning, Western Australia, in 1915. She has published poetry and short prose, and her autobiography, *The Way It Was,* was published by Fremantle Arts Centre Press in 1993.

Imelda P Smith was born in Fremantle, Western Australia, in 1924 and still lives there. She served with the Women's Australian Auxillary Air Force during World War Two. Imelda P Smith will publish her autobiography, *Outside The Fold* with Fremantle Arts Centre Press in 1997.

Justina Williams, AM, spent her childhood in Kendenup, Western Australia. She worked as a journalist with the *West Australian,* the *Daily News* and the *Workers' Star.* She is active in the feminist, civil rights and peace movements. She has published poetry and short fiction in journals and anthologies, as well as a collection of short stories, *White River,* and an autobiography, *Anger and Love*, both with Fremantle Arts Centre Press.